Xeno Tryst

Books by Troy D. Wymer

Lightyears Trilogy
Lightyears
Lightyears II: Intragalactic Terrorism
Lightyears III: Ominous Intervention

Treasures From Afar

Xeno Tryst Duology
Xeno Tryst
Feathers of Shardaa

Crystal Avarice

Xeno Tryst

BOOK ONE OF THE XENO TRYST DUOLOGY

TROY D. WYMER

Published by WymerNovels

www.WymerNovels.com

ISBN: 979-8-9916986-2-7

Second Edition: 2025, Version 2.0

Published in the United States

Preface

After brainstorming *Xeno Tryst* for two years, I had over 10,000 words put together for the framework of the novel. The structure was definitely plotter-style. I began writing the story in June 2018. In January 2019, I finished *Xeno Tryst*. I took one of my favorite metal subgenres and weaved it into the story with the symphonic metal band Maranadda. Most of the band member names were fictitious characters that I made up to joke around with when my children were young.

There is a short story in the back appendices called *Benjamin,* which is a backstory for the character Benjamin Whitmann. This short story was submitted into the 2019 Write Michigan Short Story Contest, but did not make it to the semi-finals. So, that released me to include the short story in this book.

Xeno Tryst is my first novel with a female as the protagonist. She is a badass with a kind heart. Unlike *Lightyears Trilogy* and *Treasures From Afar, Xeno Tryst* is an erotic space opera novel. It is book one of the *Xeno Tryst Duology* and it is intended for adult audiences only. Although there are explicit sex scenes throughout the novel, they are secondary to the overall story arc. In this novel, I have strived to create rich characters, detailed settings, and a fascinating plot on a galactic scale.

Appendices are located at the end of this book with the short story *Benjamin,* Maranadda band information, a select list of casinos on Salinarr Nevis, and a terminology glossary.

—Troy D. Wymer
October 24, 2025

CHAPTER ONE

"What the fuck?"

Sierra Shalinsky turned off the ship's comm, a bit upset with her bandmates for their impatience. Since she was the only band member from off-planet, she thought they should be a bit more understanding when she was running late for practice. She was the vocalist of a six-piece symphonic metal band called Maranadda. After glaring at the comm for a short time, she flicked the switch back on.

"Hey, ya bunch of Jinkins, I have a good excuse for being late."

"Yeah, you had to finish up your latest sexcapade," Arvon Estivant said.

"Don't be a smart-ass, Arvon, or I'll shove your drums sticks up your ass. I'm late because my account had recently been compromised by an identity thief. Fortunately, I fixed the situation fairly quick. Whoever did this is a fucking asshole. They better hope I never find them."

"Oh, Sierra, I'm sorry to hear that. I was just giving you a hard time. Do you know how long you'll be?" Arvon asked.

"Honestly, about four hours. I'm pushing this old fighter ship as fast as she'll go," Sierra said.

"Okay, well, don't push the *Tenebris* too hard or it might be the old war ship's last flight. Well, while we are waiting for you, we're going to celebrate my birthday and maybe go four-wheeling. Yosemite has the quads all fueled up and ready to hit the trails."

"Well, happy birthday, Arvon. How old are you now?"

"Thirty-five."

"Well, you guys have fun. Don't drink too much ale. I'll see you guys soon."

She was referring to Arvon's drinking problem. He seemed to always go past his drinking threshold. At least the rest of the band kept him in check. She looked down at the ship's controls and increased the speed of the *Tenebris* to lightspeed-plus.

It might be an old ship, but she still has a lot of life left in her, Sierra thought.

The fighter ship was from the old galactic war about one hundred years before. The Syrenthian War was fought between the Xenolfans and the humans. The humans had become aggressive against the aliens for unjust causes. When the Xenolfans started to fight back, it turned into a terrible galactic war. In retaliation, the Xenolfans had used controlled asteroids, dubbed missiloids, to assault human-occupied planets. It left very disastrous results. No one currently alive was responsible for the initial aggression toward the Xenolfans. Years ago, the human-controlled Syrenthian Government and the Xenolfan Government agreed that gaming facilities could be developed on the planet Salinarr Nevis to help the Xenolfans compensate for the previous damages done from the old war. It was all before Sierra's time. She loved her old ship, though. She had recently modified the old, black Syrenthian Government war ship with legacy parts, including laser cannons. Back in its day, the old fighter ship was one of the fastest, most maneuverable in the Syrenthian Government's fleet. It was well designed with a sleek body and tapered delta wings.

Looking out the observation window at the darkness of space, she saw blue light from the distant stars, which brightened the ship's canopy. Her reflection could be seen from the angle of the ship's side windows, revealing her blue eyes and a long black braid of hair draped over the left shoulder of her black leather jumpsuit. She had thought about moving to Red Jacket where her band, Maranadda, was based, but she loved her home on Asparr Celtarious too much. Sierra considered herself conservative, except when it came to music and sexual expression. Her feeling was that everything in life was not always black and white. She was very sexually charged and had a high sex drive. She identified herself as a bisexual unicorn in the swinger Lifestyle, a unicorn being a single female in the Lifestyle. Because of her high sex drive, it was a therapy of sorts for her. However, she had a rule not to be involved with other band members. Regardless, Maranadda's drummer, Arvon Estivant, was always trying to get into her pants. Her main career was a Galactic Emergency Medical Technician (Galactic EMT), helping out with galactic disasters across the galaxy. Her employer was Galactic Emergency Medical Services (GEMS), headquartered on the planet Relistorr. GEMS was a dedicated team of professional Galactic EMTs who responded to galactic emergencies by providing disaster relief in a timely manner. Sierra took her job very seriously, but wished her director wasn't so draconian with everything.

During her long flight to band practice, Sierra thought about how all of her efforts as a sexual freedom advocate had finally paid off. She was responsible for helping establish sex clinics throughout the Syrenthian Galaxy. Her push toward sexual freedom had opened the sex clinics, not so long ago, to help with sexual release and tension. The government finally recognized there was a need to maintain sexual health, especially for those who were either not having enough sex or who had high sex drives. The Xenolfans had their own separate sex clinics. Sex between humans and Xenolfans was forbidden only by the Xenolfan Government whose leader despised any union between the two species. It was extremely important to Sierra that Xenolfan and human lovers could be together without concerns of taboo sex and forbidden love. Part of her current objective in advocating for sexual freedom was to eliminate those restrictions on interspecies sex. Although she had yet to hook up with any of the aliens herself, Sierra had always been curious about Xenolfan sexuality. She admired their appearance. Unlike the tan humans, all Xenolfans had bluish-gray skin and white hair. After the clinics for both species had been established for some time, the galactic sexual crime rate had decreased immensely. It was also mandatory to be checked for infections regularly, which had virtually eliminated all sexual infections from the galaxy. She did receive help in all that advocating from her good friend Priscilla Stryderr. Priscilla had petitioned the Xenolfan Government on Olf Teruda to change their position on the restrictions on forbidden sex, all to no avail.

Suddenly, Sierra recalled the intimate moments with Priscilla when they would play together. She had a quick flashback of their last bisexual encounter and became aroused. Priscilla was absolutely incredible.

Mmm… Sierra savored the thought. *I didn't give her the nickname Priscilla Pussy Lips for nothing.*

Reflecting on the past threesome she had with Priscilla and her husband, Braxton, she became aroused and rubbed between her legs at the folds of her black leather jumpsuit. Sierra gave her pussy some much needed attention. Her fingers felt so good pressing against the smooth leather creases. Sierra applied pressure against her clit through the material and slowly rotated her hand in circles. She soon experienced the blissful joy of an incredible orgasm.

"Ahhh!" she exclaimed, gripping the seat with one hand.

Oh, I needed that so badly, she thought as she slowed her breathing.

She began to think about the interspecies and Lifestyle sexual freedom speech she had been working on. She also thought about the sex-positive health speech that Priscilla had been working on. Priscilla's husband, Braxton—who was a Syrenthian Government official—was very supportive to their cause. They would soon be presenting their speeches together. She was definitely looking forward to it. It was scheduled to be given on Red Jacket soon, but she still needed to put the finishing touches on her speech. She was just so busy with her work schedule, it made finishing the speech a bit difficult. There seemed to be an increase in the disasters and emergencies across the galaxy lately, putting a demand on her as a Galactic Emergency Medical Technician.

"Happy birthday to you. Happy birthday to you. Happy birthday, dear Arvon. Happy birthday to you!" the other bandmates sang to the drummer.

"Thank you. Thank you all very much," Arvon Estivant said, taking a long drink of his ale.

"Whoa. Slow down there, buddy. You need to be alert when we go four-wheeling," Yosemite McFarlin said. "Just yesterday, you scuffed up my guitar when you stumbled."

Yosemite combed his fingers through his short, spiky, brown hair. The room became awkwardly silent.

"I'm sorry, Yosemite," Arvon said.

Arvon brushed his long, brown hair aside, set his ale bottle down hard, and crossed his tattooed arms.

Arrian Trodder quickly changed the subject. "When are you going to order your new quad?" he asked.

"Right after you get your new bass, Arrian. No, I'm joking. I just ordered it from the hardware store the other day. I'm not sure how long it will take to arrive, but I'm excited about it. You all know how much I love four-wheeling."

"What color did you end up going with?" Kulu Avolium asked.

"The same color as your keyboards, black…except it will have blue stripes," Yosemite said.

"It sounds like it will be a beauty. So, what type of modifications did you add?" Kulu asked.

"Oh, I got them all. I upgraded the engine package, the suspension, and the tires for the rocky terrain here on Red Jacket. I even added a rocking stereo system," Yosemite said.

"What about the clutch?" asked Sanarith Raastarr.

"No, that is one thing I left stock. I'm joking! Of course, I did," Yosemite said.

Silence once again filled the practice room of their studio. Sanarith picked up his guitar and plucked a few strings, the lights shining off his bald head.

"This is our final practice before the big upcoming show on Salinarr Nevis. I'm very impressed with our new band manager and booking agent, Shasta Varium. It's so incredible that she was able to get this gig and have us headline the show. I'm looking forward to meeting the other symphonic metal bands that are scheduled to open for us. But waiting for Sierra is getting a bit old," Arrian said.

"Hey, just a minute," Arvon said. "Sierra may be the only one in Maranadda who doesn't live on Red Jacket, but at least she doesn't need approval from Jackie to have band practice."

Arrian turned and gave Arvon a dirty look. "Jacquelyn Enelra is just looking out for my best interest."

"Okay… The only reason why you're still with her is because of your daughter, Sophie. Seriously, you always need to get her approval for everything," Arvon said.

Arrian turned toward the picture of his girlfriend and daughter that hung next to his bass guitar. Her long brown hair was about the same length as his brown hair and was draped in front of her as she stood next to their young daughter in the photo.

"You guys suck. I love Jackie. I know she's controlling, but I still love her," he said.

"Well, I'm having one more piece of cake before we go four-wheeling," Yosemite said.

The practice room door opened and Vincent Macenburg walked in, his long brown hair in a ponytail.

"Is there any cake left?" Vincent asked.

"Plenty. Help yourself," Sanarith said.

"I'm sure it won't taste as good as Sierra does," Vincent said, grabbing a plate and fork.

"Just rub it in, Vincent. Just because she has a rule against hooking up with bandmates, doesn't mean *you* should be able to," Arvon said.

"Hey, I'm not in the band. I'm just the sound technician," he said, smiling. "Besides, my wife enjoys her too."

"I don't understand you swingers. One of these days, Sierra will accept my advances," Arvon said.

Vincent laughed. The door opened again and Vincent's wife, Shaslin, walked in, her long brown hair flowing behind her.

"Want some cake, honey?" Vincent asked her.

"Sure. Happy birthday, Arvon. What are you, thirty-five?" Shaslin asked.

"That, I am."

"Well, while you guys finish up your cake, I'm going down to set the gear on the quads," Yosemite said.

"We'll be there shortly. I need to let Arcashia know we're ready to go. She wanted to watch us," Sanarith said.

"I didn't know your wife likes quads," Shaslin said.

"She only likes to watch them, not ride them," Sanarith said.

"I suppose I should let Misty and the kids know too," Kulu said, standing up from his stool.

They finished their cake and followed Yosemite out the door. Kulu headed for home to let his family know they were about to start the quads. Sanarith walked next door to inform his wife as well. Most of them enjoyed watching or riding the ATVs, which Yosemite offered anytime.

• • •

When Kulu left the band's studio, he made his way along a shortcut and around some bushes onto an old wooden boardwalk that curved around a pond. Thick, green bushes and a few trees were on the left of the boardwalk. The water on his right looked black and deep. He loved the shortcut because it saved him a lot of time from taking the street route. The old wooden boards creaked with his weight. He soon ascended up a slight grade and into his backyard. The grass was long by design. An old wooden chair with chipped paint sat in the tall grass, a metal pail with colorful flowers setting on the ground next to it. He walked up a few gray steps and went through the back door. He saw his wife, Misty, in the living room, her beautiful blond hair braided at her temples. She was reading their two children a story. Kulu stopped and listened for a moment. As she read, she looked up at him standing in the doorway and smiled. Aaron and Shanda sat quietly on the carpet, listening to their mother read *The Ghost and the Pumpkin*. It was a story of a ghost who befriended a pumpkin that sat on the fireplace mantel of a spooky house. They were sad because no one ever came to their house out of fear. But the story ended with a big celebration when they realized they had more friends than they thought. As Misty finished the story and closed the book, the kids turned around and looked at their dad standing in the doorway, his long blond hair draped in front of him.

"Do you guys want to watch us go four-wheeling?" Kulu asked.

"Yeah!" the kids said simultaneously. They stood up from the floor, ran over to their father, and gave him a big hug.

"Okay, then. Let's go," Misty said.

When Sanarith returned with his wife, Arcashia, they stood on a patio that overlooked the rocky trail. Arcashia was a beautiful blonde with long, flowing hair. They turned their attention from where the quads sat below the patio to where Kulu, Misty, and the children approached from a patch of woods along the back of the studio.

"Hi, Misty," Arcashia said. "Are you guys ready for some ATV excitement?"

"Definitely," Misty said, looking down at the kids.

Vincent and Shaslin joined the others to watch from the patio.

They made themselves comfortable in the chairs that overlooked the trail. Vincent opened a sweet carbonated beverage called Sevis and took a long drink. Sanarith and Kulu made their way from the patio down the steps to the rusty colored, rocky trail where the five quads sat.

"Quads are fun, but I'm looking forward to hearing the band practice. I know they've been working on some new material," Vincent said.

"I think some of their best material is from their debut album, Esoteric," Shaslin said.

"Yes, the early stuff is great, but so is the Novels album and the Discord album," Misty said.

"True. I'm looking forward to the forthcoming album," Shaslin said.

"They are still in the writing process for the new album, but it's almost done. I believe they just need a couple more songs to add. The album will be called Surefire," Vincent said.

"I can't wait to hear it," Misty said, looking over the railing at the quads below.

Yosemite, Arvon, Arrian, Sanarith, and Kulu put on their helmets and the other gear that sat on each of the quads. Those who had long hair, tucked it up inside their helmets, unlike when Sierra would ride. She just let her hair flow out the back out the helmet.

"Are you guys ready?" Yosemite asked as he mounted his quad.

They each gave an affirmative answer and they all started the quads simultaneously. After making a few minor adjustments, they slowly took off. The rocky terrain of the Red Jacket trails was an interesting course for their ATV adventures. The trail wrapped around in a large five kilometer loop that ended up back at the studio. The rusty colored trails twisted and turned through some of the roughest territory on Red Jacket. There were areas of the trail that became a trench with flat, smooth rock walls on either side. Other canyon areas had cliffs that dropped far below. Unlike the pond and oasis area near the studio, a lot of the trail ran along a desert where there were very few trees and shrubs.

Yosemite twisted the throttle and sped up ahead of the others. It didn't take long for the rest of the group to catch up to him. As they approached a very rocky section of the trail, Yosemite and the others backed off on the throttle. The quads bounced and twisted over the rocks before the trail surface became smooth again.

Arrian recalled when Yosemite tried jumping over that section once. It resulted in a totaled quad and a broken arm. From that point forward, they took that section a lot slower.

As the five of them zoomed down the trail, the view to their right was breathtaking. Along the desert floor, there were small shrubs scattered about the red sand. The orange, rocky cliffs of the canyon could be seen in the distance, setting against a brilliant blue sky. The temperature was a little on the warm side, but otherwise a perfect day for riding. They rounded a sharp bend in the trail and ran along an area where there was a rock wall on their right and a drop-off on their left. Soon, they ascended a hill and the elevation plateaued. The next stretch was flat for some distance. Arvon took the opportunity to pass Yosemite. It was more about having fun than racing, but sometimes it became a bit competitive. Yosemite gunned it and attempted to catch up with Arvon. Kulu and Sanarith were side-by-side, trailing behind Arrian.

As the quads approached a ridge on the right, Yosemite and the others saw a boy of about twelve years old in a wheelchair, parked up on the flat stone slab that overlooked the rocky trail. He wore a cap on his head to keep the sunlight from his eyes. Yosemite recognized the boy. It was Benjamin Whitmann. He would always wheel himself up the ridge to watch the quads ride by. He must have sat there for hours waiting for the remote chance the quads would travel past the ridge. Yosemite waved a gloved hand up at Benjamin as they rode by. The boy excitedly waved back, his smile remaining for a long time as the quads disappeared into the distance. Yosemite wasn't sure why Benjamin was disabled. The boy's father owned the local hardware store where Yosemite always purchased the quad parts he needed.

Another rough section was ahead of the quads. They all slowed down and crawled over the large stones, the quads twisting and bouncing. The front wheels of the quad that Sanarith rode twisted beyond their limit and something snapped. The others heard the metal scrape across the stone and stopped. Sanarith stood from the ATV and looked at the damage. Yosemite, who owned all the quads, walked over to have a look.

"Whoa! That's seriously fucked up," Yosemite said. "Hey, I'll give you a ride. Let's go to the hardware store and I'll get a new tie rod."

The rest of them walked over to the ATV to have a look.

"Sorry about that," Sanarith said.

"I'm not worried about it. It's not a big deal. I can have it fixed fairly quick," Yosemite said.

They each returned to their quads and Sanarith hopped on the back of Yosemite's. Soon, they reached the main road and left the trail far behind. It didn't take long before they reached town and all parked in front of CJ Whitmann's Hardware & Supply Co. It was an old, white building that had been there as long as Yosemite could remember. He used to go there with his grandpa when he was young. It had not changed much. They always had everything he needed or could order it and have it there the next day. The others waited outside on the quads while Yosemite walked up the old, gray, wooden steps at the corner of the building. He entered the hardware, a bell on the door ringing with its movement. As Yosemite walked across the old, wooden floor, the boards creaked. He walked past the chainsaws and yard equipment. He was always astonished by how CJ Whitmann efficiently fit everything that he could possibly need into one little store. Beyond the plumbing, electrical, and hardware aisles, he stopped at the ATV parts and accessories. An older gentleman came to the counter from around a corner.

"Well, hi, Yosemite," he said.

"Hey, CJ. I am in need of a tie rod for one of my quads. One of those large rocks did quite a number on the suspension," Yosemite said.

"The new ATV you had me order from Ticrisuda Powersports will not have that same issue since you added on a beefed-up suspension," CJ said.

"Probably not."

"I'll grab you a new tie rod from the back," CJ said as he disappeared to the back room.

Yosemite looked around the old store at the tools and anti-gravitation transport supplies. He came across a picture setting on the counter. It was the store owner's son Benjamin. After a lengthy amount of time, CJ Whitmann returned with the tie rod.

"I saw your boy today watching us ride on the trail from his favorite spot," Yosemite said.

"Yeah? I told him to be careful up there. When his mother let's him go, he loves to see the quads ride by on the trail," CJ said as he rang up the part.

Yosemite retrieved his wallet from his back pocket and paid CJ the credits due.

"Do you mind if I give Benjamin a ride on the quad? I would only go at a slower speed and he could sit in front of me to be sure he's secure. I can even introduce him to Kulu's kids," Yosemite suggested.

"He would absolutely love that. Sure. He can tell me all about it when I get home tonight," CJ said.

"Okay. Thank you for the part. I will talk to you later," Yosemite said.

He left the hardware and walked back down the steps to the dusty ground. The others quietly stared at him as he approached.

"What?" Yosemite asked.

"Do you know what it says on the window?" Arrian asked.

"What?" Yosemite asked as he turned around to look at the store's front window.

"It says 'Quick Service.' We've been waiting out here forever."

"Seriously, Arrian, do you have an *Off* button?" Yosemite asked.

When the group arrived back at the trail where they had left the disabled ATV, Yosemite grabbed some tools from a compartment on his ATV. He started working on replacing the tie rod. They all helped lift it up from the rocks. Before too long, he had the new part installed and returned the tools to the tool box.

"I'll have to align it later. Let's go back to that ridge and see if Benjamin is still there. His dad said I could give him a ride," Yosemite said.

They returned to their quads, looped around in a circle, and headed back toward the ridge. In the distance, Yosemite could still see the boy in his wheelchair, sitting on the flat stone. All five of the quads slowed down and came to a stop just below the ridge. Yosemite looked up at the boy.

"Benjamin, would you like a ride on the quad?" Yosemite asked.

Benjamin grew the biggest smile.

"Yeah!"

"Okay," he said. "And we can bring you over to meet Aaron Avolium and his sister, Shanda Avolium. They are both about your age."

"Thanks, Mr. McFarlin. That would be so cool. I remember

meeting them once before, but I couldn't remember their names," he said.

"I even checked with your father at the hardware store."

"Awesome," Benjamin said as he adjusted his cap.

"Let me zoom around and head up there," Yosemite said.

The rest of the group waited on the trail as Yosemite maneuvered around a small tree and some dry brush. He swerved around and up the slope to the top of the ridge next to Benjamin's wheelchair.

"Okay, are you ready?" Yosemite asked.

The boy had the biggest smile. Yosemite carefully picked Benjamin up out of his wheelchair and gently set him on the ATV seat. He reached into the back compartment where he kept his tools and grabbed an extra helmet. Yosemite removed Benjamin's cap and replaced it with the helmet. He put the cap into the compartment, hopped on behind the boy, and fastened their seat belts.

"Okay, you hold onto this bar here in the front. Are you ready?" Yosemite asked.

"Yes, sir," Benjamin said.

Yosemite slowly backed up on the large slab of stone and turned around to go back down the ridge to the trail below. The others all greeted Benjamin as Yosemite returned to the trail where they waited. They all slowly started down the trail. Benjamin was so excited about Yosemite's offer to let him ride with them. He was also nervous and anxious about anything going wrong. He was not in his familiar wheelchair where he was in control. He put his trust in Yosemite for his safety.

This is so cool. I can't wait to tell my dad about this, Benjamin thought.

As the quads traveled past a sandy area, dust stirred up from the trail and formed a brief cloud. The boy turned and looked over the edge of a canyon, gripping the bar he held a bit tighter. Soon, they came to the rough, rocky area where the tie rod had broke on Sanarith earlier. They all took it real slow.

"Hold on tight, Benjamin. This is going to bounce us around a bit," Yosemite said.

As the angle of the quad increased, tilted, and then decreased, Benjamin held on tight. Soon, they were all past the rough area and onto the smooth trail once again.

"Can we go faster?" Benjamin asked.

Yosemite increase the speed of the ATV.

As Sierra approached Red Jacket, its bright orange, rust color lightened her ship's cockpit. Beyond Red Jacket, beautiful jeweled stars could be seen in the distance of space. She entered the atmosphere and landed the *Tenebris* on the landing pad near Maranadda's studio. Shutting down the engines, she exited the ship. Several people were on the studio's back patio. She walked toward them, her black leather jumpsuit squeaking slightly. Arrian's girlfriend, Jacquelyn Enelra, and their daughter, Sophie Enelra, had joined Vincent, Shaslin, Arcashia, and Misty and her two children on the patio. They each held a bottle of the carbonated Sevis in their hand.

"Hey, Sierra, how was the flight?" Vincent asked.

Sierra walked over to Vincent and Shaslin and gave them each a hug and kiss. The Lifestyle relationship she had with them was no secret to the rest of the group. Sierra noticed that Jacquelyn gave her a disgusted look. That was nothing new with Jackie.

"It was a long flight, as usual. Are they out on the quads?" Sierra asked.

"Yes. They came back once with little Benjamin Whitmann and then went back out again," Shaslin said. "I think Benjamin made some new friends with Aaron and Shanda here."

"That's cool," Sierra said. "So, how is everyone doing?"

"Sophie and I are leaving. My daughter doesn't need to be around a bunch of swingers," Jacquelyn said as she stood up, took Sophie's hand and left the patio.

Misty looked at her two children and then to Sierra. "Don't let Jackie get to you, Sierra. You know how she is," Misty said.

"My sex life is none of her business, the damn Jinkins!" Sierra said.

"Misty's right. You always let her get under your skin. She—" Arcashia was cut off.

"She's a bitch!" Sierra said. "The only people in the Lifestyle here are Vincent, Shaslin, and myself, none of which is any of Jackie's business!"

The sound of the five quads could be heard in the distance. As it grew louder, Sierra walked over to the patio railing and looked down at the trail. They came to a stop and turned off the engines. After removing their helmets and gear, they looked up toward the patio.

"Hey, Sierra. I'm glad to see you," Yosemite said. "Do you want to ride the quads? I'm excited about the new one I ordered."

"Not this time. They are fun, but I'm already behind schedule," Sierra said.

Arrian Trodder came up the steps to the patio first. "It's about time you got here, Sierra. Where's Jackie and Sophie?" he asked.

"Your girlfriend's a bitch. She left. The fucking Jinkins needs to stay the hell out of my business," Sierra said loudly.

Yosemite, Arvon, Kulu, and Sanarith stepped onto the patio from the stairs. They all looked at Sierra and Arrian when they heard shouting.

"What's going on?" Yosemite asked.

"She just drove Jackie away," Arrian said.

"She left on her own because she doesn't like the fact that I gave Vincent and Shaslin affection," Sierra said. "It happens every time Jackie sees me. It doesn't matter what I do. It's not like this is something new. I'm surprised she approved Arrian to come out and practice today."

"You're always starting something with her," Arrian said.

"You might want to find that *Off* button I asked you about earlier," Yosemite said.

"The Jinkins doesn't have an *Off* button," Sierra said.

"You know what? I've had enough of everyone putting down my girlfriend today. Fuck practice. I'm leaving," Arrian said and stormed off.

"Arrian, wait!" Sierra ran after him.

Shanda and Aaron looked up at their father. "Dad, what's a Jinkins?" Shanda asked.

Kulu looked at Misty. "Uh…that's a good question. You'll have to ask Sierra when she gets back," Kulu said.

"Man, she's sexy when she gets mad," Arvon said.

"Not a good time for your charm, Arvon," Yosemite said.

Sierra returned alone. The group was waiting in the studio.

"Where's Arrian?" Yosemite asked.

"We had a long discussion. I think everything is fine now. He'll be here shortly. He went to talk to Jackie."

"Sierra, what's a Jinkins?" Shanda asked

Sierra turned to the little girl with a surprised look. "A Jinkins?" she repeated. "Well, on my home planet of Asparr Celtarious, there is a group of people that have acquired a large amount of property in the Superior Mountains. They own an exclusive club in that northern mountain territory and block everyone else from seeing the beautiful mountains. They are snobs, hypocrites, and rude to others on the planet, as if they are better than everyone else. I don't put up with that shit. If you ever have a conversation with one of them, you will find they are truly stupid. They are on a committee referred to as Jinkins. So, that's why I use the term. It means idiot."

Arrian walked through the door. "Are we ready to practice?" he asked.

"Most definitely," Sanarith said.

Everyone who was not a band member stepped out of the studio and into a nearby lounge. Sierra walked over to the PA system, turned it on and made some adjustments. She then stepped in front of her microphone stand. Arrian picked up his white bass guitar and plugged in the cord as he looked at the picture of Jackie that hung next to his cabinet. Yosemite made some adjustments on his amp before plugging in his black guitar. The pointed, gothic design was one of his favorites. Sanarith took his blue guitar from its stand and grabbed a pick. Kulu activated his black keyboards and adjusted a couple of slide switches. Arvon walked behind his white drum kit and sat on the throne. He removed the long, dangling earring from his left ear, grabbed his sticks, and looked over at Vincent who was on the soundboard.

"This is our last practice before the big show on Salinarr Nevis that Shasta Varium managed to book for us. So, let's make it count," Yosemite said.

"If you're not ready for a fast-paced adventure, you might want to move over to the slow lane," Sierra Shalinsky recited her usual opening line. "Okay, let's start with Red Jacket."

They started with the song called Red Jacket, named after Maranadda's home planet. The song was from their first album, Esoteric, and covered the planet's rich mining history. It began with clean guitars, but quickly transitioned into a crunchy thrash sound, with Arvon producing an awesome double bass beat. The melodic keyboards fit in nicely as the song took a journey into Red Jacket's past. Sierra began to sing, her vocals smooth and beautiful.

"It was larger than Salinarr Nevis gold.

Red Jacket's copper tale should be told.
Desert canyon operations did impress.
Marion Calbrifae was its driving success.

"The end of an era,
Forever sealed in time.
Forlorn dissolution,
Red Jacket's history lives on.

"Historic mining proved to be strong.
Many off-worlders came along.
Laboring hard to produce red metal,
300,000 people would soon settle.

"The end of an era,
Forever sealed in time.
Forlorn dissolution,
Red Jacket's history lives on.

"Workers died and tragedies weighed.
A community was built, billions were made.
The company lived on for one hundred years.
Its epic success seldom occurs.

"The end of an era,
Forever sealed in time.
Forlorn dissolution,
Red Jacket's history lives on."

The song soon came to an end, the distorted guitar reverberating into silence.

"Vincent, increase the low end just a bit," Yosemite said.

Vincent made some adjustments.

"Next, we're going to play the much darker theme song, Alchemy," Sierra said.

Chapter Two

Gathin slowly walked along the elegantly carpeted corridor of the casino. He wore a semi-formal outfit and his shoulder-length, brown hair was styled with mousse, its natural curls full. He so badly wanted to hold Eslarr's bluish-gray hand, but it was forbidden. The love he felt for the Xenolfan female was very strong. Looking up at her beautiful face, he smiled. She wore a stylish outfit that accentuated her bluish-gray cleavage. A short, gray skirt revealed most of her long, bluish-gray thighs that were decorated with black fishnet stockings. Eslarr stood several centimeters taller than Gathin. As they walked along the burgundy corridor, Eslarr looked at Gathin and smiled back. They had met using a network platform and would occasionally meet on Salinarr Nevis to actually see each other in person, even though the two species being together was considered taboo by the Xenolfan Government.

"Our feelings toward each other are mutual. It hurts me that we have to walk around Salinarr Nevis on egg shells because of my government's prejudice against our relationship," Eslarr said.

"I know, Eslarr. But I won't let that stop us from being together. I love you," Gathin said.

"I love you too, Gathin. We must be careful on Salinarr Nevis. The walls have ears. If this gets back to the Xenolfan Government on Olf Teruda, our leader will have a fit a rage," she said.

She briefly held his hands as they stopped in the corridor. The moment was short-lived as a Xenolfan casino official walked by and gave the two of them dirty looks.

"That's a disgrace..." he said as he walked by.

They watched him disappear around a corner.

"He just killed my casino fun," Gathin said.

"Oh, no he didn't. Let's head on over to the Lucky Stone. I won some big credits there once," Eslarr said, brushing her long, white hair back.

"I love your enthusiasm, Eslarr," he said.

They continued walking down the corridor of the Blue Sapphire casino, heading for the exit. The evening sky of Salinarr Nevis was a welcomed sight. The dark sky contrasted all the bright lights of the thousands of casinos that littered the planet. The red and blue lights flashed overhead from a casino known as Auracon's Game. The streets were crowded with people, busy with their gaming and entertainment activities. The heat outside was tremendous. Gathin could not wait until they were back inside the air-conditioned environment. Many of the casinos were connected to keep exiting at a minimum. They passed Aaranix's Gold, a casino named after the leader of the Xenolfan Government. It had an impressive golden logo that lit up the evening sky. Soon, they walked past Casino 21, The Wolf's Den, and Golden Oasis.

"Do you want to stop for a bite to eat before we go to the Lucky Stone?" Eslarr asked.

"Yeah, I am a bit hungry," Gathin said.

"Okay. I know this perfect restaurant inside Lightyear's Treasure that has an awesome menu," she said.

"Nice. Lead the way, my love," he said.

Eslarr turned a corner, Gathin following closely. As they maneuvered through the crowd, they passed another casino named The Ascent. Eslarr tolerated the outdoor heat much more than Gathin, as she was accustomed to higher temperatures on her home planet of Olf Teruda. The humid air was actually pleasant to her. Soon, they entered the doors of Lightyear's Treasure. The cool air inside the casino relieved Gathin. Noise of the outside street bustle was replaced with the many games dinging and spinning. Gathin followed Eslarr to the restaurant section. They stopped at the stand and waited for the hostess to seat them.

"This is very nice, Eslarr. Thank you for the suggestion."

"You are quite welcome."

The hostess led them to a secluded area of the restaurant, most likely because it was a human and a Xenolfan eating together. The restaurant did not want the extra attention.

"They are doing us a favor," Eslarr said. "We have our own private area."

They sat down in the secluded booth and made themselves comfortable. Green plants decorated a ledge behind their booth, the vases a pleasant antique beige color. A candle was lit on the table, its aroma a wonderful fruit scent.

"Did you know that we Xenolfans used to have wings thousands of years ago?" Eslarr asked.

"Really?"

"Yes. Over time microevolution stripped them from us. There hasn't been a Xenolfan born with wings for at least a millennium."

"That's fascinating."

"The only way I can fly is in a ship," she said, laughing.

"So, Salinarr Nevis was developed to compensate the Xenolfan Government for the old Syrenthian War that happened over one hundred years ago?" Gathin asked.

"Yes, when the Syrenthian Government admitted to its wrongdoing and both governments agreed to letting my people's government have this planet to establish the gaming casinos, it was a new era for the two governments. There would have been no way for your government to financially undergo reparations. So, Salinarr Nevis was really a win-win for both governments. The Xenolfan Government is raking in so many credits from this gaming planet, you would never even believe it. Behind every casino on Salinarr Nevis, there is a powerful Xenolfan business owner who gives a large percentage to the Xenolfan Government," Eslarr said as she grabbed a menu.

"From what I read, we humans treated Xenolfans terribly back in the day. I don't know how they could have been so ignorant. Eslarr, you are totally awesome. You arouse me like no human female ever has."

"Well, these days, it seems that it has shifted in the other direction. The Xenolfan Government does not treat humans very well. My own government embarrasses me…especially for their view on Xenolfan and human unions and sexual pleasure. Sadly, I don't foresee it changing any time soon. I know a lot of work has been done for sexual freedom in recent years and even we Xenolfans have the sex clinics now as well. But until they recognize that Xenolfans and humans have the right to be together, you and I will live in tyranny," she said.

"I'll do whatever it takes for us to be together. It's not fair, Eslarr," he said as he paged through the menu.

Eslarr gazed at him with her bluish-gray face, her beautiful sapphire eyes filling with tears. "We can do this," she said, squeezing his hand.

The Xenolfan waiter arrived at their table to take their orders. He had the look of surprise when he saw them holding hands. Eslarr quickly let go of Gathin's hands and placed her order. Gathin followed with his order and the waiter left the table.

"So, how lucky is the Lucky Stone?" Gathin asked.

"They have some loose machines in there. I'm sure we will come out ahead," Eslarr said.

Soon, the Xenolfan waiter returned with their orders. He set their drinks down first, followed by the plates. His bluish-gray hands quickly let go of the hot plates. The aroma of the food was mouthwatering. Eslarr had ordered Quillexx, a popular meat from her home planet of Olf Teruda, along with some vegetables. Gathin had ordered the house salad, topped with poultry.

"Be careful of those plates; they are a bit warm," the waiter said.

"Thank you," Gathin said.

The waiter looked around the room and turned back to them. "My surprised look earlier was a good surprise. I am all for our species intermixing. It is well documented that our two species can't breed. We know it's biologically impossible. So, why not have fun trying? Do you know where all the mixed couples go to hook up for sex? Aamaress. It's kind of a secret, so be careful with that information. I got your back," he said.

"You mean Aamaress, as in the snow planet?" Eslarr asked.

"Yes. The Avalanche Resort is the name of the place on Aamaress where you can be together without fear. From what I hear, it's beautiful there. I wanted to take my human girlfriend there, but we broke up. We just couldn't handle the tension from other Xenolfans here on

Salinarr Nevis. It was just too much for our relationship. So, I wish you two the best. Go to Aamaress. Have some fun with each other," the waiter said as he left the table.

Eslarr and Gathin stared at each other with the biggest smiles. They both picked up their utensils and started eating the lavish meal.

"I can't believe we've never heard of this place before. I'm getting really excited, Eslarr," he said.

"This news is arousing me so much. I can't believe how wet I am right now. I want nothing more than to ride you right now, Gathin," she said with a reverberating purr.

"When we're all done at the Lucky Stone, I'm going to search for the coordinates to Aamaress. Maybe we can fly there soon," Gathin said.

"Yeah, but I'm sure it's not cheap," Eslarr said.

"Whatever it is, it'll be worth it," he said. "I've been fantasizing about being with you for a long time, my love."

"And I with you," she said.

As they slowly ate their meals, the endless possibilities crossed their minds.

"Do you think they marry couples there?" Gathin asked.

"I have no idea, but we will find out," Eslarr said.

The waiter came back with the bill. "There is no rush on this. Would you like a refill on your beverages?" he asked.

"No thanks. We will be leaving shortly. But we want to thank you so very much for the information. You just made our day," Gathin said.

"I'm glad I could help. Good luck. And dress warm on Aamaress. I hear it's freezing there," the waiter said.

When the waiter disappeared to the main section of the dining room, Gathin left the largest tip he had ever given at a restaurant before.

The Lucky Stone was connected to Lightyear's Treasure through a small connecting passageway. The air temperature was comfortable as they entered the Lucky Stone. The sound of many games dinging filled their ears. Eslarr led Gathin over to one of her favorite games. He followed her and sat down in the chair next to hers.

"This is my all-time favorite game," she said, putting her card into the slot. "You can set the bet to whatever you want and then you press the spin button. If you are lucky, you will get to make the big wheel spin up above. Let's try this."

She set her bet on the lowest setting and hit the spin button. The reels turned and aligned to a matching set of images. The credits began to increase. She lost a few, but gained many more credits as the reels kept lining up matching images. When she was up seventy credits, the reels aligned the big wheels across the display. She smiled at Gathin.

"Here we go. I get to spin the big wheel," she said.

A large wheel appeared above the reels. Eslarr reached up and spun the wheel. It rotated through the wedges that contained various prizes. When it stopped on the major wedge of 21,000 credits, Eslarr gasped. The machine started making a continuous beeping sound.

"Is that what I think it is?" Gathin asked.

"It sure is!" Eslarr exclaimed.

A Xenolfan female gaming attendant came over to the spin game and worked with Eslarr to transfer 21,000 credits to her financial account. Everything seemed to be going in slow motion for Eslarr. The excitement of her reverberating vocal cords caught the attention of the other patrons closest to her machine. When she cashed out her remaining seventy credits, they played a few more machines. Gathin thought it was quite fun. Before too long, they left the Lucky Stone.

"I cannot believe I won that much. This is so exciting," Eslarr said.

A lot of attention was drawn to them and it made Gathin feel a bit uncomfortable because of the mixed species situation.

"Well, one thing is for sure. We can afford to go the The Avalanche Resort on Aamaress now," Eslarr said.

The thought had not occurred to Gathin until she mentioned it. His jaw dropped and was replaced with a big smile.

"I will search for the coordinates to Aamaress as soon as I get back to my ship," he said.

Like all of the thousands of casinos on Salinarr Nevis, the Lucky Stone had cameras and microphones throughout the facility. When an informant for the Xenolfan Government picked up on Eslarr and Gathin's conversation about going to Aamaress together, he immediately reported it to the Xenolfan Government headquarters on the paradise planet of Olf Teruda. The Xenolfan Government had been trying to find the secret rendezvous planet for years. Because Salinarr Nevis was such an attraction to both species, it was the perfect place to set up operations to collect information. It was only a matter of time before they found out the secret location. One such attraction to gather information was a casino called Sex Palace where patrons could watch a theater performance of humans or Xenolfans having sex behind glass windows. The two species were always in separated theaters, but patrons from both species were allowed to sit together, unsegregated, to watch the sexual play.

The informant turned on a comm next to his desk. He gazed at the many displays in front of him as he monitored the Lucky Stone.

"I need to speak directly to Aaranix Tuvelless right away. I have some information that he has been searching for," he said.

After several minutes of waiting, the informant was greeted by the leader of the Xenolfan Government.

"Dellagg, what do you have for me?" Aaranix Tuvelless asked.

"I just learned the location of the planet where Xenolfans and humans are meeting up for the forbidden unions and unorthodox sexual relations," Dellagg said.

"Do you know how long I've been waiting for this information? Too long. What is the planet where the forbidden xeno tryst takes place?" Aaranix asked.

"Aamaress," Dellagg said.

"The snow planet with the human resort?"

"Apparently, it is not just for humans," Dellagg said.

"Thank you for the information, Dellagg," Aaranix said. "These liaisons are about to come to an end."

Dellagg could hear the anger in the Xenolfan leader's voice as he turned off the comm.

Aaranix Tuvelless turned off the comm and stood up from his large desk, his skin tone turning from bluish-gray to a mild bluish-purple. It was the result of his extreme anger. He picked up a chair and threw it across the room in a violent fit of rage. It came crashing down and slid into a shelf with a loud clatter.

Damn them and their twisted relations! he thought.

He walked from his desk across the stone floor to a large window that overlooked the outside of the government palace. Aaranix's office was on the second level of the government palace. He gazed past the ancient stone pillars along his terrace to the blue water below.

Opening the door, he stepped out onto the terrace. Olf Teruda was a paradise planet and the seat of the Xenolfan Government. Its stunning scenery was envied by many humans.

Aaranix needed to cool his temper. He breathed the fresh, humid air as he listened to the continuous, thundering crash of the distant waterfalls. Vines wrapped around the gray stone pillars and terrace railing that lay before him, matching the greens of the surrounding jungle. The Xenolfan Government palace was almost camouflaged within the Olf Teruda jungle paradise. Tall palm trees cast shadows across the stone terrace, darkening the two outdoor benches. The blue waters of the pond below were fed by the continuous flow from several beautiful waterfalls upstream. A few of the waterfalls drained over the green covered rocks across the pond, falling from a few different heights. The main waterfall was centered at the mouth of the pond, its wider span flowing out from under a couple of natural bridges. The natural bridges were decorated with greens and browns. Beyond the natural arches, a splendid 600 meter waterfall dropped from a split rock at the top where the river merged together. Above the split rock, majestic mountains could be seen in the distance, their igneous rock peaks decorated with snow.

Aaranix sat down on one of the two stone benches that overlooked the beautiful pond. His skin tone returned to its normal shade, including his patterned face. Only Xenolfan males had patterns on their faces. He tugged at his long, white hair as he looked at the scenery before him. The water was so clear, he could see the fish swimming in its depths. For many years, he had been searching for the secret location where the Xenolfans and humans were meeting up for sex, marriage, and forbidden unions.

Aamaress, he thought.

As leader of the Xenolfans, at one time, he alone had access to the ancient records in the archives below the palace. Unfortunately, the chambers were flooded by the pond many years ago, and ruined all the ancient documents and historical records. Before the archives were flooded, Aaranix was studying in the archives and had discovered the truth about the union between the Xenolfans and the humans and what it would lead to. From that point forward, he forbade his people to have sexual relations with humans. He could not prove this truth because the evidence was destroyed, but he didn't need to, for he was the leader of the Xenolfans and his restrictions were honored by most of his people. For the ones who did not honor him, they would soon learn to.

He knew the resort on the snow planet of Aamaress received shipments of snowmobiles for traveling along its trails. He also knew they received and needed thermal cubes for heat in order to keep warm on the cold planet. Both the snowmobiles and thermal cubes were manufactured in the Industrial Sector. He put his bluish-gray finger to his mouth in thought and then smiled.

Gathin settled in the pilot's seat of his ship. He found the coordinates to Aamaress relatively easy from his ship's navigation system. He transferred the location to Eslarr's ship as well. It was too risky to leave together in the same ship. Traveling to The Avalanche Resort on Aamaress separately was much less conspicuous and safer. He assumed that most interspecies couples traveled to the liaison separately. To play it safe, they first planned to travel to a decoy point in a far region of space, lightyears from Aamaress. From there, they would travel at lightspeed-plus directly to Aamaress. Eslarr settled into her large ship and programmed the coordinates that Gathin had sent her. They were both anxious during their long flights, not knowing what to expect on Aamaress. Was the waiter at the restaurant telling the truth? He seemed to be genuine. They would soon find out.

Upon arriving in the Aamaress Star System, both Eslarr and Gathin could see the bluish-white planet in the distance ahead of them, its beauty decorated by two gray moons. As they activated the anti-gravitation on their ships, they descended through the clouds and blowing snow of the atmosphere.

"It looks very cold out there," Eslarr said over the comm.

"Yes, it does. Follow me to the multi-level docking bay I discovered near The Avalanche Resort," Gathin said.

"I'm right behind you," she said.

The two ships slowly flew along the snow-covered landscape toward The Avalanche Resort. White pine tress were visible through the observation window. The pine forest extended far into the distance. The snow-capped mountains were a majestic sight. As they approached the resort, they could see the docking bay. Light snow flakes fell from the sky as they entered the rectangular opening of the docking bay. They each found an area to park. Eslarr put on some warmer clothes before exiting her ship. Gathin grabbed a warm jacket from the back of his ship.

After meeting up in the concrete facility, they took each others hand and kissed right in the bay. It was a lengthy, passionate kiss. Gathin recalled only briefly kissing Eslarr once before when they found a secluded spot on an earlier date. Her long tongue filled his mouth, its warmth a welcomed surprise. It was bluish-gray as well, but with a pink tint to it. He could feel the cold breeze blowing through the docking bay as it shifted his shoulder-length, brown hair. He looked deep into her sapphire eyes and she pulled back and smiled. The rush of his semi-erect cock made him blush.

"I'm sorry your government is so anthrophobic or xenophobic. I'm not even sure which term we should use. This connection, these released emotions…they feel so good to let out, Eslarr," Gathin said.

"That's an understatement. I'm so wet right now, Gathin. You know, you're a good kisser? Hey, let's get out of this cold and into the lodge," Eslarr said.

"Let's."

They entered a skywalk that connected the docking bay to the lodge. It was much warmer inside the skywalk with thermal cubes visibly setting along either side of the corridor, radiating their heat. From the windows, they could see some of the surrounding area. Snow covered the ground with a beautiful white blanket. Humans and Xenolfans alike could be seen in the court below, some on snowmobiles, others carrying skis. The Avalanche Resort rested at the foot of a mountain. The skywalk opened up onto a balcony that overlooked the entire grand foyer of the lodge. A large stone fireplace was directly across from the balcony. Taxidermied wolves and other wild animals were displayed on shelves located high on the stone walls of the grand foyer. The rustic log and stone design was very appealing. Eslarr and Gathin started down a wide carpeted staircase that led to the grand foyer floor. They held each other's hand tight.

Tonight is going to be absolutely incredible, Gathin thought.

The Avalanche Resort had other locations in the remote Northern Territories with cabins in wooded settings and even a separate lodge in the remote town of Winterfest. They decided against renting a rustic cabin in the snow-laden pine forest and settled with a room right in the main lodge. The human receptionist at the counter was very helpful. She gave them a room key and explained the easiest way to find it. Their room was just up a small staircase and down the corridor on the left. The resort was well decorated with an outdoors theme. They entered the room and the door closed behind them with a loud thud. The silence in their suite was deafening. It made them both feel a bit awkward for a moment. They set the bags they had each brought with them from their own ships down onto the floor.

"Are you okay?" Eslarr asked.

"Yes, yes. I'm just a bit nervous," Gathin said.

"Oh, there's nothing to be nervous about. This time we share together will be beautiful," she said.

She walked over to him and put her long arms around him. He adored her sapphire eyes. Her lips met his and their tongues merged together. The lengthy kiss aroused them both. She brushed her long, white hair back and slowly undressed Gathin. In turn, he removed her clothing to reveal a sexy, blue teddy bodysuit. It matched both the ribbon in her hair and her sapphire eyes. He put his arm around her and she rested her hand on his shoulder as they looked deep into each others eyes for a long moment. He felt the genetic remainder of bumps on her back where Xenolfan wings had been on their species once upon a time.

"I see you've found the spot where my ancestors wings used to be."

"Yes. That is fascinating. I love you."

"I love you too," Eslarr returned.

She rolled down her black fishnet stockings, tossed them aside, and then removed the teddy bodysuit. Her bare bluish-gray skin further aroused Gathin. She had never been with a human before and was in awe of his tan body. She noticed a tattoo of a beautiful wolf on his left side.

"That's a pretty awesome wolf tattoo, Gathin," she said.

"Yes. That tattoo artist does amazing work," he said.

Eslarr saw that he was well groomed below the waist. Fascinated with his erect cock, she reached out to caress his smooth balls and slowly slid her hand up his shaft, taking a moment to rub the head.

"Xenolfan males don't have heads on their cocks. This is going to feel nice inside of me," she said, tilting her head.

She opened her mouth and took his cock, wrapping her long tongue around it. The sensation Gathin felt was so intense, he grabbed the bed with both hands.

"Ahhh! Eslarr, that feels so good."

She smiled at him and he could hear and feel her low reverberating purr that vibrated down his shaft and into his balls. She began to suck up and down on his hard cock repeatedly, taking a few moments to release it and lick down its entire length to the balls below before continuing to suck. She was absolutely fascinated with the head of his cock. She could soon taste the drops of his pre-cum and knew it was time to slow it down a bit. She stood up and they kissed once again.

"That felt so good, Eslarr," he said.

Gathin began to massage her bluish-gray breasts, their purplish nipples becoming firm. He gently sucked and kissed them as he continued to embrace their smooth texture. He slowly kissed down her mid section. She moved up onto the bed and parted her legs, revealing the full view of her alien pussy. Gathin had been with several human females in past relationships, but never before had he been with a Xenolfan female. Her vulva was smooth and similar to her human counterparts, but the vaginal orifice was a reuleaux triangle shape. Like her tongue, her labia had a bluish-pink tint. Gathin slowly kissed along her thighs and then focused all of his attention on her pussy. As he licked between the folds, he found that she had a very pleasant taste. With her arousal, a drop of thin, white cream dripped down from her slit to her firm ass. He licked at her cum and slowly made his way up the thin, moist lips to her clitoris. As he concentrated on her most sensitive spot, she let out a high-pitched, reverberating sound of excitement that would have been piercing to his ears had they not been covered by her thighs.

"Oh, Gathin, eat my pussy! Oh yes!" she said in a reverberating tone.

He gently sucked at the folds of the labia and kissed along her clit, looking up into her sapphire eyes.

"You have the most delicious, beautiful pussy ever," he said with a wet smile.

She lightly held his head in place as he continued to please her. Soon, her high-pitched excitement echoed throughout their suite as she reached an incredible orgasm, her fingernails digging deep into the fabric of the bed. A small amount of milky-white cum flowed out from her pussy and dripped onto the comforter. As she lay on her back,

Gathin rubbed her thighs and moved in closer with his swollen cock. He rubbed the tip of his head in her milky-white cum and slid the bottom of his cock against her smooth, wet lips several times before slowly inserting it into the bluish-pink folds. Immediately, he could feel the heat that she radiated envelop his throbbing erection. Unlike nothing he had felt before, she squeezed his cock with an intense muscle that made him feel absolutely wonderful.

"Wow, Eslarr! That feels amazing."

"You like that?"

She squeezed some more as he slowly thrust his hard cock deep into her triangular hole. The creamy sound they made together while fucking aroused them further. She parted her mouth slightly as she looked down at the contrast of his tan shaft sliding into her bluish-pink pussy. Gathin briefly withdrew his cock from her and took a moment to bury his face between her thighs, licking at her wetness. Once again, he mounted her and they moved through the natural motions. They slowed to a stop while he was buried deep inside of her and rolled slightly on the bed, holding each other tight. He took the opportunity to kiss her breasts once again. As they casually moved their hips in perfect harmony, she rolled over on top of him and squatted, hovering over his slippery member. Slowly, she lowered herself down onto him and bounced up and down with such precision. She smiled down at him and moaned with that familiar purr. For Gathin, the moment was surreal, like a dream. He was so ecstatic that he could finally be with Eslarr, the one he loved. She soon lay down on his chest, her breasts warm against his body. She rode his cock hard, grinding down onto it with all of her might as she felt an intense orgasm rip through her entire body. Her piercing screech that followed was extremely loud. He too reached an incredible climax and groaned loudly as he burst inside of her warm, creamy pussy, his cock rhythmically pulsating. They both lay still on the bed in silence for some time, their arms embracing each other. He slowly withdrew his cock from her and lay back against the soft pillow, his eyes half closed from exhaustion. She reached over and squeezed his hand, turning in his direction. Her warm smile could have melted his heart. He looked over at her. A single tear rolled down her left cheek.

"I love you, Gathin. I've never felt joy like you have given me. Sorry if I pierced your hearing with my screams. I just… Wow!" she said.

"Eslarr, I love you too. That was so beautiful. You make me all fluttery inside. And my ears are just fine," he said, smiling.

"I wonder how many couples come her just for the sex, who are not really in it for the love, like we are," Eslarr said.

"I don't know. I would imagine that the majority is for sex only, with no strings attached. The fact that sexual infections have been eliminated from the Syrenthian Galaxy for both of our species and that it is impossible for our two species to breed makes it all the more pleasurable to fuck bareback with no worries," Gathin said.

"And pleasurable, it is," she said.

"Our stay here on Aamaress is going to be so awesome. I know we've talked about getting married. Are you up for the challenge that it will have for us?" he asked.

She sighed. "It will be tough, but I believe we can get through it. Plus, we can come here anytime to get away from the judgmental idiots," she said.

"So, are you up for some snowmobiling?"

"You bet I am," she said. "Let's clean ourselves up and go down to that store in the grand foyer to buy some warmer clothes."

Chapter Three

The distorted guitar feedback through the amp came to a crunchy halt as Maranadda finished their last song of practice. It was a song written about an uncharted, desolate, and mysterious part of the Syrenthian Galaxy called the Shardaa Sector, which was generally avoided by space travelers. Many tales of strange happenings that were reported from the Shardaa Sector over the years were incorporated into the lyrics of the song.

"Tales of Shardaa is such a dark and badass song," Arvon said.

"The whole Esoteric album is badass," Yosemite said.

"Well, that about wraps it up. I need a drink of water," Sierra said.

"The next time we meet will be here on Red Jacket to pack up for the big show on Salinarr Nevis. It's coming up soon," Sanarith said.

"At least your job didn't call you for a galactic emergency, like they have done during so many other practices," Arrian said.

"Yes. Since I'm always on call as a Galactic Emergency Medical Technician, it was nice to get through a practice for once…especially this important practice before the big show," Sierra said.

"I really like that new sound you added to the song on the

keyboards, Kulu," Yosemite said.

"Yeah, I came up with that last night and figured I would add it. It gives it a dark and ominous vibe and fits perfectly with the song," Kulu said.

Vincent killed the power to the soundboard and started organizing cords.

"Are you okay, Vincent?" Yosemite asked.

"Yes. I'm just a bit nervous about the set-up I'll need to do on Salinarr Nevis. That will be larger than any venue we've played at so far," Vincent said.

"They have a team of Xenolfans that will help with the set-up. You'll do just fine," Yosemite said.

"I hope so. I want it to sound perfect since there will be thousands of fans there," Vincent said.

"Well, the only fan we had today was the one on the back of Arrian's amp," Arvon said.

They all laughed.

"It sounds like you need to get your mind off the sound for a while. You need to relax, Vincent. How about you and Shaslin come with me to Salinarr Nevis? We can get our game on, have some fun, and check out the venue that you are so concerned about," Sierra said.

Vincent looked at Sierra's sexy smile. He knew what her fun would involve and smiled back at her.

"I think you're right, Sierra. I will go get Shaslin and we can head out soon," Vincent said.

"You guys suck," Arvon said from behind his drum kit.

"Well, Arvon, you'll always have the sex clinics that Sierra helped to establish," Kulu said.

"Ha, it's not the same," Arvon said.

Arvon knew he would never have a chance with Sierra, but also would never stop trying. Vincent left the studio and found his wife, Shaslin, in the lounge with Arcashia, Misty, and the children.

"Shaslin, Sierra invited us to go to Salinarr Nevis. Would you like to go?" Vincent asked.

Shaslin smiled. "Of course. We need to get off Red Jacket and go have some fun," she said.

She had to be careful of what she said around Misty's children. But she knew what this meant and started becoming aroused.

"When do we leave?" Shaslin asked.

"In just a little bit here," Vincent said.

"Practice sounded great," Misty said.

"Definitely," Arcashia said.

"Yes, Maranadda is ready to headline the big show," Vincent said.

Sierra popped her head in the door. "Are you two ready?"

"Yes," Vincent said.

Shaslin stood up from the couch and walked toward Vincent who stood next to the door.

"We'll need to fly separately. You know I'm always on call for Galactic Emergency Medical Services," Sierra said.

"That's fine. Would you like to meet at our usual casino and hotel?" Shaslin asked.

"You know it," Sierra said.

The three of them left the lounge.

Sierra could see the bright lights of Salinarr Nevis in the distance of space as she looked through the observation window of the *Tenebris*. She would arrive in two lightminutes. Vincent and Shaslin were not far behind her. As she approached the planet, she made some adjustments on the control panel and the anti-gravitation was enabled. Passing through the thin, gray clouds, she flew toward her favorite gaming district. Ahead of her, she could see the specific docking bay that she usually parked in, its evenly-spaced lights surrounding the opening. She entered the bay and found an open spot to land. After she finished the power-down cycle, she exited the old fighter ship canopy and headed for the casino.

Moments later, Vincent and Shaslin settled their ship on a different level of the same docking bay. Once they grabbed a few things from the back of the ship, they stepped out and onto the concrete floor of the docking bay. They walked to the entrance of the casino. After walking through several corridors, they spotted Sierra waiting for them on a bench outside the gaming room. She saw them coming and smiled.

"Fancy meeting you here," Sierra said.

"Yes, what a coincidence," Shaslin said, laughing.

"We always seem to meet at the Sex Palace. I wonder why," Sierra said, jokingly.

Sierra stood up and walked toward them. Vincent brushed his long, brown hair aside and they gave each other hugs. Then their mouths joined, their warm tongues merging together in a hot, three-way kiss.

"Mmm, you two turn me on," Sierra said.

"And you turn us on," Shaslin said.

"I've already checked us into our hotel," Sierra said.

"Wonderful. Thank you," Shaslin said.

As swingers in the Lifestyle, they enjoyed the Sex Palace casino because every game had a sexual theme to it. There was a section in the casino where scheduled sex events would take place. The patrons were able to view the sex shows through windows from the observation seating area. Of course, the humans and the Xenolfans had their own separate sex show theater rooms. The voyeuristic patrons of either species could observe either of the two sex show theater rooms.

"So, what do you guys want to do first?" Sierra asked.

"Let's play some games, eat dinner, watch some live sex, and then have some fun of our own," Vincent said.

"That sounds good to me," Sierra said. "We can check out the venue where Maranadda will be playing before we leave Salinarr Nevis."

"Most definitely," Vincent said.

They turned around and opened the doors to the gaming room. The familiar sound of the games filled their ears with dinging and chimes, but was distinctively accompanied by arousing electronic sounds of sex emitting from many of the games. The game themes were a huge turn-on for the guests.

Sierra walked over to her favorite game and inserted some credits. The object was to have the reels line up across the machine, completing the penis insertion into the spinning vagina. She spun the reels. They spun around and slowly came to a stop, revealing balls, tits, and more balls.

"Damn Jinkins!" Sierra exclaimed.

She spun it again and it stopped at tits, tits, and more tits. Vincent and Shaslin stood next to her.

"Nice. Three tits in a row," Vincent said.

They all looked up at the display toward the top of the machine. A large set of boobs became a live video and bounced around for a bit, celebrating the small win of a few credits. She spun the reels again and they stopped at a cock, cum, and a pussy.

"It looks like you got a coitus interruptus. Oh well. Keep trying,"

Shaslin said.

The two-seater game opened up next to Sierra. Vincent and Shaslin took advantage of the opening and sat down to play the game. It was a progressive game with a bondage theme. It already had a large jackpot of 54,000 credits. Shaslin inserted some credits into the machine and selected max bet. A Xenolfan female member of the staff walked by in a very sexy and revealing outfit, offering drinks. The ladies were too busy playing their games, but Vincent accepted drinks for all three of them. For himself, he received the sweet carbonated beverage, Sevis, and for the ladies, a couple of ales. He took a long drink and focused on Shaslin's second play. The game had five lines across the screen. It stopped and the first line had an image of a tall, sexy woman bent over, getting spanked with a flogger. The second and third lines were the same image. That meant she would receive ten free games. The fourth line was the image of a woman in an elegant mask and the fifth was of a man in leather. The free games started as Shaslin took a drink of her ale. Vincent and Shaslin sat and watched the machine flow through its series of bondage images. When the ten free games ended, the display revealed a flogger, a pinwheel, a ball gag, a rope, and a slapper.

"You're up fifty credits, Shaslin," Vincent said.

"I'm not really into this game," Shaslin said, hitting the collect button.

Suddenly, they heard Sierra shout in excitement and looked over at the game next to them. Sierra's reels lined up to the balls, cock, and pussy for the major prize of 800 credits.

"Now that's a good fuck," Vincent said.

They all laughed and Sierra hit the collect button as well. She quickly finished her drink and stood up.

"Are you guys getting hungry?" Sierra asked.

"I'm starving," Shaslin said.

"Yeah, me too," Vincent said. "All I had was cake earlier."

"Would you like something from the intoxication joint in here, or would you prefer a nice restaurant?" Sierra asked.

"The intoxication joint," Vincent said.

"A nice restaurant," Shaslin said at the same time.

"I'll let you two work that out, but dinner is on me since I won 800 credits," Sierra said.

"Awesome!" Shaslin said.

"Okay, fine. We'll go to a nice restaurant," Vincent said.

"There is a great restaurant toward the back of the casino, not far from the Sex Palace Theater," Sierra said.

They headed in that direction, passing a large spinning penis game. The large, inflated penis that was connected to the game came around and swung close to the walking path of the isle as they passed by. Vincent turned around and looked at the guy playing the game who had full control over the direction of the penis.

"Don't be a dick!" Vincent said to the guy.

Both Vincent and the man started laughing. The three of them continued toward the restaurant at the back of the Sex Palace. When they arrived, there was no wait for seating. They were led to a booth near a fountain of flowing water in the center of the restaurant's dining area. Statues were evenly spaced around the circular fountain. The off-white marble sculptures represented several different sexual positions. They alternated between human couples and Xenolfan couples. The closest statue to their table was of a human couple and had the woman on top facing backwards. Both of their legs were spread open to reveal a full view of his cock inside of her as she leaned back toward him. They tilted their heads at the Xenolfan sculpture beyond. The other sculptures around the fountain were just as arousing. A refreshing mist of water sprayed over them from the fountain. They all looked at each other.

"That looks fun," Sierra said.

"Yes, it does. You two need to do that and then I can easily get between your legs and give you both a licking that you won't soon forget," Shaslin said.

"Nice. I can't wait," Vincent said with a smile.

They looked over the menus that lay on the table before them. Soon, the Xenolfan waitress came by and took their orders.

"The Sex Palace is the only sex-themed casino on Salinarr Nevis. And as an add-on to the casino, they recently opened up a new sex mall that we absolutely need to check out," Sierra said.

"I heard there are stores and shops all along the mall corridor relating to sex," Vincent said.

"They also have sex carriage rides along the mall corridor where you can get in and have some sexy fun while riding up and down the mall corridor," Shaslin said.

"That should be our next stop after we eat," Vincent said.

"You missed a good swinger party, Sierra," Shaslin said.

"Yeah? Was that the one over on Enax Port?" Sierra asked.

"Yes, it was. What an awesome party!" Vincent said.

"Well, I was broken that week. It seems like my damn monthly always flows when there's a good party," Sierra said.

"And we thought you missed the party because you wanted to hang around vanilla people," Vincent said. "I'm just joking!"

"You better be, ya damn Jinkins! Now that you mention it, I was around a bunch of vanillas that evening. I had previous obligations with my non-Lifestyle friends," Sierra said.

"Well, you'll just have to go to the next party. Enax Port is such a fun planet for Lifestyle parties," Shaslin said.

"And there were several unicorns at the party. One of them was this hot blonde. Mmm," Vincent said.

"She was hot, but I'm not into squirters," Shaslin said.

"It all eats the same," Vincent said.

"Speaking of eating, our food's here," Sierra said.

The waitress soon approached with their orders. As she set the plates in front of them, the mouthwatering aroma rose to meet their senses.

"Mmm, this stuffed pie smells so good," Vincent said.

Sierra smiled at the waitress and studied her bluish-gray figure as she walked away. Shaslin noticed Sierra's gaze.

"You want that Xenolfan, don't you?" Shaslin said.

Sierra smiled and said, "I've never been with a Xenolfan before, male nor female. I think it would be fun. It is one of my desires. Priscilla Stryderr and I have advocated for Xenolfan and human interspecies sex and relationships for some time now. Priscilla even went to Olf Teruda to convince the Xenolfan leader that the forbidden relationships are nonsense. Of course, it did no good. Part of the sexual freedom speech I will soon be presenting on Red Jacket covers precisely that."

"The human government doesn't forbid the interspecies relationships. It's only the Xenolfan Government, correct?" Vincent asked.

"Yes. Mainly, their leader, Aaranix Tuvelless, and his close dignitaries are the ones who forbid it," Sierra said, taking a bite of her food.

"You know you have done great things across the Syrenthian Galaxy in the name of sexual freedom, Sierra," Shaslin said. "Like the sex clinics for both species, for instance."

"Well, I appreciate the kind words. I have advocated for sexual freedom for a long time, but there has been collaboration on many of the projects. I'm only one person and I can't advocate for everything. I stick to the things I feel most passionate about, like health, the swinger Lifestyle, bisexuality, and interspecies sexual freedom. There are other people that can advocate for all the things that I don't cover. I can't do it all," she said.

"You deserve better recognition for all that you've already done…more than you've received," Vincent said.

"It's been fun, but seriously, I'm very tired of being blacklisted by people because of our Lifestyle. It gets old, you know," Sierra said. "Especially when we have do deal with haters like Jackie and my boss, Madison."

"Hang in there, Sierra. You have plenty of support," Vincent said.

"Hey, we are here to have some fun. Let's stay positive," Shaslin said as she ate her meal.

After dinner, they made their way to the new sex mall, which was adjacent to the main Sex Palace casino game room. As they slowly walked along the corridor, they noticed many of the stores had specific sexual products they specialized in. Vincent and Shaslin followed Sierra into a store that sold personal massagers of all sorts. There was an assortment of vibrators, dildos, artificial vulvas, and more. Sierra slowly browsed at the displays and picked up one of the smooth Xenolfan male dildos and studied it for a brief moment before putting it back. It was bluish-gray and looked similar to an ovipositor with an angled end. The reuleaux triangle shaped dildo was quite interesting.

"That looks like it would feel really good inside of me," Sierra said.

Shaslin looked at a human double-ended dildo. "Mmm," she said, looking at Sierra.

The Xenolfan female store clerk walked over to the three of them and smiled.

"Can I help you find anything specific?" she asked with a slight reverberating tone.

"What is the cost of this Xenolfan male dildo?" Sierra asked.

"I'm sorry. We can only sell human toys to humans and only sell

Xenolfan toys to Xenolfans. It is our law. I apologize for any inconvenience. Perhaps it will change some day, but for now, that is our policy."

"Well, I aim to change that Xenolfan law. Anyway, you have a great day," Sierra said.

The three of them left the store and returned to the large corridor. Sierra's boots echoed as they made contact with the stone floor tiles.

"That's a bunch of fucking shit. Damn Jinkins! Who gives a shit what my dildo looks like!" Sierra exclaimed.

"The Xenolfan leadership is pretty fucked up," Vincent said.

"That, it is," Shaslin said.

They continued along the mall corridor and stopped in front of a leather and bondage store. Sierra looked at Vincent and Shaslin and smiled.

"Okay, I'm not into the whole bondage scene, but we have to check this out," Sierra said.

"You are both planning to tie me up and whip my ass, aren't you?" Vincent asked, jokingly.

Sierra turned to him and gave him a dead-serious look. "Yes."

Vincent's smile faded.

"I'm joking. Lighten up," Sierra said.

Shaslin laughed and looked at the many stylish floggers that hung along one of the aisles. She picked one up and snapped Vincent in the ass.

"Damn!" he shouted, rubbing his right asscheek.

Shaslin returned the flogger to the hook.

"Blindfolds, collars, crops, gags, leashes, masks, shackles, clamps, paddles, pinwheels, rope… Whether you're a top or bottom, they have everything you would need for your kink," Vincent read the list along the aisle.

"These belts are nice," Sierra said, looking a some studded black leather belts. "I think I'm going to get one."

She picked her size and removed one of the studded black belts from its hook. Vincent and Shaslin continued to browse while Sierra made her way to the counter to purchase the belt. When she was finished with the transaction, she met them at the entrance with a bag in her hand.

"So, where to next?" Sierra asked.

Shaslin pointed across the corridor to a lingerie store. "Let's check that out," she said.

They made their way across the stone tiled floor toward the intimate apparel store. Upon entering, Sierra gasped. Vincent and Shaslin looked at her.

"What?" Shaslin asked.

Sierra pointed to a display on their right side, by the wall. They followed her gaze.

"Those are the coolest corsets and bustiers I've ever seen," Sierra said.

They made their way to that section. A variety of corsets and bustiers decorated the mannequins, including brocade, taffeta, and leather. There were many colors and patterns to choose from.

"Oh my... I really like a lot of these. I need to get a couple of them," Sierra said.

She inspected a red and black brocade corset with crisscrossed laces on either side as well as in the back. She made sure it had metal boning. Pulling the hanger from the rack, she moved on to another one that sparked her interest. It was a black leather bustier with a zipper in the front and a black lace pattern on the sides. She also took that one from the rack.

"I'm sure you will look sexy in either of them," Vincent said.

"That reminds me, I need to get some new fishnet stockings while we are here," Shaslin said.

They made their way to the stockings section and Shaslin grabbed a couple of pairs. The store was fairly busy with customers, both human and Xenolfan. As they made their way to the counter, Vincent stopped and looked at the men's leather vests. He picked up a black leather vest with crisscrossed leather ties on the sides. Two chains decorated the front.

"You two are getting stuff, so I might as well get something I like as well," he said.

"That will look good on you," Shaslin said.

The line at the counter was short. Soon, they paid and left the store, all three carrying bags. As they walked into the mall corridor, one of the coach rides slowly made its way by them and came to a stop. The horses that led the carriage were a beautiful brown color. Attached bags prevented any mess from reaching the mall floor. The driver looked down toward the attached carriage. The door opened and a laughing human couple retreated from the carriage, kissing each other.

They stepped down onto the stone floor. The woman waited while the man paid the coach driver. Afterward, the couple made their way along the mall corridor, disappearing from sight. The driver then looked at the three of them, interested in finding his next customers. Sierra looked at Vincent and Shaslin.

"Let's go for a sexy ride," Sierra said.

"Sounds fun," Vincent said.

"Okay. Just give me a minute to clean up the carriage and change the sheets," the driver said as he stepped down from the front.

He stepped up into the carriage as the three of them waited next to a fountain of continuously splashing water that decorated the center of the mall corridor. Soon, the driver stepped down from the carriage.

"You three are all set. There are beverages in the refrigerator if you are interested," he said.

"Thank you," Shaslin said.

They walked over to the coach, stepped up into the carriage, and closed the door. Once the driver climbed back up to his front seat, the coach began to slowly move forward along the mall corridor. The inside of the carriage was spacious with seating and a large bed with fresh sheets. Vincent noticed a linen closet to the left of the door. There were mirrors at several locations around the inside of the carriage. A beverage bar was fixed along the front of the carriage. They each set their shopping bags down near a side cabinet. Vincent walked over and opened the refrigerator. He found an ale and opened it.

"Do you two want anything?" he asked.

"I want to suck your cock. That's what I want," Sierra told him.

Vincent took a quick sip of his drink and set the container down on the counter. They all started to undress.

"These rides aren't very long, so we'll have to make this quick. Let's just keep it oral for now. We can do more when we get to the hotel," Sierra said.

"Sounds fun to me," Shaslin said.

The two nude women dropped to their knees and both caressed Vincent's erect shaft. Sierra started licking on his smoothly-shaved balls while Shaslin took the hard cock into her mouth. Vincent looked down at the two beautiful women, closed his eyes, and moaned with pleasure. The two ladies soon joined together in licking up his shaft in unison. As they slowly reached the tip, their tongues wrapped around the underside of his cock at the frenulum where the tips of their tongues came together in an open sexual kiss. The kiss became more passionate, trapping the head of his cock between their lips. The sensation he felt was incredible. Once more, they slid their tongues down his wet shaft. This time, Sierra took his cock into her mouth and sucked with rhythmic motions, pulsating her tongue on the warm underside. They kept alternating the blowjob, sucking on his cock until Vincent couldn't take it anymore.

"I'm coming!"

He staggered where he stood and grabbed the counter as a powerful orgasm drove him to ejaculate several centimeters into the air. The white fluid landed on Sierra's right tit as more cum squirted out and flowed down his cock to meet Shaslin's mouth.

"Ohhh, was that awesome! You two are amazing," he said, breathing heavily.

Shaslin walked over, grabbed some wipes from the headboard, and brought them back to where Vincent stood. She wiped her mouth, Sierra's right breast, and then used another of the wipes to clean up Vincent's wet cock and balls. She discarded the wipes into the trash can. Sierra and Shaslin both walked over and sat at the edge of the bed. They gave Vincent a look that said they were ready to be pleasured. He followed them over to the bed and fell to his knees as the two women spread their legs. He started with Sierra, taking a moment to enjoy the beautiful sight of her smoothly-shaved labia folds. He took the time to lick upwards precisely between each of the outer pussy lips before licking up the center from her hole up to her little, erect, pink clit, which stood out proudly. He remained there, flicking his tongue intensely at her most sensitive spot. With one hand, Shaslin leaned over and began to palm Sierra's breasts and suck on the pink nipples. With her free hand, she reached down and stroked her own pussy, rapidly moving her fingers back and forth across her clitoris. Sierra grabbed Vincent's head and held it in place as she ground her pussy up onto his mouth. Her hips pumped against his face faster and faster, until she held her pelvis up off the bed against his mouth for a long moment. Quivering with excitement, she reached a deep orgasm.

"Ahhh!"

Shaslin changed her position on the bed and took the opportunity to go down and lick at Sierra's creamy pussy.

"Your turn," Vincent told Shaslin.

She returned to her former position on the bed and spread her legs. Vincent slowly kissed along her thighs until he came to her smooth, parted lips. He proceeded to bury his mouth on her cunt and repeatedly slid his tongue down against her slit rapidly. As she moaned, he increased the pressure of his tongue. Suddenly, the three of them could feel the coach slowly turn around and head back down the mall corridor from which they came. Sierra turned around and lay on her stomach, joining Vincent at Shaslin's pussy. Sierra's tongue flicked Shaslin's clit from the top while Vincent's tongue plunged into her creamy hole. With the two of them licking simultaneously, it didn't take long for Shaslin to reach an orgasm. Her pussy queefed as the muscles contracted, followed by a drip of cum that flowed out of her vagina and down toward her ass.

"Oh fuck!" Shaslin groaned.

Vincent quickly licked at the drip and looked up at the two women. All three of them were breathing heavily and smiling at each other.

"That was fun," Sierra said.

Vincent and Shaslin agreed. They slowly found their clothes that were flung about on the inside of the carriage. When they were fully dressed, Vincent finished his ale. The coach came to a stop near the fountain in the center of the mall corridor, where they had started. They each grabbed their shopping bags and stepped out of the coach. Vincent walked over and paid the driver for the ride.

"Thank you," Vincent said.

"I hope you three had an enjoyable ride. Now, I need to change the linens and feed my horses. Have a wonderful day," he said.

"You as well," Vincent said.

The three of them walked along the mall corridor. They passed a store that sold sex furniture. There were different sex chair designs, a variety of chaise lounge chairs, couches, and suspended swings.

Looking in the window, Sierra said, "That looks like one of the rooms I have set up at home."

"Your slate blue chaise lounge chair is better than those ones," Vincent said.

"I don't know. Those look pretty nice to me," Sierra said.

"So, what do you want to do next?" Shaslin asked.

"Let's head over to the Sex Palace Theater. That's always so arousing," Sierra said.

They maneuvered back through the casino game room to a

secluded area near the rear of the facility. A large, white, arched doorway opened up to reveal the Sex Palace Theater. Two separate sex show theater rooms were located next to each other, one for humans and one for Xenolfans. Large glass windows that stretched from floor to ceiling would reveal each of the theater occupants once the show started. Until then, the tall, burgundy curtains were drawn shut. Rows of guest chairs were located in front of the theater rooms. Many of the seats were already occupied with both humans and Xenolfans alike. The two different species were a mixed crowd in the seating section. Some guests chose to stand and watch instead of sitting. Sierra, Vincent, and Shaslin made their way to a few chairs in front of the theaters. The next scheduled event was about to start.

The host made an announcement over the speaker. "Welcome to the Sex Palace Theater, where you can enjoy live sex show entertainment. Thank you for visiting. In the theater to your left, you will have the pleasure of observing a human couple new to Salinarr Nevis. I'm told they have something extra special planned for this evening that is sure to delight you. In the theater to your right, you will have the pleasure of observing a married Xenolfan couple. You may have seen them perform here before. Shalarr and Fioness are regular performers at the Sex Palace Theater and long-time residents of Salinarr Nevis.

"Are you searching for an uninhibited, liberating adult experience? You have found the right place. The Sex Palace is home to Salinarr Nevis's one and only live sex show entertainment theater. Our guests enjoy a fun social atmosphere, hot dancing after the show, flirting with other open-minded people of the same species, and much more! This is one erotic sex show you won't want to miss. After both shows are complete, feel free to enjoy the music on our spacious dance floor. The DJ has a variety of music to keep you dancing. We also have separate human guest and Xenolfan guest playrooms available for your own sexual pleasure. There is no pressure, only fun. Make some new friends and enjoy the show."

After the announcement, Sierra noticed a dance floor off to the left of the theaters. The tall, burgundy curtains slowly parted on the left theater, while the curtains on the right remained closed. A human couple occupied the theater room. White leather sex chairs were fixed at several locations throughout the large room. A large mattress sat on the floor as well. The woman was a tall, petite blonde. She wore a sexy black and white outfit that revealed a tight, smooth ass. She had average breasts, which protruded from the low cut design. The man wore a loosely-fitted, white shirt and black pants. His short, black hair was styled and sleek. They slowly circled around each other in a theatrical fashion. It became a game of cat-and-mouse, as they danced around the sex furniture. Suddenly, the man scooped her up from her back and held her close to himself, her breasts resting on his chest. They stared into each other's eyes for a long moment and quickly engaged with a passionate kiss. The lengthy kiss became an open-mouth kiss. The man licked down her neck. As she parted her lips and looked up toward the ceiling, the man picked her up and carried her over to one of the nearby sex chairs. He proceeded to remove her outfit and lay her back into the chair. She raised her feet and settled them onto the padded rests on either side of the chair. The man removed his white shirt and it settled to the floor, his muscular body smooth in the warm light. The woman's spread thighs revealed a very defined vulva with large, open inner labia. She bit at her lip with anticipation as he removed his black pants. His large phallus sprung forth. He sat down on the low padded cushion of the sex chair and began to perform cunnilingus. As he flicked his tongue against her clitoris, her moans immediately fill the theater. She squirmed in the chair, his mouth planted hard against her moist pussy lips. As he continued to eat her, her breathing became heavier. Suddenly, she spasmed in the chair with her toes pointed outward. She pushed her pussy hard against his face and screamed with excitement. The man stood up, wiped his mouth and inserted his hard cock into the warmth of her sexy, pink pussy. After several thrusts, the man turned around and looked directly at the audience.

"And now for something extra special..." he said.

He clapped his hands and seven other people came into the theater room from the rear entrance. There were four females and three males. The group of seven were also dressed in black and white. Their clothing quickly came off as they began to engage in a group sex scene. Two of the males lay on a large mattress and were mounted by two of the females who sat reverse on top of them, facing the audience. The full view off their genitals in action caused a stir from the crowd. Both men's balls rhythmically shifted as the women slid up and down on their hard shafts. The sight of their cocks disappearing into the two pussies was very arousing. One of the two women reached her hand down, caressed the man's balls, slowly slid her fingers up his wet cock, and rested her hand against her wet pussy. She stroked her clit back and forth. The woman next to her squatted down hard onto the other man's cock, her tits circling around in a continuous bounce.

Two of the other newly arriving females started playing with each other in one of the sex chairs, grinding their pussies together in some hot tribbing action. The remaining male walked over and joined the original couple, his erect cock swaying back and forth as he walked toward them. The woman in the chair grasped his member and wrapped her mouth around it while being fucked hard from her first partner. As she sucked his cock, he arched backwards slightly and looked upward, groaning with pleasure.

Creamy, wet sounds from the group were mixed with moans of pleasure and grunts of ecstasy. They mixed it up by swapping partners several times and eventually all joined together in a group orgy. Their tangled bodies moved through rhythmic motions. Two of the women were lying on top of each other with their smooth pussies facing one of the men. He penetrated the one on the bottom first, burying his hard cock deep inside of her. After pumping her for a brief time, he withdrew his cock and then inserted it deep into the woman on top. Sliding it in and out for some time, he then withdrew. He continued to alternate between the two women, their pussies pulsating on each withdrawal. Bending down, he licked both of their pussies and then continued with the alternating penetration. Next to the trio were two of the other men, lying on the spacious mattress with their backs down and one had his legs up and over the other's. Grabbing the bases of both men's cocks, a woman squatted down onto them together in a double vaginal penetration. It took her a few tries, but soon she managed to fit both of their hard shafts inside of her pussy at the same time. She moved up and down very slowly, her breasts bouncing slightly. The two cocks rubbed together in a tight fit. All three of them moaned with pleasure. One of the men on his back leaned over and started sucking on the left tit of the woman next to him. She was on the bottom of the two stacked women that were being alternately fucked. Next to the two sets of trios was the remaining three performers. They lay in a circle of oral sex. The man rested on his side, licking the pussy of one of the two females, his tongue repeatedly lapping the moist folds. The woman receiving his playful tongue had her face buried into the vulva of the remaining woman, sucking the labia into her mouth and moving her head back and forth quickly. She then continuously glided her tongue down hard with pressure against the other's clit. The woman receiving her tongue, in turn, took the man's rigid cock into her mouth and sucked, swirling her tongue around and around. A hand reached over and cupped her right breast. It belonged to the woman who was stacked on top of the first trio.

The entire group of nine were in very close proximity to each other on the mattress, their body heat adding the their arousals. After the two stacked women reached orgasms, the man alternating between them finally came, his cum squirting up into the air and landing onto both of their pussies. The white liquid dripped from one pussy down to the other pussy below and finally came to a rest upon the mattress. The woman squatting on top of the two men in the second trio reached an incredible climax that sent a stream of creamy cum down onto both shafts. She continued to slide up and down on the men until they finally burst at the same time, shooting a double load of hot cum up into her. The three of them could feel the intense pulsating of the two cocks together. As she pulled away, the full pussy-load of cum dripped down onto their cocks and continued dripping down to their balls. In the circle of oral sex, the man came first, his large load squirting into the mouth of the woman giving him pleasure. She licked around the head of his penis and cleaned up the drops. She spit some out and then swallowed a small amount. She then pushed her hands hard into the mattress as she reached a great orgasm. Looking down at the other woman, she smiled, white cum dripping from her mouth. The woman eating her smiled back just before reaching her own orgasm. For a long moment, they all just lay there and relaxed, enjoying the sexual afterglow.

The audience began to clap and express their enjoyment of the show.

"Oh my! That was incredible," Sierra said. "I am so horny right now, I could fuck a horse."

Vincent looked at her with an odd expression. "I hope you're not serious. But if you are, there's one in the mall," he said.

They laughed.

"I'm not. But I can't wait to fuck you," she said.

"I do like stuffed pie," Vincent said.

"I like it when you stuff my pie," Sierra said.

"I think I'm so wet that it's soaking through my pants," Shaslin said.

Sierra and Vincent both looked down between Shaslin's legs.

"Yep," Sierra and Vincent said in unison.

The three of them smiled at each other.

The nine performers stood up from the large mattress and started cleaning themselves up with wipes and gathering their clothes as the curtains slowly closed. Once the crowd finished clapping, there was a brief pause before the burgundy curtain on the right parted to reveal a similar theater room. The two Xenolfans had not entered the room yet.

"Do you think it's odd that the Xenolfan Government doesn't want interspecies sex, but they allow both species to sit together at the same sex show, where everyone is getting aroused? You would think if they are so concerned about it, they would have totally separate shows," Vincent said.

"Perhaps they think just because they have a law in place that all the Xenolfans will obey it. I don't know," Sierra said in a low tone.

A man with short, black hair sitting next to them looked up at Sierra. He looked to be in his early forties. "I'm pretty sure I know why," he said in a low voice.

"Why?" Sierra asked.

"Because they are trying to seek out interspecies couples that hook up and follow them to the secret planet of tryst. I don't think they know where it's at. That is precisely why couples must go to a decoy point first before they reach their destination. That is a planet that should never be mentioned while on Salinarr Nevis because the walls have ears," he whispered to Sierra.

"That's a good theory," Sierra said.

"Rastall's the name," he said, putting his hand out to Sierra.

"Nice to meet you, Rastall. My name is Sierra Shalinsky and these are my friends Vincent and Shaslin Macenburg," Sierra said.

"Hello," Shaslin said.

"Hi, Rastall," Vincent said.

"You guys are going to enjoy this Xenolfan show. I've seen it multiple times. I would love to hook up with this Xenolfan couple so very much," Rastall said.

"Maybe you should try," Sierra said.

"They wouldn't be interested in me, especially since I'm human," Rastall said.

"You never know until you ask," Sierra said.

Rastall pondered the thought for a long moment. "Perhaps you're right. I think I will ask them after the show," Rastall said.

Rastall looked over at some other members in the audience. He caught a glimpse of a human female wearing a wide brim hat decorated with a colorful floral splash. She sat next to a Xenolfan male and briefly squeezed his hand, smiling at him.

Rastall turned back to Sierra, Shaslin, and Vincent. "I'm certainly glad they now have the sex clinics to go to on a regular basis," he said.

"Well, I'm thankful the health clinics promote positive sexuality," Sierra said.

"Actually, Sierra here is the main reason why they now exist," Shaslin said.

"The main reason why they now exist? What are you, super horny or something?" Rastall asked.

Sierra looked at Shaslin with a tilted head and then laughed. "Okay, I was pretty much the driving force behind their success. But I like to remain humble about it. I advocate for sexual freedom for both interspecies couples and the swinger Lifestyle. At some point soon, I will be giving my sexual freedom speech on Red Jacket."

"Oh wow! Well, thank you. The sex clinics really help me out. But last time I was there, my regular nurse was gone and I was assigned a male nurse. I didn't expect that, but it was a nice experience," Rastall said.

At that moment the two Xenolfan performers, Shalarr and Fioness, entered the theater room. They also wore the black and white themed clothing, which contrasted their bluish-gray skin. Shalarr was a very muscular Xenolfan male. His arms were quite impressive. Fioness was fairly petite in comparison. As they entered the room, they began to act out an ancient Xenolfan mating ritual. Once upon a time, when Xenolfans had wings, they would leap slightly in the air and circle around each other in flight until they came to settle and would wrap their wings around each other. The act that Shalarr and Fioness performed had them circling around each other on the tips of their toes. They stopped and embraced each other, wrapping their arms around each other in a long hug. Shalarr backed away and slowly undressed, the black and white clothing piling onto the theater floor. Fioness watched him with delight, his nude bluish-gray body now fully visible. She began to slowly remove her own outfit. As she kicked her stockings aside, her small breasts wiggled slightly, their bluish-purple nipples erect with anticipation. Shalarr admired the beauty of his wife and soaked it in for a long moment as he watched her finish undressing.

Shalarr picked up Fioness completely off the floor and carried her over to the sex chair. Setting her down on the chair, he gripped her ankles with either hand and slowly penetrated her moist, reuleaux triangle hole. Sliding his cock deep within her, he adjusted her bluish-gray legs apart a bit farther. The high-pitched, reverberating purr that escaped from her mouth would have pierced the ears of the audience through the insulated glass windows had the sound been any louder. The ecstasy that she felt was revealed in her facial expression. Her sapphire eyes told a story of love and admiration for her husband. Shalarr continued for a long while before suddenly pulling out. As he did, a drip of her cream fell onto the chair. He knelt down and buried his face into her bluish-pink pussy lips, quickly shaking his head side to side. Fioness made such a high-pitched moan the second time that a few of the audience members quickly covered their ears.

"Damn!" Sierra said, reaching for her own ears. "That must feel so fucking good. Look at her."

"We need to get to our hotel room soon. I'm about to burst," Shaslin said.

"I hear ya," Vincent said.

After licking her wetness, Shalarr stood up and began to pound her pussy with hard thrusts that shook the chair. In a short time, he exploded inside of her. As he pulled away, she bent down on one knee and cleaned him off with her mouth.

"Mmm, that was awesome," Sierra said.

As the curtains closed, the audience's applause once again filled the Sex Palace Theater. This time, it was for a sustained period of time. Sierra clapped and shouted with her enjoyment of the shows.

Rastall looked up at Sierra and whispered, "Shalarr and Fioness usually come to the dance floor after the show. I'm going to take you up on your advice and ask them if they are interested in an interspecies threesome."

"Just in case you are correct about your theory, be careful," Sierra advised.

"Definitely," he said.

The host began to make another announcement over the speaker. "Thank you all for attending both shows at the Sex Palace Theater. I hope you enjoyed the excitement. And without further delay, the DJ is ready to start with some music that is sure to get you on the dance floor. Don't forget the playrooms are available in the back for each separate species. And as a token of our appreciation, all of our guests here at the Sex Palace Theater will receive sixty-nine credits of free slot play in the casino. Have a great evening."

An electronic trance music began playing from the nearby dance floor speakers, its subwoofers vibrating their seats.

"Wow, that bass feels good," Shaslin said.

Sierra and Vincent looked at the wet spot in the crotch of her pants and smiled. They stood up as the audience began to disperse.

"Okay, one dance and then we'll head to the hotel room," Sierra said.

"It's not metal, but it will do," Vincent said.

As they made their way through the crowd toward the dance floor, Sierra noticed the black-haired man they had met in the audience maneuvering his way toward the back of the dance floor where the two Xenolfan performers emerged from the back. She saw him start a conversation with them and knew exactly what Rastall was proposing to them. The loud music was the perfect cover, if his theory was correct. The theory totally made sense to Sierra.

When they finally reached the edge of the dance floor, Sierra, Shaslin, and Vincent began to move their bodies to the beat with a sweet lustfulness. The experienced swingers had a connection that most others didn't. The sexy ambience of the dance floor heightened their arousals because they knew what was coming next when they got back to their hotel room.

Rastall approached the Xenolfan couple at the rear of the dance floor. The music was much louder there. He took the opportunity to ask his question without being heard by others.

"Hello, Shalarr and Fioness. My name is Rastall. I thoroughly enjoyed your performance. It was very arousing, as it always is."

"Well, thank you," Shalarr said over the music. "So, you have seen the show on multiple occasions?"

The dance floor lights revealed the pattern on Shalarr's bluish-gray face.

"Oh, yes. Yours is one of my favorite shows. And..." he said in a low voice, "I am wondering if you two would consider a threesome with me."

Fioness looked around. The music was far too loud for anyone to hear them. "We need to have a private conversation in our ship. But you mustn't stay aboard for more than a few minutes. We can discuss it there. Remember, they monitor social activity to enforce the law, so be careful," she said.

Shalarr gave Rastall the location of their docked ship. The Xenolfan couple smoothly passed by Rastall, as if no conversation took place, other than a quick congratulations on their performance.

Rastall made his way to one of the many docking bays on Salinarr Nevis. The location that Shalarr had given him was not the nearest one to the Sex Palace casino. The corridors were empty for the most part, with just an occasional person walking along. He turned from one corridor onto a concrete ramp that led down into the docking bay. Many different styles of ships became visible as he continued along the ramp. He made his way to their ship and knocked on the hull, near the ship's door. The ship was a medium-sized, modern vessel with a white hull and a sleek design. The door slowly opened with a hiss. Rastall made his way up several stairs to the main floor. His shoes echoed on the diamond-plated metal floor as he walked along to meet Shalarr and Fioness. A light gray robot peeked around the corner at the arriving guest.

"Hi, Rastall. Welcome aboard the *Celestial Frost*. Don't mind our robot, XT-B5. He's just a bit nosy. We have about five minutes before the Salinarr Nevis surveillance team kicks you out of the ship. So, listen. We would love to hook up with you. The only way that will happen is on Aamaress. But we must both fly separately to different decoy points first and then to the destination. We can leave here shortly. Does that work for you?" Shalarr asked.

"Yes. I will be careful," Rastall said.

Fioness walked over to Rastall, grabbed the front of his pants, and gave his cock a squeeze. "I look forward to sucking this," she said.

Rastall smiled. "Yes. And I look forward to being with you two as well," Rastall said as he turned toward the door.

"The surveillance team may question you. If so, just tell them you came to get an autographed theater poster," Shalarr said, handing

Rastall a signed poster.

"Right. I'll see you two soon," Rastall said.

Poster in hand, Rastall made his way out of the ship and onto the docking bay floor. He headed toward the concrete ramp. Their ship could be heard in the distance as it slowly made its way toward the exit. He unrolled the signed poster and smiled at the risqué pose of Shalarr and Fioness on the theater chair. As he rolled it back up, two Xenolfan males approached him. They were dressed in black uniforms.

"What was your business aboard a Xenolfan ship?" one of them asked.

"Oh, hi. Well, I enjoyed the show at the Sex Palace Theater. So, after the show, I asked the performers if I could get a signed poster. They were kind enough to give it to me for free," Rastall said.

"In the future, have them bring it out of the ship and hand it to you. The Xenolfan Government has laws that require the segregation of our species in private settings. Do you understand that?" the other one asked.

"Understood," Rastall said.

"Have a good day and enjoy your stay here on Salinarr Nevis," the first one said.

"Thanks," Rastall said.

He finished the ascent up the ramp and into the corridor.

What a bunch of assholes! he thought.

They followed him down the corridor for a short distance before turning off into a different direction. He made his way toward the docking bay where his ship was located. He started thinking of what decoy point he could travel to first, before jumping to lightspeed toward Aamaress. As he pondered the thought, he saw two other Xenolfan security officers, also dressed in black, walk past him at a quick pace before disappearing around a corner into another corridor.

I wonder what that's all about, he thought.

He passed several rows of ships and then turned toward the row his ship was on. A short distance away, he stopped in front of his ship and looked up at it. A comfort came over him as he stared up at the imperfections of the dark gray hull. *Cosmic Disturbance* was an older ship, but it still functioned well. After unlocking the ship, he stepped aboard, set the poster down on a shelf, and headed for the bridge. He engaged the ship's engines and slowly maneuvered it toward the exit. He punched in the coordinates of his decoy point and prepared the ship for lightspeed.

Shaslin moaned from their hotel suite as another intense wave of orgasmic pleasure rippled through her. Sierra looked up, saw Shaslin's expression, and continued to perform cunnilingus. Shaslin's long brown hair partially covered her breasts. Sierra gently brushed the hair aside and caressed them.

"That's absolutely incredible, Sierra. Damn!" Shaslin said, breathing heavily.

Vincent positioned himself behind Sierra and slipped into her. He reached around under Sierra and cupped her breasts. Vincent groaned as he felt the warmth deep inside of her. Aroused by the wet, creamy sounds of coitus, Sierra continued to moan and rotate her hips rhythmically.

"Ohhh…that's nice," Vincent said.

"Fuck my pussy," Sierra moaned.

He continued for a while. Soon, they all changed positions. Shaslin and Vincent lay in a side-by-side position with their legs spread open. His smooth phallus parted the moist folds of Shaslin's labia. Sierra reached down between both of their legs and gently stroked them with her fingers, gliding them across the wetness. She put the tip of her finger to her mouth and enjoyed the warm taste of their sex. She then began fucklicking them, kissing and licking their genitals as they fucked.

"Ahhh yeah," Vincent groaned.

"Oh, Sierra, that's incredible!" Shaslin said.

Shaslin panted repeatedly before her whole body tensed up with a relieving orgasm. Vincent pushed Shaslin's left thigh outward slightly before withdrawing. Moving down, he grabbed her ass from beneath and pushed her vulva toward his mouth, licking at her juices. Breathing heavily, Shaslin cried out, her fingers grabbing his arms as she came again. The scent of their sexual secretions fill the air.

"Oh, my pussy feels so good," Shaslin exclaimed.

After changing it up, Vincent once again buried his erection deep into Sierra. She lay on her back and he rode her pelvis high, rocking against her clitoris. She parted her legs wide, toes pointed outward. Shaslin sucked on Sierra's right breast as Sierra felt a flood of nerve endings engulf her entire body from head to toe. Both Vincent and

Sierra exploded with simultaneous orgasms. Vincent continued thrusting several times before withdrawing, his ejaculate dripping from her. Exhausted, the three of them lay with their legs interlaced for a long while.

Walking along the casinos, Sierra, Shaslin, and Vincent had a spring in their step and smiles on their faces. They made their way toward the large venue where Maranadda was scheduled to play in the near future. After seeking permission to view the Silver Star Concert Hall, a Xenolfan official opened the doors and turned on the lights. Revealed before them were rows upon rows of seats, a massive floor area, and a large empty stage. They had played many venues in the past, but the Silver Star Concert Hall was one of the largest, most elegant venues they had been offered to perform at. They stood there for a long moment, soaking it all in.

"So, this is it..." Sierra managed.

"Wow. This is a huge place to perform! The show will be awesome," Shaslin said.

Vincent walked over to the sound booth in the center rear of the facility and browsed at the equipment from a sound tech's perspective. Until now, he had some concerns with how things would work out, but after seeing the sound booth, he was relieved. He spotted where his computer would connect into the system. It was far better than he expected.

"So, does it meet Vincent's expectations?" Sierra asked.

"Definitely," he said, looking at the two women. "This show will be awesome indeed."

"You know, I'm surprised your job hasn't contacted you with some galactic emergency lately, like they usually do," Shaslin said to Sierra.

"Yes, I know. As busy as we've been, the quiet seems strange," Sierra said.

As they left the venue, they thanked the Xenolfan official and he locked up behind them. After walking past the box office, Sierra spotted a woman that she recognized from the audience of the Sex Palace Theater. She wore a wide brim hat, decorated with a floral splash. She remembered the woman being with a Xenolfan male. They were both stopped across the corridor and surrounded by the black uniformed Xenolfan security. As they passed the confrontation, they overheard one of the security officers saying something about the Xenolfan law that forbids the two species to have a relationship. After continuing down the corridor for some distance, Sierra stopped. Vincent and Shaslin came to a stop next to her.

"Damn it! That there…that right there pisses me off. That is why I continue to fight for sexual freedom. That's a bunch of shit. Fucking Jinkins! This is the worst I've ever seen them with their enforcement of the damn law," Sierra said loudly.

The three of them stopped and looked back down the corridor at the scene. A casino owner and several other Xenolfan businessmen stood before the interspecies couple. One of the security officers placed handcuffs on the Xenolfan male. A frightened look was revealed on his patterned face.

"You know our law strictly forbids interspecies relationships. You cannot be with this human! You will be placed in a holding cell until we get a judgment from our leader on Olf Teruda. And you…" He turned toward the woman. "Take that hat off. You are going to be deported directly to the Syrenthian Government capital on Exandra. You will be permanently banished from Salinarr Nevis."

"Your law makes no sense," the woman said.

"Why were you spying on us?" the Xenolfan male asked.

"Our leader, Aaranix Tuvelless, wants to crack down on violators of the law. We also overheard you both mention the resort snow planet of Aamaress where your unlawful tryst would take place. That information just confirms what we already know. The supplemental information will be documented and sent to our Xenolfan Government on Olf Teruda," the casino owner said.

One of the other Xenolfan businessmen stepped forward. "I am outraged by you two, flirting with each other in the casino corridors and planning to hook up. You two disgust me! I've seen others like yourself in the corridors, at the casinos, in the restaurants. It's time we crack down on this disgrace," he said.

The security officers escorted the two of them away.

"No fucking way!" Sierra said.

Sierra thought about the theory that Rastall told her about in the Sex Palace Theater.

I believe Rastall is right. They are spying on couples and getting information, Sierra thought.

She started walking after them. Vincent and Shaslin grabbed her arms and held her back.

"What are you two doing? We can't let this happen!"

"Sierra! Sierra! You cannot do this right now. You will just get us banned from Salinarr Nevis too. Hello! No concert… You and Priscilla Stryderr are already fighting this law the right way. You will do no good in all your advocating if you get into trouble here," Vincent said.

Vincent and Shaslin could feel Sierra release her tension and relax as they held her arms.

"I know it frustrates you, but Vincent is right. You will do more good with the way you are already advocating. Just work on your sexual freedom speech," Shaslin said.

"Yes, you're right," Sierra said as she glared at one of the businessmen. "Let's get the fuck out of here."

Chapter Four

GATHIN AND ESLARR entered the main lobby of The Avalanche Resort from the cold outdoors. They both shivered as the electronic doors closed behind them. Snowflakes decorated their cozy outfits, but quickly melted in the warmth of the lobby. Heat from the lobby's stone fireplace was a welcomed comfort, the sound of its fire crackling. Removing their hats and gloves, they made their way to the front desk to turn in the snowmobile keys. They had been snowmobiling on the trails, which ran through the nearby pine forest.

"That blizzard sure is getting bad out there. It was almost a total whiteout on the trail getting back to the resort here. The snow is getting pretty deep as well," Gathin said to the young man at the counter.

Gathin read the desk clerk's name tag as Max.

"I'm freezing," Eslarr said.

"You look a bit frozen. And it's supposed to get worse. This snowstorm is supposed to set a record here on Aamaress," Max said.

"That will give us a good excuse to cuddle later," the young female worker next to Max said.

She flung her blond hair back, walked up to him, and squeezed his ass.

He smiled back at her. "I'm looking forward to it, Mauve, but we need to behave in front of our guests. By the way, would you two like to try some Sipathrott? It's an aphrodisiac we are giving out to our guests. We bring it out on special occasions…like this winter storm," Max said to Gathin and Eslarr.

"Of course, we would," Eslarr said.

"You referred to it as winter. Isn't it winter all the time on Aamaress?" Gathin asked.

"It's always snowy, but in actual winter, it's worse," Max said.

Eslarr took the vials of Sipathrott and put them into her pocket.

"Keep in mind, those are very potent. You two will be aroused in no time. And it lasts for hours. I think my co-worker here already had one," Max said.

"Actually, I did," Mauve said with a smile.

"Yes, I know it's potent. I've had it before some years ago on Olf Teruda. It will be a wonderful evening," Eslarr said.

"Well, Eslarr, shall we warm up by the fireplace?" Gathin asked.

"Yes," she said.

They walked over to one of several large, white leather couches located in front of the stone fireplace. Other guests sat near the fire, enjoying the warmth. They sat next to a Xenolfan couple and Eslarr removed her scarf.

"Hello," the other Xenolfan female said to Eslarr. "My name is Fioness and this is my husband, Shalarr."

"Hi, I'm Eslarr and this is Gathin. It's nice to meet you."

"This is our first time on Aamaress. The Avalanche Resort is an awesome accommodation and I'm glad to have a place where Eslarr and I can finally be together. They have great amenities here. So, where are you two from? You both look familiar," Gathin said.

"We are from Salinarr Nevis. You may have seen us in the Sex Palace Theater," Shalarr said.

"Yes! That's were it was. In the past, we've watched you two in the theater sex acts. You two are amazing. But I have to ask, since it's not a problem for two Xenolfans to be in a relationship anywhere in the Syrenthian Galaxy, why would you come to Aamaress to hook up?" Gathin asked.

Shalarr's husky laugh filled the grand foyer. "Oh, we are here with a human male. He should be down here any time now. Well, that's quite a storm out there, isn't it?"

"Definitely," Gathin said. "It's nice to meet you both."

"Did you two get some Sipathrott at the desk?" Fioness asked.

"We sure did. I'm looking forward to drinking it and having some fun tonight," Eslarr said.

"So, how long are you two here for?" Fioness asked.

Eslarr looked at Gathin. "We're not sure yet. We have to check in to a couple of things. From what I understand, if an interspecies couple get married here, The Avalanche Resort will make an offer for a housing deal to live here on Aamaress. It's just so damn cold and icy here, I'm turning blue," Eslarr said.

They all laughed.

"I love your blueness," Gathin said, smiling.

"But living here may be well worth it. I don't like to be harassed by my own government because of who I'm in a relationship with. It's just plain wrong," Eslarr said.

"I didn't know the resort offered that. That's great," Shalarr said.

A man with short, black hair approached them and sat on the couch next to Shalarr and Fioness.

"This is Rastall. Rastall meet Gathin and Eslarr," Fioness said.

"It's so very nice to meet you both. Are you enjoying your stay here on Aamaress?" Rastall asked.

"Yes, we are," Eslarr said.

"Things are getting pretty bad on Salinarr Nevis…and the Syrenthian Galaxy as a whole, when it comes to the Xenolfan Government enforcing the law regarding interspecies sex and relationships. I was approached by security officers on Salinarr Nevis after I was on their ship for only five minutes," Rastall said.

"They followed the *Celestial Frost* for a short distance as we made our way to the decoy point," Shalarr said.

"Yeah, I think our leader, Aaranix Tuvelless, has increased his enforcement of the law recently. I'm not sure what is going on, but I hope someone puts a stop to it. It's ridiculous," Fioness said.

"I met a woman during your show at the Sex Palace Theater who is advocating for our sexual freedom. Her name is Sierra Shalinsky. She plans on giving an important speech on Red Jacket sometime in the near future," Rastall said. "I have a theory that the Xenolfan Government uses the Sex Palace casino, the Sex Palace Theater, and the new mall to spy on interspecies couples."

"You know what? I think you are correct. Mixing our two species in an arousing atmosphere when we have this law has never really made sense to us, but that theory sounds about right to me," Shalarr said.

"Wow! We should consider ourselves lucky that we never got into trouble on Salinarr Nevis, as much as we were together," Eslarr said.

"I know," Gathin said.

Rastall adjusted himself in the crotch and tried to get comfortable.

"Are you okay?" Shalarr asked him.

They all noticed a large bulge in his pants.

"Umm…I may have already drunk my vial of Sipathrott."

"Oh. Well, we better head on to our room, then," Shalarr said.

The three of them stood up from the couch.

"You three have fun," Eslarr said.

"That, we will do," Fioness said. "It was nice to meet you two. Take care."

Gathin and Eslarr watched the three of them go up the carpeted steps and disappear around the corner.

"Did I mention that I love you?" Gathin asked.

"I think once or twice," Eslarr said, smiling.

They stood up to head for their room and passed the front desk. To their surprise they heard the young human resort workers giggling from the back office. Gathin peeked around the corner of the office doorway to ask for more room towels when he saw Max with his head buried between Mauve's legs.

"You two might want to save that for later before you get into trouble with your supervisor," Gathin said.

The young man looked up. "Perhaps you're right," he said. "The aphrodisiacs are only supposed to be for our guests anyway."

"Sorry," Mauve said.

She pulled her panties back up and straightened up Max's hair.

"I'll have Housekeeping send those extra towels to your room right away," Max said.

Shalarr, Fioness, and Rastall arrived at their room. The Sipathrott that Rastall drank was intense. He was relieved that he could finally remove the constricting pants he wore. Shalarr and Fioness grabbed a few drinks from the refrigerator and made themselves comfortable on the bed.

"So, Rastall, have you ever been with a Xenolfan before?" Fioness asked.

"No. But I have certainly enjoyed watching you two in the theater many times. I find the slight difference in color and in genitalia to be quite arousing," Rastall said.

"We have been with humans in the past—both male and female—on occasion and find it very arousing as well," Shalarr said.

"Rastall, are you okay with bisexuality?" Fioness asked, sipping her drink.

"Well, I don't identify as a bisexual, but I'm open-minded and flexible, as long as it doesn't involve kissing or anything anal," Rastall said. "I had an oral experience with a human male last time I went to the sex clinic."

Rastall remembered the human male nurse he was assigned last time he went to the sex clinic. His usual female nurse had the day off and he was pleasured by the male nurse instead. The oral scene replayed in his mind.

"Did that arouse you?" Shalarr asked.

"Yes, it did. I'm open to that," Rastall said.

"Well, we have a treat for you, then," Fioness said.

The three of them set their drinks down and undressed. Rastall was used to observing the bluish-gray Xenolfans from a distance in the theater. He was fascinated and further aroused to see them up close. Fioness had small breasts with bluish-purple nipples. Rastall noticed her vulva was similar to her human counterparts, except the vaginal orifice was slightly triangular in shape. He turned to look at Shalarr's bluish-gray cock. It was also slightly triangular in shape. The round-cornered reuleaux triangle was stepped down to a smaller girth toward the tip and had an angled end without a head on it. Both males focused their attention on Fioness as they stood nude before her. She knelt down between them and slowly massaged their hard cocks. She brushed her white hair back and put her mouth around Shalarr's stiff cock, sucking ever so slowly. With a free hand, she stroked Rastall. Switching to the human cock, she licked up the shaft to the head and remained there for a long moment, circling it with her long tongue.

"I've always found human cock heads fascinating," Fioness said, "not that there is anything wrong with Xenolfan cock, by any means."

She continued to alternate between the two of them, enjoying the very different qualities of each.

"Why don't you two lie down, scoot close, and put your cocks together? Rastall, put your legs over Shalarr's. I want to suck both of your cocks at the same time in a double barrel blow job," Fioness said.

Without hesitation, both followed her instructions. They slid together on the bed and Fioness made herself comfortable between them.

"Look at that," she said.

As she grasped her bluish-gray hand around both cocks, she stroked them together in a frotting action. After enjoying the visual contrast of the two different penises, she took both of them into her mouth at the same time. Shalarr and Rastall could feel the heat of their cocks pressing together. They felt her tongue glide along their shafts, down to their balls, and back up to the tips. She could feel the two cocks pulsate in her mouth as she sucked them both.

"The heat of his cock on mine and your warm, wet tongue… This is amazing!" Rastall said.

"Thank you," Fioness said as she continued.

Shalarr groaned with pleasure. After some time, Fioness pulled her mouth away and smiled.

"Let's try something…" she said. "You two stay in that position."

She swung one leg over them and squatted down onto the two cocks. Reaching underneath her, she grabbed them both and slowly inserted them together into her wet pussy.

"Ohhh, that's tight. I like that! That's a nice full-of-cock feeling," she said.

She slid up and down very slowly, leaning on Shalarr's chest.

"Damn, it *is* tight," Rastall said.

Fioness pulled away and the two cocks fell apart.

"Sorry, I can't do that for very long. Rastall, why don't I fuck you from on top, facing Shalarr, and he can fucklick us?" Fioness suggested.

"That sounds fun," Rastall said.

The three of them shifted positions and Fioness sat down on Rastall's cock, in reverse, facing Shalarr. Both of their legs were spread open enough for Shalarr to get in between them.

"I noticed that you are much more wet than human females," Rastall said.

"Yes, we Xenolfan females secrete about twice as much as human females."

"And we Xenolfan males ejaculate about twice as much as you do," Shalarr said.

"Interesting," Rastall said.

Shalarr rubbed both of their thighs as he enjoyed the contrast of the two different skin colors engaged in coitus. His hands moved from their thighs to their genitals. The erotic, creamy sound of their sex turned Shalarr on. The tan cock and balls were so sleek and defined. He caressed Rastall's balls and slowly massaged them, sliding his hand up the shaft to where it disappeared inside his wife. He removed his hand and replaced it with his tongue, starting at Fioness's moist, bluish-pink labia folds. He circled around her clit and back to the labia. Gliding his tongue down farther, he licked the exposed underside of Rastall's cock as it went in and out of Fioness. He continued licking down the shaft to Rastall's smooth balls. As he continued to fucklick them, he could taste their wet, musky sex.

"Ohhh, that feels so good, Shalarr," Fioness said.

"Yes, it does," Rastall said.

"Oh, Shalarr, put your mouth up on my pussy. Oh, keep it there. Oh fuck!" she screamed with a high-pitched, intense, reverberating cry.

"Damn," Rastall said, holding his ears.

A noticeable amount of vaginal fluid dripped out of her pussy and around Rastall's cock. Shalarr quickly licked it up. The sudden warm gush of Fioness's orgasm along with Shalarr's tongue sliding across his inserted cock was all that Rastall could take. His thrusts quickened.

"Come inside of me!" Fioness said.

Shalarr backed away as Rastall buried his cock deep into the Xenolfan. It was his fantasy and he could not believe it was happening. He moaned loudly as he came deep inside of her. She could feel the warm burst of his cum.

"Oh, Fioness, that was so nice," Rastall said as he pulled out.

"Yes, it was," she said.

Fioness shifted to her back and Shalarr mounted her, holding her legs apart. She welcomed his familiar cock and pushed upward with her hips. As they fucked, Rastall began sucking on her tits, alternating each one.

"Would you two like me to return the favor and fucklick you both?"

Rastall asked.

"I would, but I'm about the come," Shalarr said.

As he pounded her pussy hard, the whole bed shook. Moments later, he erupted inside of her, mixing his cum with Rastall's. Although it was not as high-pitched as Fioness's was, he too made a reverberating moan as he reached an orgasm. The three of them sat there on the bed for a long moment, exhausted.

"This threesome was positively awesome," Rastall said.

Sierra Shalinsky sighed. She could hear the faint sound of the *Tenebris's* engines at the rear of the ship. Space travel was never quick enough for Sierra. As she traveled home to Asparr Celtarious, she thought of the fun she had with Vincent and Shaslin back on Salinarr Nevis. They were always fun to hang with and to play with. She smiled to herself. In her mind, she started piecing together her forthcoming sexual freedom speech. The more she thought about it, the more she felt blacklisted because of her sexuality. She felt it was easy to advocate for interspecies sex, but when it came to her own swinger Lifestyle and her bisexuality, she just felt blacklisted. On the long flight home, she also had the time to work on a song. Writing songs always helped her keep things in perspective.

In the distance, the sphere of Asparr Celtarious could be seen, its white, blue, and green colors bright against the darkness of space. She disengaged lightspeed and maneuvered the old fighter ship toward the planet's atmosphere. Her coordinates took her near the Superior Mountains toward her property on Lake Serenity. She skirted the airspace of the Superior Mountain Club, just to piss off the club members.

"Fucking Jinkins," she mumbled.

As the *Tenebris* approached her property, she settled the ship onto a landing pad next to her house. Two blue adirondack chairs sat on a smooth, brown rock slab that overlooked Lake Serenity. White pine trees surrounded the lake, their reflection seen in the calm, clear water.

As she exited the ship, she paused and took a deep breath of the fresh air. Sierra absolutely loved her home on Asparr Celtarious. It was so peaceful...well, except for her discord with the Superior Mountain Club.

"Fucking Jinkins!" she shouted across the water, her voice echoing.

She turned and walked toward her house. It was a beautiful rustic home with a large stone front and beautiful slate blue siding. A spacious deck overlooked Lake Serenity. She unlocked the door and entered her living room. The scent of a clean house welcomed her. She walked over to her comm to check any messages that may have been left. There were three. The first message was from the company that she ordered her ship parts from.

"This message is for Sierra Shalinsky. This is the Accounting Department at Flux Ship Mods. We have frozen your account due to suspicious activity. If you could contact us at your earliest convenience, that would be great. Thanks."

She forgot to erase that message. It had to do with her identity theft. She had already secured all her accounts, including Flux Ship Mods, so there was nothing more she could do, except curse the bastard who did that to her. She erased the message. The second message was from Priscilla Stryderr.

"Hi, Sierra. This is Priscilla. I miss you. I just wanted to let you know that I went to Olf Teruda again to protest against the Xenolfan Government's unjust interspecies relationship law. I gave them the signed petitions that we gathered. Their leader, Aaranix Tuvelless, is an asshole, along with some of his close dignitaries. Most of the Xenolfan population seem to be great. Anyway, how is the speech coming? We have that seminar coming up here pretty soon so I'm just checking with you. Braxton says 'hi.' The three of us need to hook up again. That was fun. Anyway, I hope all is well with Maranadda and your work. Take care. Bye."

Sierra looked at the third message. It was from her boss, Madison Stephard. She was the director for her unit of the Galactic Emergency Medical Services.

"Sierra, this is Madison. When I ask you to fill out paperwork, you better leave it on my desk. Do I have to hold your hand? Next time you get an emergency call and arrive here at GEMS headquarters, we need to go over something."

Madison made Sierra's job as a Galactic Emergency Medical Technician very difficult. There was always something that Sierra didn't do good enough to please Madison. Sierra recalled Madison getting in her face when she found out that she was a swinger. That incident replayed in Sierra's mind often. There were so many things about working for Madison that she couldn't stand. There were other units in the Galactic Emergency Medical Services that would be a lot better to work under, but they were difficult to get into. So, she just bit her tongue for now.

Sierra grabbed a carbonated beverage from the refrigerator and walked over to her slate blue chaise lounge chair. She sat down and tried to relax, but was antsy for some reason. She couldn't put her finger on why. After taking a long drink, she set the beverage down on a stand next to the chair and stared at the cathedral ceiling for a long moment.

Her upstairs bedroom overlooked the living room and kitchen areas. It wasn't designed for privacy, but she didn't have to worry about that, since she lived by herself. If she did have guests over, most likely they were in the Lifestyle and bedroom privacy wasn't an issue. There was the convenience of a large upstairs bathroom next to her bedroom. The rest of the house was spacious as well. Another bathroom was located beyond the kitchen and featured a comfortable hot tub. Sierra's office was adjacent from the living room. Its large desk, full bookshelves, and stone fireplace made it a cozy retreat. Many of the books on the shelves were self-learning books of various subjects.

What the hell is bothering me? she asked herself.

Sierra had a lot on her mind. She thought about Madison's comm message. She also thought about the petitions that she and Priscilla had gathered on many planets across the Syrenthian Galaxy. That was a daunting task. And all for what…just so Aaranix Tuvelless could ignore them? She had copies in her office, but that wasn't the point. The incident on Salinarr Nevis of the Xenolfan male being arrested and the human female with the wide brim hat being deported played in her mind over and over. What more could she do? She suddenly became inspired to organize her sexual freedom speech. Sierra stood up from the chaise lounge chair, grabbed her beverage and headed for her office.

After printing the first draft of her speech, the comm sounded.

"Sierra here," she answered.

"This is Madison. We have a galactic emergency to respond to in the ominous Shardaa Sector. Let's meet up at GEMS headquarters."

"The Shardaa Sector? Damn. People usually don't go there," Sierra said.

"Well, someone did. Be here soon," Madison said.

Well, that's a creepy place to go, Sierra thought.

Sierra left the speech on her desk. She walked toward the door, stepped outside, and locked it behind her. Turning toward the *Tenebris,* she quickened her pace.

So much for sleeping in my own bed for once, she thought.

When the *Tenebris* reached space above Asparr Celtarious, she set a course for Relistorr at lightspeed-plus.

Sierra awaited clearance to approach Relistorr. A large hospital ship could be seen orbiting the planet. Surface lighting revealed its gray hull. Two docking bays were located on either side of the ship. It was the *Deliverance,* the Galactic Emergency Medical Services hospital in space. Multiple levels and numerous facilities weaved their way through the ship. A state-of-the-art surgical center was one of its many features. The ship was continually staffed by a multitude of doctors, surgeons, nurses, therapists, and emergency personnel. Most staff worked in shifts, but others worked on an on-call basis, such as Sierra's unit. Part of the emergency services division had some military personnel in the mix, as well as a salvage unit. The majority of people working for GEMS were human, but there were some Xenolfans as well. All of Sierra's unit were human.

"You are cleared for landing, *Tenebris,*" a voice said over the comm.

"Roger that," Sierra said.

Sierra could not wait to land so she could use the rest room. She adjusted the anti-gravitation controls and flew through the atmosphere of Relistorr. As the white clouds drifted aside, the green and brown surface came into full view. Most of Relistorr was flat with brown rocks and green moss. There were a few beautiful mountainous areas with lakes and waterfalls, which sparkled in the light. The planet was extremely secure and only medical and other emergency personnel had access to and from its surface. As Sierra flew around a large outcrop, the Galactic Emergency Medical Services headquarters appeared on a distant hill. The colossal facility, with its many boxy sections and towers, was decorated with brown concrete and tinted windows. She flew around the side to the landing pad and parked the *Tenebris.*

Response times during many emergency relief calls was very long, due to the extent of galactic distances. It was just a fact of space travel. There were times when victims of disasters and other emergencies did not survive the wait. On-call personnel added to the response time because they first had to travel to Relistorr before continuing on in the *Deliverance.* The hospital ship was currently the fastest ship in the galaxy, with the ability to achieve speeds many times faster than lightspeed.

As Sierra exited her ship, she was greeted on the landing pad by Madison Stephard, her unit's director. Madison had long, curly red hair. Also on the landing pad were Sierra's fellow Galactic EMTs, Alex, Aurora, Blaze, and Rachel. She noticed that Aurora had already grabbed her EMT bag from her office.

"We've been waiting. We *do* have a distress signal to respond to," Madison said.

"I came as quickly as I could. My ship can't go any faster," Sierra said.

"We need to get on the transport shuttle and dock with the *Deliverance* right away. How about you get a faster ship?" Madison said.

How about fuck you? Sierra thought.

"What is it that you wanted to talk to me about when you left your message for me?" Sierra asked.

"Our incident commander will be giving a motivational speech. I just wanted to make sure you're at HQ when he does," Madison said.

"Okay. When is that?"

"After this run," Madison said, "assuming you're not running off to do more sex advocating."

Fuck you, bitch, Sierra thought.

"You know…I have to take a piss. I'll be right back," Sierra said, walking toward the building.

"The transport shuttle is leaving. I don't care if you piss your pants," Madison said. "Forget it. Let's go, team. We'll wait for Sierra's slow ass in the shuttle."

Unlike the larger medical shuttles, transport shuttles did not have rest rooms. Sierra entered the headquarters building and made her way down a corridor and passed her office toward the rest rooms. A few people could be seen in that section of the building, but for the most part, it was quiet.

I hate that fucking bitch! Sierra thought as she entered the women's rest room.

She finished in the rest room as quickly as she could.

And of course the paper towel would be out! she thought.

"Screw it!" she said.

She flung the water off her hands and ran for the exit and toward the transport shuttle.

The flight to the *Deliverance* was quiet. The rest of the team could feel the tension between Madison and Sierra and no one spoke.

The docking bay could be seen through the transport shuttle's observation window as they approached. Flashing lights were evenly spaced around the entrance. The gray, metal docking bay floor was painted with yellow markings for shuttle parking. Crew members could be seen attending to their tasks. As the transport shuttle came to a stop, each of them unfastened their seat belts and stood up.

"I need to go have a word with the captain of the *Deliverance*. I will meet you all in the briefing room shortly so that we can go over the details for this run," Madison said.

Madison Stephard walked across the docking bay and made her way up a yellow painted, metal stairway that led to the observation deck. From there, she started walking down a corridor toward the bridge of the *Deliverance*. The rest of the team made their way across the docking bay floor in the opposite direction, toward the briefing room.

"Don't let Madison get to you, Sierra," Aurora said.

"She does know how to push my buttons, the Jinkins!" Sierra said, smiling at Aurora. "Thanks for getting my EMT bag from my office."

"No problem," Aurora said.

The tall blonde had her hair in a ponytail. Sierra was quite attracted to Aurora, but like the policy she had with her bandmates, she also did not permit herself to get involved in relationships with co-workers. Those in her unit knew she was in the Lifestyle and they respected her choice, except for Madison.

"I'm going to change into my uniform before we go to the briefing," Alex said, heading for the locker rooms.

"Yeah, that's a good idea, since we now have to wait for Madison," Rachel said, brushing her brown hair aside.

"We're supposed to be getting new uniforms at some point soon," Blaze said.

"Yeah, they are kind of getting worn out," Sierra said.

They all headed toward the locker rooms. The corridors were busy with many other personnel attending to their tasks. A few medical assistant robots could be seen on occasion. The locker rooms were two levels below their current location.

"Elevator or stairs?" Blaze asked.

They all stopped on the landing and looked at each other.

"Stairs," Sierra said, heading for the steps.

The others followed her. As Alex and Blaze followed down the steps behind the others, Sierra turned back to see the two brown-haired men looking at a picture that hung on the wall of the next landing. She followed their gaze.

"That's the Syrenthian Government capital on Exandra," Sierra said.

"Since we usually take the elevator, I've never seen that picture before. That's a nice photo of the capital at night, with all the lights," Alex said.

"Have you been to Exandra before?" Aurora asked Sierra.

"Yes. That's where my friends Braxton and Priscilla Stryderr live. Braxton works for the Syrenthian Government as an investigator and he also does some other administration stuff too," Sierra said.

As they turned toward the next flight of steps, two nurses passed them, heading up the stairs. Soon, they reached the locker rooms and changed into their Galactic Emergency Medical Services uniforms. The GEMS logo, with its spiral galaxy and heart, was embroidered into the shoulder of each uniform.

When Madison arrived in the briefing room, she immediately noticed the team had already changed into their uniforms.

"Sorry for the delay. Captain Linex Railler and I were discussing navigation of the *Deliverance* through the Shardaa Sector. Let me brief you on the run. We received a distress signal from a space traveler who ventured into the Shardaa Sector. As you know, it's not recommended for anyone to travel to the Shardaa Sector because of all the strange occurrences and disappearances over the years. The captain is hesitant to take the *Deliverance* into that system, so we will only be going to the edge of the Shardaa Sector in this ship. We will be taking a large medical shuttle the remainder of the way to where the signal is emitting. Our technicians believe the signal is emitting from one location and echoing or bouncing off from a different planet in close proximity to the other. So, at this point we are unable to pinpoint which one is the source. The *Deliverance* has just left the orbit of Relistorr. We should be there in several hours at top speed. If the technicians are unable to determine the source by the time we reach the edge of the Shardaa Sector, we are on our own to figure it out. Since the medical shuttle does not have that type of detection equipment on board, it'll have to be by trial and error. Along with the distress signal, there was a faint message from the space traveler, but they could not distinguish exactly what he was trying to say. He mentioned that he saw something or someone. We are not sure. His name is Dennon Cobalt. We believe he may be unconscious or dead. Something happened out there. Other than the salvage team, our team is the only one going in. The salvage team will be behind us to retrieve Dennon Cobalt's ship. I will admit, I feel a bit uneasy about this run, but it's our job. I want everyone to be very alert out there. We *will* be bringing weapons. Do any of you have questions?" Madison asked.

Madison could see the uncomfortable looks come across each of their faces. Madison had been the unit's director for years and she never had a run into the Shardaa Sector before. It was not normally her territory.

"Maranadda has a song about the Shardaa Sector called Tales of Shardaa. It's about all the strange occurrences and stories from there that have circulated through history," Sierra said. "I never thought I would actually be going there."

"Well, this isn't one of your songs, so stay sharp," Madison said. "The Shardaa Sector is virtually uncharted space. We do know from long range scans that there are at least six planets in the Shardaa Star System. The closest to us is also named Shardaa. The other five planets are simply referred to as S2, S3, S4, S5, and S6. The signal could be coming from Shardaa or from S2. We're not quite sure."

"What weapons will we be taking with us?" Alex asked.

"We will each carry a high-powered laser rifle. Hopefully, we won't need to use them," Madison said.

The medical shuttle departed from the *Deliverance*, leaving the docking bay far behind. The salvage team was right behind them in the *Mossenberg*, exiting from a separate docking bay. The *Mossenberg* was equipped with a ship extractor, a tractor beam, and other technologies used to retrieve and haul ships.

"Since the *Deliverance* technicians were unable to decipher which of the two planets the distress signal is transmitting from, we will be checking Shardaa first. It is the closer of the two. We don't know a lot about Shardaa, but our scanners are not detecting air. We'll be there in ten lightminutes, so let's suit up now," Madison said.

Each of them went to the rear of the medical shuttle and began to put on their spacesuits. Sierra adjusted her long, black hair into the helmet. She could not leave her hair out, like she did with the ATV helmets back on Red Jacket when she would ride the quads. They grabbed some EMT bags, oxygen tanks, and their laser rifles. Shardaa loomed ahead in the observation window. It looked dark and desolate. The pilot of the medical shuttle slowed down and gently settled it in a gray, rocky clearing. Most of the planet's surface was dark gray rocks and jagged cliffs. A few areas of shallow, frozen liquid could be seen in the distance. A gray wall of stone was not far from the ship, hidden in the shadows. Madison looked on the computer at the coordinates the technicians had given her.

"The signal seems to be coming from that rock wall area, according to the coordinates we were given," Madison said.

As they headed for the exit, they heard the *Mossenberg* settle onto the ground next to their ship. They cautiously exited the medical shuttle's airlock and stepped out of the ship and onto the dark gray, rocky ground of Shardaa. Sierra held her laser rifle tight in her hands. The EMT bag was slung over her shoulder. A team of five men from the *Mossenberg* joined them. All eleven of them slowly walked toward the rock wall.

"There is no sign of a ship here," the salvage team leader said into the helmet comm.

"No. I'll bet the signal from S2 is skipping off that rock wall," Madison said.

"It looks like there is some sort of reuleaux triangle cave over there. It seems to be a rock crevice that advances upward from the cave," Rachel said.

As they neared the wall, they found that it was not a cave, but a rock crevice that was carved into the side of the rock wall. Sierra noticed a symbol chiseled into the stone above the carved opening. She came to a stop next to the others. An inscription of a feather symbol was fixed above the crevice with two diagonal feathers, forming a cross. The feather leaning to the right was chiseled as a broken feather and was pointed downward from just above the intersection point. Suddenly, an ominous, foreboding feeling came over Sierra and she gasped and became weak in the knees. She reached out and grabbed Blaze's arm to prevent herself from collapsing.

"Sierra, are you okay," Aurora asked.

"Yeah, I think so. I think it's just this spacesuit," Sierra said.

"If you can't handle the mission, perhaps you should stay in the shuttle," Madison said.

"That is an odd feather symbol," Alex said.

"Yes. Well, we need to find Dennon Cobalt. Let's head to S2," Madison said.

The two teams turned around and headed toward their own ships.

"I'm sorry, Madison. I'm fine. I just had a strange feeling overcome me when I saw that feather symbol. This is a weird place," Sierra said.

"Indeed, it is," Madison said.

They all boarded the medical shuttle and removed their spacesuits. Sierra went to the back of the shuttle and rested on a bench. Aurora followed her and sat down next to her.

"Are you sure you're okay?" Aurora asked.

"I…don't know. It was weird. I can't really explain it. Did you feel anything at that rock wall back there?" Sierra asked.

"No, not really. It is a creepy place, though," Aurora said.

"I wonder what that feather symbol means and who carved it there," Sierra said.

"I wonder… Well, I'm going back up front where it's warmer. I just wanted to check on you," Aurora said.

"Thank you, Aurora. I'll be right behind you," Sierra said, holding the blonde's hand for a long moment.

Sierra watched Aurora's ass as she disappeared down the corridor. Her warm smile made Sierra feel better. Sierra stood up and followed her toward the front area where the lounge was located.

The two ships lifted from the surface of Shardaa and set a course for S2. Soon, a similar planet came into view. Madison checked the computer scan of the planet.

"S2 has air. There are no traceable toxins in the air, so we will be fine to go out without spacesuits," Madison said, looking at Sierra. "This is definitely the stronger of the two signals, so the other must have been a phantom signal."

Sierra frowned at Madison. She did not know how much more she could take working in Madison's unit. She often thought about all the things that bothered her about working under Madison, but now was not the time to think about such things. Being focused on the current mission in the Shardaa Sector was her main priority.

The pilot of the medical shuttle followed the other set of coordinates the *Deliverance* technicians had calculated for S2. For the most part, S2 looked similar to Shardaa with its dark gray, rocky landscape. The difference was in the monoliths and spires that protruded from the surface of S2. In the distance ahead, they spotted a ship that had crashed into the rocks. The *Mossenberg* and the medical shuttle settled onto the ground near the crashed ship. The Galactic Emergency Medical Technicians again cautiously exited the shuttle with laser weapons drawn. They slowly made their way around to where the ship had impacted onto the surface of S2.

"That's going to need some repair," Alex said.

"Rachel, Blaze, and Aurora, I want you three to check for Dennon Cobalt inside the ship. Sierra and Alex, scout the parameter," Madison said.

Soon, the three Galactic EMTs stepped out of the damaged ship and reported to Madison.

"There is no one on board," Rachel said.

Madison gave the salvage team a signal to begin the process of extracting the ship from the rocks. She led Blaze, Rachel, and Aurora to scout for Dennon Cobalt in a different direction than Sierra and Alex had gone. The team was relieved not to have the restrictive spacesuits on.

"We have something!" Sierra said over the comm that was attached to her arm.

Sierra and Alex ran over to where a human man lay on the rocky ground. He was in a narrow opening between two monoliths. Sierra dropped to one knee next to the man, setting down her laser rifle and EMT bag. She began to check his vitals.

"The patient appears to be in his forties. His respiration rate is normal. I have his heart rate at 110 beats per minute and a blood pressure reading of 150/95. His pupils are dilated," Sierra said.

Alex removed a natural aromatic inhalant from his EMT bag and broke it under the man's nose. The man took a deep breath and opened his eyes wide. He looked from Alex to Sierra.

"Help me! I saw her. She's here! She's here!" he shouted.

The frightened man fell back into a state of unconsciousness. Soon, the rest of the team arrived with a transfer board.

"He's alive, but appears to be having an acute stress reaction," Sierra said.

"Let's get him back to the medical shuttle for further assessment and monitoring," Madison said.

They carefully positioned him onto the transfer board and lifted it from the rocky ground between the monoliths.

"He has a cut on his upper left arm. It looks like it's from the sharp rocks," Rachel said.

"When we tried to wake him, he said something about seeing 'her' and that 'she's here.' Do you think he was looking for someone in the Shardaa Sector?" Alex asked.

"Good question," Madison said.

They passed the salvage team as its workers prepared to tractor beam the extracted ship into the docking bay of the *Mossenberg*. After boarding the medical shuttle, they moved Dennon Cobalt to the infirmary.

"Let's get him hooked up to the monitors. Sierra and Alex, I want you both to take a look around the vicinity. See if there is another person out there that Dennon was talking about," Madison said.

"We're on it," Alex said.

The two of them left the ship. The salvage team already had Dennon Cobalt's ship in the docking bay of the *Mossenberg*. They walked past the ground that had been disturbed from the ship crash. Rocky outcrops and monoliths were numerous. They passed the area where they had found Dennon. Making their way along the jagged rocks, they saw a cliff to their right and a rock wall to their left. Sierra peered over the edge of the cliff and into a dark chasm. She slowly walked back toward Alex, near the rock wall.

"There doesn't seem to be anyone around here," Sierra said.

"Take a look at this," Alex said.

Sierra joined Alex around the corner of the rock wall. She followed his gaze.

"Wow! Another rock crevice with a reuleaux triangle opening at the bottom…but this one actually has a cave," Sierra said.

"And look, another feather symbol inscription is chiseled into the stone above the cave," Alex said.

Sierra walked closer to the opening. It was indeed the same exact feather symbol, with its crossing feathers, and a broken one on the right side.

"Oh wow. I just noticed that the crevice in the rock wall looks like a vulva," Alex said.

"Wow! You're right. Why didn't I notice that before on Shardaa? I would have thought that I would be the first one to see something sexual like that," Sierra said.

"I know, right?"

Sierra turned her head sideways and looked at the rock slit, realizing that Alex was correct. After a closer look, she noticed the labia and clitoris that was roughly carved into the stone.

"With a reuleaux triangular vagina, it must represent a Xenolfan pussy. This is suddenly amazing and creepy at the same time. The feather symbol is up where the mons pubis would be. Very strange…" Sierra said.

"Shall we take a look inside the cave? I have an illuminator," Alex said.

"I suppose. I never thought I would be walking into a rock pussy," Sierra said.

They both laughed. Suddenly, the planet's daylight dimmed considerably as night set in. It quickly became darker as they entered the cave. Alex enabled the illuminator and they made their way in. The tunnel soon ended.

"If there is some female that Dennon was searching for, she does not seem to be here," Alex said.

"No. Let's check a bit more on the outside and then we need to get back," Sierra said.

Alex led the way out with the illuminator in hand. As they neared the opening, Sierra turned around and looked into the darkness. She thought she caught a quick glimpse of two small, blue lights. They exited the cave and Sierra shook her head side to side. As she looked back up at the feather symbol above the opening, the same eerie feeling she had felt on Shardaa overwhelmed her once again. Alex could see her distress. She collapsed onto the ground. She looked up at the night sky, the starlight surrounding her field of vision. He knelt down to help Sierra and inadvertently dropped his comm and it slid down between two rocks. He quickly reached between the rocks, but it had slid too far and was out of reach.

"Shit, I dropped my comm and can't reach it," Alex said.

"Forget it. You can get another one in the shuttle. Get me out of here, Alex."

He helped Sierra to her feet and kept her steady. They made their way toward the medical shuttle.

"It wasn't your spacesuit the first time. Something here in the Shardaa Sector is stressing you," Alex said.

"I saw something in the cave when I turned back…like blue lights. And these feathers of Shardaa… I'm just overwhelmed for some reason. Maybe I shouldn't have come on this run," Sierra said.

On their walk back, Alex scanned the surrounding area with his eyes. It was a bit difficult to see in the dark, but he did not see anyone else and didn't have time to investigate further. He needed to get Sierra back. As they neared the medical shuttle, they noticed the *Mossenberg* had already departed from S2. Madison was waiting for them at the shuttle entrance. Sierra straightened her composure the best she could.

"We didn't find the additional person that Dennon spoke of," Alex said.

"I didn't think you would. After he awoke again for a brief moment, he said she was a tall, sexy woman with black wings and blue eyes. What we have is a delusional space traveler. We'll get him back to the *Deliverance* and then get ourselves back to headquarters on Relistorr," Madison said.

In the conference room of the Galactic Emergency Medical Services headquarters, Madison and her team sat in soft, comfortable chairs made of light gray fabric. The incident commander was about to make a motivational speech. It was just a reminder that Sierra had to put the finishing touches on her own speech. She wondered how Priscilla was coming along with her sexual health part of the speech for the upcoming seminar. A man in his fifties walked up to the front of the table. His hair was all gray. He wore a uniform with his name and title on the front.

"Hello. My name is Elliss Millott. I am the GEMS incident commander. I oversee most of the runs that the different units are assigned to. Today, I want to share a motivational speech with your unit. You see, GEMS is in desperate need of Galactic EMTs. We need more of you, but we're not getting what we need. A lot of people are getting degrees and becoming doctors and nurses. If we don't get more Galactic EMTs, the doctors and nurses won't have enough patients to make a career out of it. So, let's talk about education and experience.

"One can follow in the traditional educational process, but the harvest of self-learning is boundless. Don't be discouraged and lose the will to forge ahead against the grain. Detoxing one's self from the avaricious system and unlearning the protocol can set one free. Vocational training and certifications are a great value and I recommend them over college for GEMS. Educate yourself and don't be brainwashed and ripped off by institutions that don't have your best interest in mind. Be true to yourself. And if you can, help others as well. That's what we are all about here. Take charge of your life and stop relying on these failed institutions to do it for you. Don't become a life-long slave to that system. Get motivated, take charge, and be in a position to make a difference. There is no degree that will give you that kind of power. If you know anyone that would like to go through vocational training, we could use the help.

"Step-by-step tutorials can certainly bring a result, but a skill set and technical working knowledge that is not a recipe-style formula is priceless. This can only be achieved through experience. It is only through applying a foundation and specific techniques that these skills can truly become a value. You can educate yourself all you want, but you will only become a valued asset through years of hands-on experience. We've all made mistakes along our journey. Learning from those mistakes forges your experience. Keep in mind that no one is perfect. Just keep moving forward. I would not only like to get some new Galactic EMTs in here, but I would like to keep them here for years to come. Let's go out and save the galaxy."

The team clapped their hands. With the conclusion of the speech, each of them stood up from their chairs and departed the conference room. Sierra stayed back and waited for Madison to leave. Once she was gone, Sierra quickly approached Elliss Millott as he finished organizing his speech papers.

"Hi, Elliss. My name is Sierra Shalinsky. I totally agree with you on the self-learning and vocational education. I do a lot of self-learning. So, since there are so many current Galactic EMT openings, I am wondering if I can transfer to a different unit. Madison and I don't do well together and it's been affecting some of our runs. I think this mission to Shardaa was a bit more than I could take from Madison. If you could at least look into it, I would appreciate it. Teams need to all work together, like a well oiled machine. If you have gears with a different pitch, it's not going to work out. She is very draconian and I'm surprised I've dealt with her this long. Perhaps now is the perfect opportunity..." Sierra said.

"Well...you are not the first one to complain about Madison. She is a bit rough around the edges. And it seems that you are too. So, I get it. You two are not compatible. I'll tell you what... I will look for another opening for you in a different unit. I know you have a lot of experience and GEMs can't afford to lose you. As I said, we need more people like you...and soon. Our response times have gone down because of the personnel shortage. We're thinking about implementing a policy where on-call first responders don't travel to HQ first, but instead meet up with the *Deliverance* at the incident location. In theory, it would save precious time and probably someone's life. But that is still in the works... Anyway, I will look into it and see what I can do for you," Elliss said.

"That's all I ask. Thank you, sir," Sierra said as she departed the conference room.

Chapter Five

As he did on many occasions, Aaranix Tuvelless walked along a stone path that led through the jungle paradise of Olf Teruda, near the government palace. The warmth of the humid air was comforting to him. He brushed a hanging vine from his long, white hair as he followed the path around a curve. Ahead of him, the trees cleared to reveal a stone patio with two stone benches, similar to the ones on the terrace outside of his office. The government palace could be seen in the background, vines and green foliage covering the majority of its stone walls. He noticed one of his sexy lovers sitting on the farthest of the two benches, facing the palace. Her bluish-gray skin peaked through her open-back shirt.

"Well, hello, my love," Aaranix said.

She turned around, surprised to see him there. A smile suddenly appeared, her sapphire eyes sparkling. It didn't bother her knowing that she was just one of many lovers the Xenolfan Government leader had. He took very good care of all of them.

"Aaranix, what a surprise. It's nice to see you get out of your office once in a while," she said.

"Malanaa, you are looking lovely. I like the style of your top," he said.

He sat on the bench behind her and began to massage her back and shoulders through the shirt's open back.

"Oh, that feels good. Over to the left… Oh, don't stop," Malanaa said.

"You are tense there. I will rub it as long as you want me to," Aaranix said.

She leaned back against him. He continued to massage her tight back muscles. He lightly traced around the genetic bumps where wings had once been on their species many generations before. As he worked his way down, he lightly reached around and caressed both of her breasts. Gently squeezing them, he started kissing along her neck, her white hair brushing against his bluish-gray, patterned face.

"Finger my pussy," Malanaa said.

The patio was in an isolated area of the government palace grounds and was rarely frequented by anyone else. But as leader, he didn't much care if anyone was around or not. He would do damn well what he pleased. He reached down beneath her thin dress and began to massage her pussy, softly rubbing at her smooth labia. He inserted two fingers into her reuleaux triangular opening and Malanaa's pussy became very moist. He shifted around in front of her and she lay back on the stone bench, opening her legs for him. As the dress fell away, Aaranix pulled her damp panties to one side and began to lick at the warm folds of bluish-pink skin. Her familiar high-pitched, reverberating purr filled his ears. He could distinguish between his different lovers by the tone of their voice when they reached orgasm. It was all music to his ears, each of them a different delicate instrument. His polyamorous relationships were no secret to his people. All of his lovers were spoiled with everything he had to offer in his position as leader of the Xenolfan Government.

"Let me suck that nice cock of yours," she demanded, removing his pants.

The bluish-gray member flopped out before her. Its rounded triangular shape was stepped down to a smaller girth toward the tip. She put her mouth around it, her long tongue wrapping around its surface. Moving her head up and down, she slowly sucked his hard shaft. She caressed his smooth balls as their eyes met in a lustful moment. He soon bent her over and she straddled the stone bench.

As he entered from behind her, she let out a long moan of sexual bliss. He moved her dress up and over her back. Holding her hips with both hands, he pounded her blue cunt hard. The sound of the wet slaps from their genitals colliding together filled the patio area, followed by their audible sounds of joy. Aaranix moaned as he reached an orgasm, his cock pulsating deep inside of her. He pulled away, his cum dripping to the stone patio.

"Mmm, that was very nice, my love," Malanaa said.

"Yes. It was a lovely surprise to see you here," Aaranix said.

She adjusted her panties and dress as he pulled up his pants.

"I'll see you around. I have a hair appointment to go to," she said.

She flung her long, white hair aside and headed toward the palace.

As Aaranix entered the government palace, he decided to visit a part of the palace he had not been to in many years. He turned into a desolate corridor that rarely saw any traffic. The marble floor reflected the limited lighting in the area. The echo of his shoes was the only sound to be heard. Although they were no longer used, old candles were fixed along the corridor. Pictures of former Xenolfan Government leaders decorated the walls, going back to leaders from more than a thousand years before. The illuminators were much dimmer in that area of the palace, casting dark shadows. The corridor turned perpendicular and narrowed. The narrowed corridor was decorated with a burgundy carpet that had many gothic patterns woven into the design. Aaranix soon stood before a large set of double doors. They emitted a slight squeak as he manually opened them. After entering the room, the pneumatic doors closed behind him. The room was darker yet, a musty odor lingering in the air. He walked across the marble floor to another set of doors. Before continuing, he hesitated for a long moment and let out a deep sigh. He slowly opened the heavy doors that led down into the lower levels of the palace. The marble steps curved downward in a spiral to a landing where the ceiling opened up to a wide room. Sunlight brightened the area from a skylight window that was designed to emit light all the way from the roof of the palace to the basement. The light revealed the standing water that occupied the old archives room. Aaranix could not go past the landing without getting soaked with the algae-laden water.

On several occasions after the archives had been flooded, Aaranix had a team try to extract the water and try to find the source of the leak, but they were unsuccessful and the water would always return. So, he gave up.

As he stood at the landing, he gazed down into the water-filled archives. Pieces of the old books could be seen floating in the water and at the bottom, along the floor, their paper goo serving no purpose. It had been years since the pond flooded the lower levels. He had not been down there since they tried extracting the water, but he felt moved to see it again, as it had been on his mind lately. Only the sitting leader of the Xenolfan Government had access to that section of the palace. As he looked at a piece of floating paper goo and the remainder of book bindings, he wondered which piece of paper mush belonged to the book that he discovered on that day so many years ago.

After sneezing twice, he turned around and headed back up the curved stairs.

Aaranix Tuvelless sat in his office and read the report from Salinarr Nevis. Another interspecies sex violator would be arriving on Olf Teruda to stand trial. The violator's human counterpart had been sent to the Syrenthian Government on Exandra. The reports angered him every time he saw one. Perhaps it was the lack of respect that bothered him more than the interspecies sex, but he didn't know for sure which one bothered him more. People were going to pay for the unorthodox abomination. He had his military officers on a couple of missions to disrupt the madness and put and end to their dangerous practices. Respect of the law is all that Aaranix Tuvelless had going for him and he knew it. The ancient proof of the problem with the forbidden unions had been destroyed all those years ago when the archives in the lower levels were flooded. He was glad he went down there again to see it.

He remembered back to that day when he discovered the truth. Aaranix had been sitting down in the musty archives, studying Xenolfan history from a different perspective than the history taught to the public. The archives in the lower levels were the Xenolfan Government's top secret texts that only the sitting leader had access to. He had sat in disbelief after reading one of the ancient books. The book was titled *Anathema Strain*. According to the book, the Xenolfan and human relationships would cause a host of problems, but the worst was their offspring. He didn't know what to think of the book he had held in his hand that day. One of his predecessors, Siiteper Affelum, had written the book a thousand years before. The fact that it contradicted what he knew about the biological make-up of the two species made him wonder, since it was impossible for the two species to breed. So, he didn't know what to make of it. It wasn't until he woke up from a nightmare, covered in sweat, that he decided to create the law of forbidden interspecies sex. He recalled the nightmare of hellish monsters. But in all the interspecies relationships that the government intervened in, there had never been a pregnancy nor offspring produced. He often doubted the context of the book he had read and its accuracy. It angered him to question himself. It was not something that he was willing to take a chance on, so he implemented the law. He had always been curious about his people's history, but after that discovery and subsequent nightmare, he stopped going into the lower levels. From all the hundreds of secret government books that had been in the archives, he wished he had taken that single book, *Anathema Strain,* up into his office. When the pond flooded the lower levels, it destroyed every book, every scroll, every text. Although the water had receded over the years to its current level, most of the archives were still under water. If he had mentioned to his people what he had read, they would think of him as mentally ill.

He often thought the implementation of the forbidden interspecies sex law was really just because of his disdain for humans. He certainly did despise humans because of the Syrenthian War, which took place over one hundred years before. The only territory the Xenolfans had to show for it was Olf Teruda and Salinarr Nevis, although they were much more wealthy than the Syrenthian Government. His hatred for them seemed to be growing. He had always thought humans should assimilate to Xenolfan culture more than they did.

How dare they come here to our capital and protest their disgraceful and immoral relationships! Aaranix thought.

Aaranix believed that humans had no respect for Xenolfans, just like one hundred years before. If humans disrespected his people in any way, didn't treat them equally, discriminated against any of them, they were not welcome on Olf Teruda nor Salinarr Nevis. He had no allegiance to the humans and his only loyalty was to his own people. The sexual freedom protesters were driven off. After their contemptuous petitions sat on his desk for a week, he finally threw them into the trash can. Some of his top dignitaries, along with another female government officer, Phensiarr Charseaa, had seen them beforehand. Aaranix had noticed that Phensiarr Charseaa seemed a little upset when he discarded the petitions. Oh well… What an incredible waste of time they had spent gathering them from all across the Syrenthian Galaxy. The amusement made him laugh.

Garrious folded his bluish-gray arms and stood in the hangar watching the engineers make the final adjustments to a massive ion engine. The illuminators overhead brightened the facility adequately. Large tool boxes and other equipment could be seen all around. Other uniformed Xenolfan workers began to roll the platform the ion engine rested upon toward the open bay of a large ship. As Garrious looked on, one of the engineers walked over to him.

"So, Garrious, are you ready for your upcoming mission?" Keddaa Doraa asked.

"Well, Keddaa, when the asteroid is ready, I will be ready as well. I hope it is well worth dying for. I'm not sure why Aaranix Tuvelless wants this, but I am loyal to our leader and I will obey," Garrious said.

The engineer patted Garrious on the shoulder and continued on toward the hangar exit. They were at a military base on the Olf Teruda satellite called Dalaa. Garrious was selected by Aaranix for the suicide mission. The ion engine would be fixed onto a small asteroid in space, along with a controller cockpit. The engineers followed the same instructions that were used one hundred years before, during the Syrenthian War. Rigging the asteroid with a directional ion engine, controlled remotely from a different location on the same asteroid, was exactly how the Xenolfans retaliated against the human-occupied planets during the old Syrenthian War. During the war, the missile asteroids were dubbed missiloids. They had left very disastrous results. And now, Aaranix Tuvelless felt compelled to assault a planet in the Syrenthian Government's territory. Garrious would man the missiloid on a collision course for Aamaress. The mission was one of two different types that the Xenolfan leader had put into place.

In space, not far from Olf Teruda's military satellite of Dalaa, a shuttle docked with an asteroid using a docking claw. The asteroid was to be used on the mission to assault Aamaress. The ion engine and cockpit had been mounted to the asteroid. Both the lead engineer, Keddaa Doraa, and Garrious exited the shuttle in spacesuits and slowly drifted toward the missiloid to review the controls and his mission. They began at the ion engine in the aft section of the missiloid.

"This is the powerful engine that will transport the asteroid to Aamaress and has enough power to make a devastating impact. It is controlled remotely from the cockpit," Keddaa said into the helmet comm.

"Remotely? Okay," Garrious said.

They floated along the rocky asteroid toward the front section.

"Here is the cockpit where you will remotely control the speed and direction of the asteroid's ion engine. The cabin is comfortable and will have just enough air supply to get you to Aamaress and complete your mission. There are no additional weapons on the missiloid. It is not meant to be very maneuverable. We have followed the engineering drawings from back in the Syrenthian War. This is exactly how they used to do it," Keddaa said.

"So, once I get in and seal the canopy, the air supply will fill up the cabin and I can remove my helmet?" Garrious asked.

"That is correct. There is a small cubby behind the seat to store the helmet. Also, the observation window is made with a special heat resistant glass for atmospheric entry. It will shield you adequately from the heat…well, at least until the impact," Keddaa said.

"Okay. I appreciate you going over all this with me in person. I will head back to Olf Teruda tonight and say my goodbyes to my relatives and then head back out here tomorrow to start the suicide mission," Garrious said.

"You have my utmost respect, sir," Keddaa said.

"Thank you."

They made their way back into the shuttle airlock. At the shuttle's controls, Keddaa released the docking claw. The two of them did not notice what came next. When the docking claw was released, it scraped along the rocky surface of the asteroid and came into contact with the left front anchor plate of the cockpit. The force of the claw's contact disturbed the threaded stud that was driven deep into the rock.

The return flight to the Olf Teruda moon of Dalaa was fairly quiet. Garrious's ship was parked in the hangar on Dalaa. From there, the flight back to Olf Teruda would not take long. After the shuttle settled into the hangar next to Garrious's ship, the two Xenolfan men exited.

One of the technicians walked over to them.

"So, what did you think of our marvelous missiloid?" the technician asked.

"Very impressive. They must have had hundreds of those during the Syrenthian War," Garrious said.

"Oh, yeah…at least," the technician said, looking at the shuttle docking hook. "Whoa, you two must have scraped that asteroid pretty hard."

They both turned around and noticed a small amount of damage to the end of the claw.

"It was rock. What do you expect? Throw a fresh coat of paint on there and it will be good as new," Keddaa said.

"Well, I'm not getting into the middle of this one. I'll see you tomorrow, Keddaa," Garrious said.

"Yes. Have a very meaningful evening," Keddaa said.

"That, I will," Garrious said, heading for his ship.

Chapter Six

Priscilla Stryderr pushed her husband's head down between her legs as he sucked at the pink lips of her pussy. She absolutely loved her pussy eaten by her husband…and on occasion by their unicorn lover, Sierra Shalinsky. She parted her legs farther and pushed up with her hips, forcing her cunt against his mouth.

"Oh yeah! Eat that fucking pussy," Priscilla groaned.

He continually put pressure on the down-lick and alternated the tip of his tongue side to side across Priscilla's clit. Every once in a while, he would stick his tongue deep into her vagina and swirl around before changing it up to sucking her inner and outer labia into his mouth. He knew how much she enjoyed cunnilingus. She could go for a long time with multiple orgasms and he enjoyed every bit of it.

"I'm coming again!" she said as her body stiffened up.

A drip of cum rolled from her vagina and he quickly licked up the musky cream. Her wet pussy juice covered his mouth as he smiled up at her beautiful face and long, blond hair.

"You taste delicious," he said.

"I love you, Braxton."

He moved up and kissed her.

"Mmm, I love the taste of my own pussy," she said.

The comm at the side of the bed rang.

"Shit, who the hell is that at this hour?" Priscilla asked.

Braxton leaned over Priscilla's beautiful breasts and looked at the comm.

"It's the office," he said, picking up the comm. "Braxton here."

Priscilla looked up at him and then down at his half-hard cock and frowned.

"Okay. I'll be there shortly. Bye," Braxton said.

"Don't tell me you have to leave…" Priscilla said.

"Yes. We have a situation. It's kind of a galactic emergency. I'll fill you in when I know more," he said.

He quickly searched for his clothes on the floor and got dressed.

"Don't forget to wash your face," she said.

"Oh, good idea," he said, heading for the bathroom.

When he left the bedroom, she began to finger herself. She was going to have sex with or without him. She grabbed one of her sex toys on the headboard and rubbed it back and forth against her wet vulva. Slowly inserting the dildo, she closed her eyes and pushed up with her hips. It wasn't Braxton, but it sure felt good. She continued moving the smooth phallus in and out. As she felt a deep orgasm build, she pushed the dildo in as far as possible and rode the waves of her nerve endings from head to toe.

"Ahhh!"

That is the last thing Braxton heard as he shut the house door. He smiled.

Damn, I hate my job at times, he thought. *I will definitely have to finish that later.*

Priscilla Stryderr worked in the health care industry at a hospital on Exandra. She also helped Sierra Shalinsky advocate for interspecies sexual freedom. Priscilla and Sierra had gathered petition signatures from all across the Syrenthian Galaxy. She personally delivered them to Olf Teruda and presented them to Aaranix Tuvelless and his officials. Priscilla protested on Olf Teruda twice. She had just completed the finishing touches on her healthy, sex-positive speech that she would be presenting with Sierra during their upcoming Sexual

Freedom Seminar on Red Jacket. She was very excited about the opportunity to present the health-side of sex at the seminar. Her relationship with Sierra was a close one. They were in the Lifestyle together…sort of. Sierra was a unicorn and played with others, but Priscilla and Braxton only played with Sierra exclusively. Priscilla considered Sierra her best friend. She was sexy, smart, tough, an awesome vocalist, loved to help people as a Galactic Emergency Medical Technician, and really knew how to use her tongue. The first time Priscilla met Sierra was when the *Deliverance* hospital ship arrived in the shipping lanes above Exandra to transport a patient down to the hospital that she worked at. Sierra was one of the Galactic EMTs assigned to that patient transfer. They hit it off right away and have been friends and lovers ever since.

Braxton hated leaving his wife in the middle of sex, but this was urgent. They lived outside of the city in a beautiful country setting. He flew his anti-gravitational transport down a hill that overlooked the Syrenthian Government capital city on Exandra. The beautiful city lights brightened the night sky. There was not much traffic at that hour. The night view of the city lights was absolutely fabulous. Many photographers would take their photo shots from the top of the hill.

Braxton Stryderr had short, brown hair, but was starting to get a touch of gray throughout. He was an investigator and administrative clerk for the Syrenthian Government. Being in his position meant that he had to respond to the call of duty at any hour they needed him. Fortunately, it did not happen very often in the middle of the night. He made his way through the city toward the administrative center. Soon, the government building lay before him, its many large pillars bright with lights shining up on them in the darkness of the night. The building was a unique and spectacular design that mixed both modern and ancient flavors into the architecture. After clearing with security at the gate, he parked his anti-gravitational transport and headed for the entrance at a quick pace. Braxton was pleased with the tight security at the administrative center. When he reached the building entrance, he said hello to the security guard and proceeded to enter his security clearance code in the electronic door panel. It swiftly slid aside and he made his way to his office on the third floor. His investigative partner was already there waiting for him.

"Okay, what kind of galactic emergency is this? Do you realize I was making love to my wife?" Braxton asked.

"Sorry, Braxton. I'm sure that was hot, but this bit of information is much hotter," Tellaris Whitestone said, rubbing his hand along his grayish-white hair.

"And as my investigative partner, I have faith that you are correct. At least I hope so because, damn, Priscilla was hot," Braxton said.

"Okay, our Communications Department has picked up chatter on Xenolfan channels that is disturbing. They discovered that the Xenolfan Government is planning something against an unknown target. It's highly unlikely they would strike one of their own two planets, neither Olf Teruda nor Salinarr Nevis. So, the only conclusion is they plan to assault the sovereign territory of the Syrenthian Government, and that would be an act of war. I'm not sure what Aaranix Tuvelless is up to, but this is a bit alarming. Our government leader is on his way to this meeting as we speak," Tellaris said.

"Edward Sirlain is coming here tonight? Okay, this shit just got real," Braxton said.

"This is definitely—" Tellaris was cut short from the office door opening.

A tall, thin man with long, grayish-blond hair tied into a ponytail, walked through Braxton's office door. He wore an elegant black and burgundy suit. A small security detail of four men followed him into the office.

"Good evening, gentlemen. There hasn't been this much concern with the Xenolfan Government for almost one hundred years. Aaranix Tuvelless has been increasingly angry in recent years regarding interspecies relationships, of all things. Protesters were driven away from Olf Teruda on a couple of occasions. A lot of arrests have happened on Salinarr Nevis. Xenolfan Government officials have deported both male and female humans from Salinarr Nevis and had them transported directly here to Exandra on multiple occasions while their Xenolfan lovers were arrested back on Salinarr Nevis. So, we believe this new chatter we have discovered on the Xenolfan frequencies could be related to their leader's disdain for humans. So, where is their target and how will they deliver the assault? Those are questions I need you both to find the answers to. I had a meeting with two of my top aides regarding this before I arrived here," Edward Sirlain said.

He handed both of the men file folders.

"Enclosed in these files, you will find your investigative assignments. We must find out what the Xenolfans are up to. Tellaris, we're sending you to the Xenolfan Government capital on Olf Teruda as the official Syrenthian Government envoy. You are to confront and inquire. They need to know that we know. Braxton, I need you to work directly with the Communications Department and piece together any clues you can get from the Xenolfan channels. Follow up on any leads. Both of you contact me with anything you find," Edward said.

"We're on it," Tellaris said.

The Syrenthian Government leader, Edward Sirlain, and his security detail left Braxton's office.

"Well, I better get home and change into something a bit more alien," Tellaris said.

Tellaris Whitestone stood up from the chair.

"Good luck, Tellaris," Braxton said.

"Thanks," he said, heading out the door with the file folder in his hand.

The Communications Department was in another section of the government administrative building. Braxton Stryderr sat in a comfortable chair deep inside the complex. Surrounding him was a vast array of communications detection equipment with LEDs flashing, displays lit up, and multiple chatter sounds emitting from speakers. Braxton sat with two communications technicians, one of which had a set of headphones on. The man removed the headphones and set them down on the bench.

"Anything new?" Braxton asked.

"Nothing," the man said.

The three of them looked up as a woman came through the door with an urgent announcement.

"We just received a report from the planet Shar Nefalis in the Industrial Sector. Garnell Meshtief, owner of the manufacturing facility, Ticrisuda Powersports, witnessed two Xenolfan males messing around in his warehouse. He said they were spotted in the snowmobile and ATV section of the warehouse with some large duffel bags. The company's security team chased them off," she said.

"Okay, that sounds like a lead to me. I'll be on my way to Shar Nefalis. If you guys hear anything else, let me know," Braxton said.

After passing through security, Tellaris Whitestone settled his ship onto the landing pad of the Xenolfan Government palace on Olf Teruda. When he exited the ship, he immediately felt the humidity of the jungle paradise planet. He quickly felt the dampness affect his hair. As he stood on the landing pad, he gazed at the marvelous stone palace, with its many vines growing up the side of the walls and wrapping around the pillars. He proceeded toward the building's main entrance. He contacted them ahead of time to let them know he would be arriving to discuss an urgent matter. It did not surprise Tellaris that no one was there to greet him. It just reinforced Aaranix's contempt for humans. Upon entering the palace, Tellaris made his way to an information center that sat in the middle of a large marble floor. A Xenolfan woman sat at the desk.

"Hello. My name is Tellaris Whitestone. I'm the envoy from the Syrenthian Government. I'm here to speak with Aaranix Tuvelless regarding an urgent matter. I believe he is expecting me," he said.

"Yes, of course. I will let him know you have arrived," she said.

She activated the comm. "Tellaris Whitestone is here to see Aaranix," she said.

"Send him up," one of Aaranix's dignitaries said.

"Right away," she said.

"If you would like to follow the stairs to the second level, turn left and follow the corridor to the last door on the right. There, you will find an office where someone can assist you," she said.

"Okay. Thank you," Tellaris said as he turned toward the stairs.

The staircase and railing were both made of stone and curved upward toward a mezzanine. Once Tellaris reached the top of the stairs, he turned left and made his way across the open mezzanine to the corridor beyond. It was a very long corridor, which ran the entire length of the palace. Tellaris could see a window at the far end. Soon, he came to a stop at the window and looked out and down to a beautiful pond. He saw the door on his right that the receptionist had referred to. Turning toward the door, he took a moment to gather his thoughts and took a deep breath. He knocked on the old wooden door. After a pause, the door opened and a tall Xenolfan stood before him.

"Come in," the dignitary said. "Have a seat."

Tellaris entered Aaranix's office and sat in a chair in front of his desk. They were accompanied by two of Aaranix's dignitaries. It was a spacious office, but very disorganized. The Xenolfan leader sat at his desk in front of Tellaris. The desk was in the middle of the room on a large decorative carpet. Various stacks of papers and other items sat on the desk. Along the wall to the right, Tellaris noticed a series of bookshelves that made up the leader's private atheneum. Several of the books were pulled from the shelves, leaving empty spots. The pulled books sat on the ledge of a half wall that ran along the side of the office. A couple of the books were open to a particular page and left upside down on the ledge. Beyond his desk was a window and door that revealed an outdoor terrace. The stone terrace overlooked the pond below and was decorated with two stone benches and pillars that stood at equal intervals along the stone railing. Green vines wrapped around the pillars.

"So, Tellaris Whitestone, what urgent matter brings you to Olf Teruda?" Aaranix asked.

"We have evidence that the Xenolfan Government plans an assault on the Syrenthian Government's sovereign territory," Tellaris said.

The two dignitaries looked at each other and then to Aaranix. Aaranix shifted in his seat.

"What evidence do you have of such nonsense?" Aaranix asked.

"That's classified information. We have reason to believe this pertains to interspecies relationships," Tellaris said.

"Well, it's no secret that we have a Xenolfan law that forbids our species to be in any type of relationship with yours, but I'm afraid your accusation is preposterous," Aaranix said.

"I'm not sure where you Xenolfans plan to assault our territory, but I can assure you that if any such assault leads back to you, it will be an act of war. And war is something that you will not want," Tellaris said, standing up from the chair.

"Is that a threat?" Aaranix asked.

"I'll see myself out," Tellaris said, leaving the office.

The two dignitaries looked at Aaranix.

"Make sure he does not leave Olf Teruda," Aaranix said.

One of the two dignitaries ran after Tellaris. Aaranix turned to the remaining dignitary.

"Kill him and throw the body into the flooded archives in the lower levels. Yes, you have my permission to enter the lower levels of the palace for this task. And then get rid of his ship," Aaranix said.

The remaining dignitary quickly left Aaranix's office.

Braxton Stryderr arrived on the planet Shar Nefalis in the Industrial Sector. As his ship descended, he could see factories and industrial areas extend far into the distance, disappearing beyond the horizon. Many pipes and smoke stacks could be seen along most of the buildings. Parts and other miscellaneous items sat on hundreds of skids that lined the outside of the buildings. Many forklifts could be seen loading anti-gravitational transport semis and freight train boxcars, all destined for the spaceport. Containers were stacked high along many of the industrial areas. Braxton settled his ship onto a landing pad and shut down the ship's engines. Upon exiting, Braxton was greeted by a man with black hair.

"You must be Braxton Stryderr from the Syrenthian Government," the man said.

"Yes."

"Thank you for coming, Braxton. My name is Garnell Meshtief. I'm the owner of Ticrisuda Powersports."

"It's nice to meet you, Garnell."

"Let me briefly tell you about the history of the Industrial Sector. Aomium Swith is the second largest planet in the Industrial Sector. It was the planet that gave the Industrial Sector its name from the large industrial empire that was first developed there. A multitude of products were forged within the factories of the early Industrial Sector. Railways began to sprout across the planet with numerous freight lines. The Industrial Sector has been well engineered with superior construction and extraordinary maintenance through the years. Prosperous businessmen, brilliant negotiators, and successful visionaries have always been abundant here, some of them have even become legends. Soon, the manufacturing facilities sprouted to the other planets in the Shar Nefalis Star System. Here on Shar Nefalis and on Aomium Swith, factories stretch as far as the eye can see. Distribution channels were devised across the Syrenthian Galaxy for product delivery. In later years, Chelliss and Ardellia were the remaining planets in the star system that were added to the ever expanding Industrial Sector," Garnell said.

"That's very interesting. Well, we definitely want to get to the bottom of this investigation. So, what do you do here at Ticrisuda Powersports?" Braxton asked.

"We are the galaxy's largest manufacturer of snowmobiles, ATVs, and other recreational sport vehicles," Garnell said.

"So, tell me what happened," Braxton said.

"Let me take you to the warehouse and show you," Garnell said.

Together, they walked toward the entrance and entered the building. After passing through a large office area, Garnell led Braxton to the manufacturing center. Assembly lines stretched as far as Braxton could see. Snowmobiles were being assembled on several lines. Across the cement floor several more lines displayed ATVs being assembled. Workers went about their jobs efficiently, paying close attention to detail and quality. Labor robots were seen helping with heavy lifting at some of the work stations. As Garnell and Braxton passed that section of the facility, the noise level increased slightly. They were heading into an engine testing area. Soon, it quieted down as they entered an extremely large warehouse. Braxton saw an incredible amount of ATV crates setting to his right. Farther down on the left, a similar display of snowmobile crates were stacked high into the racks and far down the isle.

"They were right about here," Garnell said, stopping near the snowmobile crates.

"Describe what you saw," Braxton said.

"There were two Xenolfan males looking at these crates. They both had large duffel bags. One of them had his bag on the floor. He knelt down and started to grab something out of the bag when I spotted them. I yelled at them and asked what they were doing as I ran closer to them. The one Xenolfan dropped whatever he was about to take out of the bag back into the bag and closed it. He grabbed the bag and they both ran off very quickly. I called our security team to chase them down, but we lost them. We inspected in and around many of these crates, but could not find anything out of place. We have no idea what they were doing here," Garnell said.

Braxton walked over to the snowmobile crates and ducked under the rack, peering behind the shelving. He looked at the markings and stamps on the wooden crates. One thing stood out to him. They were all stamped with a destination of Aamaress.

"Who purchased this group of snowmobiles?" Braxton asked.

"There are about two hundred or so snowmobiles on these racks that were purchased by The Avalanche Resort on Aamaress," Garnell said.

"Aamaress? Hmm," Braxton said.

He pondered the information for a long moment.

"We inspected the area very well after that and our security team is being extra vigilant. I don't know what else to do," Garnell said.

"Well, that's about all you can do. Be sure your employees are aware of the incident. If you see any other suspicious activity, let me know right away. Here is my contact information," Braxton said, handing Garnell a card.

"We will definitely—"

Garnell was cut short as the cement floor beneath their feet suddenly shook and a deafening explosion sound rocked the foundations of the facility. One of the ATV racks across the isle suddenly collapsed, sending many crated ATVs to the warehouse floor.

"What the hell was that?" Garnell asked.

They both ran toward a nearby exit to see what happened. They stepped out onto a small roof section of the building. In the distance, a massive cloud of fire and smoke reached up into the sky. Several kilometers away, a factory had erupted. A secondary explosion suddenly engulfed the sky once again, the concussion knocking both men to the rooftop. Several alarms started blaring throughout the industrial area.

"Braxton, are you okay?" Garnell asked.

Both men sat up and looked at the blazing fire in the distance.

"Yeah, I think so," Braxton said.

They both stood up and brushed themselves off.

"What manufacturing facility is that?" Braxton asked.

"That's the thermal cube factory. They mine a substance from beneath Shar Nefalis and make thermal cubes that keep people warm. I wonder what the hell happened," Garnell said.

"They keep people warm…as in people in cold places, like Aamaress?" Braxton asked.

Garnell looked at Braxton for a long moment. "Yes," he said. "They mine a natural warming element from beneath the surface and encase it in portable cubes."

Braxton removed his comm from his pocket. He contacted the administrative building on Exandra.

"This is Braxton. I may have just discovered the Xenolfan's target. A thermal cube factory on Shar Nefalis was just destroyed. I believe they also tried to destroy Ticrisuda Powersports here as well. I need you to send in first responders immediately, both fire and medical. We need the Galactic Emergency Medical Services here as soon as possible. It doesn't look like it's going to be pretty. I'm going to see if I can find the owner of the thermal cube factory…if he is still alive. I'll keep you updated, Edward," he said, turning off the comm.

"His name is Bradford Smith," Garnell said.

"Who?" Braxton asked.

"The man that owns the thermal cube factory. Most likely he was not there. He's never there. He has other people run the facility and do mining for him. You will probably find him at the local intoxication joint," Garnell said.

"Okay. I will see if I can track him down," Braxton said.

They both went back into the building. Several employees came up to Garnell. They all wanted to know what was going on. Garnell walked over to the intercom and made the announcement.

"The violent explosions that you all just heard and felt came from the thermal cube factory. There is some damage to our warehouse where ATV crates fell from several of the racks. I want our reclamation team to assist with correcting that immediately. I want all of you to just look over your areas and be sure everything is operating correctly. Emergency personnel have been called in to assist with victims of the explosion. There is reason to believe this was no accident and that it could have been us. Our security team has recently chased two suspicious Xenolfans out of our warehouse. If any of you see anything odd, please let the security team know immediately. Thank you," Garnell said, turning off the intercom.

The employees walked back to their stations.

"Well, good luck with your investigation. I will say their alien presence here on Shar Nefalis was very out of place. Unlike the other planets in the Industrial Sector, the workers here on Shar Nefalis are primarily human. The other planets, Aomium Swith, Chelliss, and Ardellia, have a mix of our species," Garnell said.

"That's good to know. Thanks for your help. And again, if you discover any other information, let me know," Braxton said.

Garnell walked Braxton back to his ship.

"Where can I find this intoxication joint?" Braxton asked.

"It's just down the street to the right, within walking distance. You can't miss it," Garnell said. "Look for a man named Bradford Smith. He has gray hair."

CHAPTER SEVEN

Sierra Shalinsky was excited. She couldn't remember the last time she looked forward to something as much as the big concert that Maranadda was about to perform on Salinarr Nevis. She started humming with her voice and sang a few lyrics in the cockpit of her old fighter ship, *Tenebris.* Breaking into song helped exercise her voice and prepare for the show. It was going to be one of their biggest shows to date. Sierra could not contain her smile. She turned on the comm.

"This is Sierra. I'm en route to Red Jacket now. Are we ready to kick some ass tonight? This is going to be a phenomenal show. I'm very excited," she said.

"Hi, Sierra. This is Yosemite. We are packing all the equipment into the ship now. Which mic do you want us to pack?" he asked.

"I can grab it when I get there. Actually, just pack my two favorites. You know which ones they are," Sierra said.

"Yes, I do," Yosemite said.

"Our new manager and booking agent, Shasta Varium…is she there yet, or is she going to meet us on Salinarr Nevis?" Sierra asked.

A new voice came over the comm. "Shasta Varium is very, umm, hot!" Arvon Estivant said.

"Arvon, get off the comm," Yosemite said. "Shasta will be meeting us at the venue on Salinarr Nevis."

"You guys crack me up. I'll see you soon. I'm just going to land on Volum to grab a bite to eat. I'm starving," Sierra said.

"Okay. We'll see you soon," Yosemite said.

Sierra turned off the comm and set a course for Volum. She knew of a little intoxication joint and cafe that she loved to stop by every once in a while. It was the Eccentric Elixir and they had excellent food.

Sierra remembered visiting Volum by herself when she was about nineteen. She had been extremely interested in the sex museum they had at the time. She laughed at the thought of how she had a high sex drive even back then. She wondered if the museum was still there. Someone years ago had told her it was closed. She recalled seeing all the sexual artwork on display there. One erotic sculpture from her visit stood out in her mind. It was of a couple fucking, both laying on their backs with the male beneath the female. Both of their legs had been spread open to reveal a very detailed cock half inserted into a very detailed pussy. She remembered that guests were not allowed to touch anything. Many times over the years, she recalled the visual of that sculpture and it always aroused her.

The intoxication joint and cafe was a jaunt off from the main space lanes and was not well-known, but Sierra liked the cafe's food enough that the extra distance was worth it. She was so excited about the gig Maranadda was about to perform on Salinarr Nevis, but that was not going to happen on an empty stomach. After exiting the ship, she entered the quiet intoxication joint. The old wooden floors were well worn and stained. There were a few patrons sitting at tables around the small room. Along the counter, all the barstools were empty. She decided to sit at the counter. As she walked across the creaky floor, she could smell old, musty scents of various ales and liquors. She sat at an old, worn barstool on the far right of the counter. The ambience was quiet with very low music in the background. A display of exotic liquors, imported from many planets throughout the Syrenthian Galaxy, could be seen behind the bar. As the bartender walked over to her, she recognized him from the last time she was there.

"Sierra! It's been a while. How are you?" the bartender asked.

"Remywian Yort! I'm great. I'm on my way to Salinarr Nevis. Maranadda is about to perform a huge gig with other symphonic metal bands in front of thousands of fans. And we're the headliner!"

"That's great. Congratulations! So, what can I get for you?" Remywian asked.

"Can I see a menu? I'm starving."

Remywian Yort grabbed a menu from the counter and handed it to her. She looked at it for a brief moment.

"I'll have a filet mignon steak and an ale," Sierra said.

"I'll get right on that," Remywian said.

He poured her an ale, set the tall glass on a square napkin in front of her, and then disappeared around a corner into the cafe's kitchen. She sipped at the foamy ale and looked around the room at the other patrons. The few that were there were occupied with their own conversations, reading newspapers, or fiddling with their comms. As she lifted her glass for another drink, the napkin stuck to the bottom of the glass and came up with it.

"You know how to solve that?" Remywian asked, grabbing a salt shaker.

"Yes, I do," Sierra said, crumbling the napkin and tossing it across the counter. "Problem solved."

Remywian smiled and shook his head, setting the salt shaker back down. Sierra's comm went off and startled her.

"Sierra here," she said.

"This is Madison. We have a call that we need to respond to immediately. There was a terrorist attack on Shar Nefalis in the Industrial Sector and a thermal cube factory was destroyed, killing at least a dozen and wounding many more. They have the fire under control. There are a few miners trapped in a mine there. It's pretty bad. I need you on Relistorr as soon as possible," she said.

"Oh shit! I was just on my way to Salinarr Nevis to one of our largest shows ever, where thousands of fans from all across the galaxy will attend," Sierra said.

"You need to be on your way to GEMS headquarters right now. You don't have time right now for your band, your swinger Lifestyle, or whatever the hell else you do. Take your job serious if you intend to keep it," Madison Stephard said, ending the connection.

Sierra looked at her comm in disbelief.

You have got to be fucking joking! she thought. *This cannot be happening!*

Remywian Yort brought out her steak and set the plate in front of her. He grabbed a napkin and utensils and set them next to her plate. He could see the look of disappointment on her face.

"You look like you're about to cry. Is everything all right?" Remywian asked.

"No. As you know, I'm a Galactic EMT and they just called me to an emergency run. I'm supposed to be on my way to our big concert. This really sucks!" Sierra said.

"Oh, that does suck. Good luck with all that," Remywian said. "You probably don't want another ale, then?"

"No. I need to eat and run."

"Good luck, Sierra," he said as he straightened up behind the counter.

"Thank you, Remywian."

She picked up her comm to make the dreaded announcement to her bandmates. A tear rolled down her right cheek.

"Yosemite, this is Sierra. GEMS HQ just called me. I have to go to an emergency run and I cannot make the show. I am so sorry. I don't even know what to say. Madison was a bitch. I don't—"

"Are you fucking kidding me? What the hell are we supposed to do in front of thousands of fans that have traveled from all across the galaxy to see us play and we have no vocalist?" Yosemite shouted.

Sierra had never heard him that angry before.

"I'm sorry," she said.

"Our new manager and agent, Shasta Varium, has worked very hard to get us this gig on Salinarr Nevis. I don't even know how I'm going to explain this to her," Yosemite said.

Her other bandmates started to complain over the comm.

"I'm sorry," she repeated.

She turned off the comm and ate her steak in silence as tears fell from her eyes. An anger started flowing to the surface. Sierra understood the ultimatum. The emphasis on her job was more important, or at least the more responsible choice. But why did Madison always have to be a bitch to her? And now her bandmates were angry at her too.

I've been with GEMS for many years and, it gets thrown in my face that my ship's not fast enough, or my music's not important, or that I'm a swinger, Sierra thought.

Remywian heard her conversation on the comm. "This is on the house today, Sierra. Good luck with everything," he said.

"Thank you," she said.

A man walked into the intoxication joint and made his way over to the counter. He sat down a couple of barstools over from Sierra. She looked over at him as he removed the hood to his jacket.

"What can I get for you?" Remywian asked.

"Umm, just an ale," he said.

The bartender quickly poured him a drink and set it down in front of the man. The new patron briefly looked over at Sierra and then back to his drink. He looked very fidgety as he sipped his ale. He kept looking around the room, over his shoulder, and then back to the amber liquid in his glass.

Sierra noticed another man walk into the intoxication joint. He was a large man, dressed in all black and his black leather jacket had an insignia embroidered onto it. He casually walked across the room and came up behind the patron that had just sat down a couple of barstools over from Sierra.

"I've been looking for you," the large man said.

The fidgety man swirled around on the stool in surprise.

"You are the identity thief that has fucked with the wrong person," the large man said.

The man dressed in black took his large, gloved fist and began to pummel him about the face. He lifted the man up off the barstool, ripping his hooded jacket open. From the inside pocket of the hooded jacket, a long accordion-style identification folder flopped out and unraveled to the floor, revealing many different identity cards. The large man pointed at one of the fake IDs.

"That's my ID and so it's confirmed," the large man said.

Sierra looked over at all the IDs that were rolled out onto the floor and noticed that hers was among them. Her jaw dropped. The man in black beat the identity thief in the face a few more times.

"No, no, please! I'm sorry," he cried, blood dripping from his mouth.

"You've been marked for death by the Syrenthian Brotherhood Knights of Darkness," the large man said.

The man in the black leather jacket, pulled a knife from his side, flicked it open, and then sliced the identity thief's throat. With a quick roll of the eyes, the man fell over from the barstool to the wooden floor, blood gushing from his throat. A few gurgling sounds could be heard as the man tried to scream. The large man in black leaned over and used the tip of the blade to carve "ID X" into the thief's forehead.

"Fucking little man boy," the large man said, spitting on him.

As the man bled out onto the wooden floor, the large man in black stood up, wiped off his blade, and threw a coin onto the counter to compensate for the mess. He turned around and walked out of the intoxication joint. Remywian looked at the coin on the counter and realized it was an Asparell coin. The coins were used in ancient times and were now worth about 2000 credits each. There was only one group of people who currently used Asparell coins in the galaxy, the Syrenthian Brotherhood Knights of Darkness. They certainly were not a group to mess with. Sierra just stared in disbelief. It was a disturbing scene, yet knowing the man had been responsible for her compromised identity as well, it was also morbidly satisfying. As a Galactic Emergency Medical Technician, she knew there was absolutely nothing she could do to save the man anyway. Remywian picked up the Asparell coin and put it into his pocket.

"Well, it looks like he fucked with the wrong person," Remywian said.

"I was one of his victims as well," Sierra said.

She pointed at the ID cards in the accordion-style folder on the floor next to the man.

"Wow!" Remywian said.

One of the other patrons must have called the local authorities. Suddenly, the door flew open and three officers rushed in to assess the situation. They walked over toward the counter and stopped where the man lay on the floor. The pool of blood beneath him had already seeped into the wooden floorboards.

"What happened here?" one of the officers asked the bartender.

"One of the Syrenthian Brotherhood Knights of Darkness came in here and killed him for stealing his identity," Remywian said.

They checked the man on the floor against their database.

"Well, it looks like he was wanted by many agencies across the galaxy for identity theft and other crimes. It looks like someone else got to him first," the officer said.

One of the other officers walked over to Sierra. "Can you describe the man who killed him?" he asked.

"No. I'm sorry, I cannot. I was eating my steak and didn't see anything," Sierra said. "Besides, I need to go. I work for GEMS and need to respond to a galactic disaster on Shar Nefalis in the Industrial

Sector."

Sierra stood up from the stool and walked out of the intoxication joint.

Chapter Eight

Yosemite McFarlin had just received the bad news from Sierra Shalinsky. She had to go on to the Industrial Sector for her job with GEMS. Maranadda arrived on Salinarr Nevis and began to move their equipment from the ship to the back of the large stage in the Silver Star Concert Hall. Not only were they without a vocalist, but they were also slightly behind schedule. The first opening band, Frozen Solstice, had already started to play. The crew for the second act were tending to the many tasks required for setting up a large show. Maranadda's sound technician, Vincent Macenburg, began to prepare his monitoring equipment that would soon be plugged into the sound system. The band's new manager and booking agent, Shasta Varium, was backstage with the band going over their strategy of how to handle Sierra's absence. The symphonic metal bands that were opening up for Maranadda included Frozen Solstice and Enchanted Resonance.

"I am so pissed at Sierra right now, I could scream," Arrian Trodder said as he removed his bass guitar from its case.

"Yeah, I'll have to agree with you on that," Yosemite McFarlin said. He put two of his guitars on their stands.

"Do you guys know how hard it was for me to book this gig?" Shasta Varium asked.

"Yes, we do, Shasta. And we appreciate all of your hard work and effort. Perhaps we could ask one of the other bands if their vocalist would be willing to fill in for Sierra," Sanarith Raastarr suggested as he grabbed a box of guitar picks.

"I'll go ask our friends from Enchanted Resonance. Hey, grab my keyboard stand from the cart, will you?" Kulu Avolium asked, walking toward the members of Enchanted Resonance.

"Look, we all know Sierra is on call all the time to respond to galactic disasters across the galaxy. When we hired her as a vocalist, we knew she was a Galactic EMT. We all said that was an awesome and commendable career. You all should be a lot more understanding. Listen to yourselves! What about the people that she helps? What about the lives she helps save? Is this show more important than that? I don't think so," Arvon Estivant said. He threw his drum sticks across the backstage room and they landed against his drum kit with a loud clatter.

"Yes, I agree with you, Arvon, but the fans who have traveled from distant worlds all across the galaxy to see Maranadda play may not be as understanding. They spent a lot of credits on this show and traveled a great distance," Shasta said.

"We don't dare cancel. Can you imagine the rage the crowd would go into? We'll have to stall or come up with something clever," Yosemite said.

Arrian grabbed Kulu's keyboard stand from the cart and set it next to his keyboards. They all looked across the backstage area as Kulu returned.

"Well?" Sanarith asked.

"No. She doesn't feel comfortable filling in and doesn't want to piss off the crowd. She also said she is not familiar with all the lyrics and vocal parts of our songs. We'll probably get the same response from Frozen Solstice," Kulu said.

"Maybe we could say this is our instrumental set," Arvon said.

"Oh, that'll go over real well," Arrian said.

"Well, you guys will just have to improvise," Shasta said.

A young, blonde woman came from the side of the room and walked over to Arvon. She kissed him on the lips.

"Hi, babe," she said.

"Hey, umm, we're kind of in the middle of a meeting. I'll meet up with you shortly," Arvon said.

"Oh, sorry. I'll just be around back," she said.

She walked across the back of the stage, her very sexy short shorts ever so noticeable, and disappeared around a curtain.

"Who the hell was that?" Yosemite asked.

"Just a young woman that I'm dating. Her name is Rosheil," Arvon said.

"How old is she, seventeen?" Sanarith asked.

"Actually, she's twenty," Arvon said.

"She's fifteen years younger than you. What a fucking hymen hacker," Arrian said.

"You mean you finally gave up on Sierra?" Yosemite asked.

"Look, I haven't been this happy in a long time," Arvon said.

"I'll bet," Kulu said.

They all laughed.

"We'll improvise the best we can, Shasta," Yosemite said.

From backstage, they listened to the sound of Frozen Solstice. The gothic keyboards, crunchy guitars, and very rhythmic drum beats, combined with the beautiful female vocals, created an awesome synergy of sound. Soon, they finished their set and the crowd cheered. Enchanted Resonance was up next. Enchanted Resonance scrambled to get their stage props set up and remove the black tarps that lay across their equipment. When the vocalist of Frozen Solstice came backstage, Kulu asked her the same question he had asked the vocalist of Enchanted Resonance. He received the same answer. The members of Maranadda became anxious as Enchanted Resonance started to play. What were they going to do with no vocalist?

Arrian Trodder's girlfriend, Jacquelyn Enelra, along with Sanarith Raastarr's wife, Arcashia, Kulu Avolium's wife, Misty, and Vincent Macenburg's wife, Shaslin, were all in the hall's segregated box seating area, high above the floor and close to the stage. There was a narrow corridor that connected between the box seating and backstage. Acquaintances of the other two bands had their own box seating as well.

Yosemite walked over to the front curtain at the side of the stage and peeked out at the crowd. He stood in disbelief at the sheer number of fans that were out there. There were humans and Xenolfans alike. The sea of people was certainly an awesome site to see. It was the largest crowd Yosemite had ever seen at any of their concerts. The others joined him next to the curtain.

"Wow!" Sanarith said.

"I'll be back shortly. I'm going to find my girlfriend," Arvon said.

The rest of them listened on at the amazing sound of Enchanted Resonance. The rich tones and melodic compositions of the band were very impressive. The mixed sound of string instruments and wind instruments from the keyboards was magnificent. When the second band's encore was finished, they began to tear down their set and remove their instruments.

"We're up next, guys. The venue crew will get your equipment set in place," Shasta said. "Do the best you can. Delay as long as possible. At some point we're gonna have to inform the fans."

"Just let us know when that point is," Yosemite said.

"I will give you a signal," Shasta said.

Sanarith walked by and handed an amp to one of the venue crew. "Where the hell is Arvon?" he asked.

"I don't know. It's too bad we were running behind schedule, or we could have had our entire set already onstage and covered with tarps," Arrian said.

They continued to roll equipment out and had the venue crew set it up onstage, the crowd cheering each time one of the venue crew members appeared with the equipment.

The *Tenebris* landed at the Galactic Emergency Medical Services headquarters on Relistorr. Sierra quickly ran into her office to grab her EMT bag. The rest of her unit waited in the lobby.

"Why are we always waiting on you?" Madison asked.

Sierra did not respond and walked out the door toward the transport shuttle. The others followed. As they boarded the transport shuttle, Madison glared at Sierra.

"Our incident commander, Elliss Millott, has informed me that this will be the last time we meet here at HQ before a run. In the interest of saving time and lives, it has been decided that we will meet up with the *Deliverance* at its destination instead of coming here first. They have opened up an extra docking bay to park our personal ships. So, you need to keep your EMT bags with you in your ship at all times. Be sure to restock your supplies at HQ when necessary. The coordinates for where you will meet for those future runs will be sent to you over your comm," Madison said. She looked at Sierra. "I expect that this new system will see you arrive with the rest of us."

Madison walked up to the front of the transport shuttle and sat next to the pilot.

"I literally arrived two minutes before you, Sierra, and Madison said nothing to me. I think you got here very quickly," Aurora said in a low voice.

"It doesn't matter if I was here before any of you. Nothing I do will ever be good enough for that bitch. I'm looking into transferring to another unit. It's about time I executed an exit strategy," Sierra whispered.

"No, no. Tell me it's not true," Alex said.

"Don't let her get to you, Sierra," Rachel said.

"We need you in this unit. You are awesome at your job," Blaze whispered.

Sierra looked up into Aurora's brown eyes and then looked at the floor in defeat. Aurora squeezed Sierra's hand. Aurora's hand felt warm against hers. Their eyes met once again.

"Hang in there," Aurora said.

Suddenly, Sierra felt a surge of hormones rush straight to her pussy. She held Aurora's hand for a few moments and continued to look into her eyes. She began breathing heavily. Sierra began to rethink her position against having sex with her co-workers.

Well, if I leave the unit, it won't matter anyway, she thought.

Sierra squeezed Aurora's inner thigh and tried to calm her own mixed emotions. The others didn't notice the energy connection occur between them.

"So, do you guys want to hear about a murder that I just witnessed?" Sierra asked.

The *Deliverance* arrived at the shipping lanes of Shar Nefalis. Three medical shuttles departed from one of the docking bays and flew through the atmosphere toward the remains of the thermal cube factory. In the distance ahead, they could see the smoldering ruins of the thermal cube factory through the observation window. Madison handed each person in her unit a respirator mask to wear and then looked at her hand-held computer. The shuttles settled and members of each unit stepped out onto the ground. The nasty smell of burned materials enveloped them. Two men approached from beyond the parked shuttles. They also wore masks.

"Okay, paramedics from the other shuttles are going to set up a triage center in the first medical shuttle. We need to find the survivors and move them there. The local firefighters have already removed some of the dead. The coroner is removing more as they are found. We need to check for survivors on the surface and then go down into the mine shaft with our recovery effort. The second unit will come in behind us to transport survivors to the medical shuttle," Madison said.

The two approaching men stopped next to Madison. Sierra recognized Braxton Stryderr and grew a big smile beneath her mask.

"Hi. My name is Braxton Stryderr. I'm an investigator for the Syrenthian Government. This is Bradford Smith. He is the owner of the thermal cube facility and mine shaft," he said.

"There should have been twenty people in the factory and another five down in the mine. They have recovered twelve bodies from the factory so far. We still need to locate eight more, plus the five miners," Bradford Smith said, adjusting his gray hair around his mask.

"Sierra!" Braxton said.

He walked over to her and gave her a hug.

"You don't know how much I need a hug right now. It's nice to see you, Braxton," Sierra said.

"It's nice to see you as well. You guys be careful in there. Stay sharp and watch for falling debris. Contact me over the comm if you see anything odd," Braxton said.

"Okay, let's move out," Madison said.

Madison scowled at Sierra as she walked past her.

You're just envious that I know someone in the Syrenthian Government, bitch! Sierra thought.

The coroner and his team could be seen in the distance. The paramedics began their work on the first medical shuttle's triage center. Madison's unit split into teams. Sierra went with Alex and Rachel while Madison, Aurora, and Blaze looped around in the other direction. The second medical shuttle's unit was not far behind with transfer boards.

"Over here," Sierra said.

She saw a pair of legs sticking out from behind a wall. When she reached the wall, she turned the corner and then backed up in horror.

The others caught up with her and gasped. The only remaining part was the legs. The rest of the person was missing.

"We need the coroner over near the rear of the building," Sierra said over the comm.

They continued searching through the rubble. Water puddles were numerous from the firefighters quenching the fire. Charred remains of the structure were visible everywhere, the burned odor very intense. Several metal beams had collapsed from the explosion and blocked most of the path ahead of them. Sierra squeezed through the small opening, the others following. Since the roof was completely gone, daylight brightened most of the area. Some shadows darkened the area under the collapsed beams. They sloshed through a puddle of water toward a metal stairway. Most of the yellow railing was all twisted from the explosion. When Rachel took the first step, the stairway fell several centimeters from its original position. She quickly grabbed the wall.

"Be careful, Rachel," Sierra said.

"Damn!" Rachel said.

They carefully made their way down the small set of steps and onto the lower level. The blast had pushed a lot of debris in that area, covering a large portion of the floor. As Alex walked near a collapsed wall, a hand suddenly reached out and grabbed his boot, startling him.

"Over here," Alex said. "Help me lift this wall."

Sierra and Rachel ran over and helped Alex lift the wall piece from the victim. A woman crawled out from beneath the rubble and then collapsed in a puddle of water at their feet. They lowered the wall back down. Sierra set her EMT bag up on the wall to keep it out of the water. Alex helped the woman to sit up. Her hands were bleeding and she had a laceration across her forehead. Sierra began checking the woman's vitals while Rachel reached into her bag and grabbed some irrigation solution and bandages.

"We found a survivor, toward the center of the building," Sierra called over the comm.

"We found a couple of survivors as well," Aurora said over the comm.

"What happened?" the woman asked.

"It is believed to be a terrorist bomb," Sierra said. "I have no idea why they would want to destroy a thermal cube factory."

"I saw two Xenolfans in here the other day. I told security, but they thought I was crazy. Can I get a drink of water?" the woman asked.

"Sure thing," Alex said, grabbing a bottle of water from his EMT bag.

"Once we get you over to the medical shuttle triage center, I would like you to tell an investigator friend of mine what you saw," Sierra said.

"Okay," the woman said.

The second unit came in behind them with the transfer board. They carefully strapped her onto the board, gave her a respirator mask, and carried her back toward the medical shuttle.

"Braxton, this is Sierra. The woman the second unit is bringing to the shuttle now saw two Xenolfans in the factory the other day. You may want to question her," she said over the comm.

"All right. Thanks, Sierra," Braxton said.

Sierra, Alex, and Rachel continued the search-and-rescue mission. They looked under more debris, cleared an area, and moved on to the next. Several hours had passed by the time they had rescued and recovered the remaining victims.

Braxton questioned the conscious patients and found that the woman with the bandage on her forehead is the only one who had seen the two Xenolfans. The information was consistent with what Garnell Meshtief from Ticrisuda Powersports had seen. He did want to continue his investigation by inquiring with other nearby factory personnel.

Chapter Nine

Arvon Estivant was around behind the backstage area of the concert hall with his new girlfriend, Rosheil. She had his pants down and smiled up at him. He shifted his long, brown hair.

"Oh, Rosheil, you're so good at that. Oh shit," Arvon gasped.

"I enjoy giving head."

"Well, I'm glad you do."

She slowly slid her lips up the underside of his shaft and flicked the tip of her tongue against his frenulum. The sensation sent his hips forward. Once again, she took it into her mouth and began sucking. Her warm tongue pressed against the bottom of his cock as she sucked, bobbing her head up and down. She continued for a long time and Arvon could feel the eruption of nerves and was ready to explode.

"I'm coming!" he shouted.

She continued sucking his cock as it pulsated in her mouth, squirting his hot load to the back of her throat.

"Oh fuck, that's nice," Arvon said, breathing heavily.

"Mmm," Rosheil moan as the cum dripped from her mouth.

Yosemite came from around the corner. "There you are. We have to— Seriously? We're on in five minutes. Put your pants back on," he said. He looked at Rosheil. "You may want to use the rest room and wash your face."

The crowd began chanting "Maranadda, Maranadda, Maranadda" as the band gathered backstage.

"Listen to them out there," Kulu said.

"Are you guys ready? Start with a jam session and take it from there. Do some long solos or something. I'll signal you when we reach the inevitable," Shasta said.

Arvon Estivant adjusted his crotch before walking out onto the stage. He was the first band member out and the crowd went wild. After maneuvering around the set and behind his drum kit, he sat down and grabbed his sticks. A few minor adjustments had to be made with the drum positions. He beat the double bass drum a few times to check the sound. The subwoofer thud sent vibrations throughout the venue. The crowd cheered. The rest of the kit sounded great as well. He looked toward the sound booth at the back of the venue and gave Vincent a thumbs-up.

Arrian Trodder walked onstage next, carrying his bass guitar. As he walked toward far stage right, the crowd cheered once again. He strapped on the bass guitar, walked over to the amplifier head, and flicked on the switch. The low, reverberating sound of his strings filled the concert hall. The fans looked toward house left of the stage at Arrian and roared with anticipation.

Yosemite McFarlin and Sanarith Raastarr walked out onstage together with their guitars strapped over their shoulders. The sustained cheering from the audience was quite loud. The two of them waved at the crowd and took their positions onstage, with Yosemite standing on stage right in front of one of the microphones.

Kulu Avolium was last to arrive onstage and strolled over to his keyboards. The crowd raised their voices in applause.

"How are we doing tonight, Salinarr Nevis?" Yosemite shouted.

The response was thunderous.

"Thank you all for coming to the show. We appreciate it. Let's make some noise to thank our friends in Frozen Solstice," he said.

The audience cheered.

"We also want to thank our friends in Enchanted Resonance. What a stunning performance!"

Once again, the audience cheered. When the applause died down, there was an awkward silence as Yosemite looked over at the lonely microphone stand at the front and center of the stage. Yosemite began to play a slow melodic guitar riff and the others joined in. It was an improvised jam session, but it sounded amazing. With the freedom of their wireless guitar connections, Yosemite and Sanarith began to walk toward each other and met in the middle of the stage. They alternated shredding with blistering guitar solos while Arvon gave a thunderous drum beat and many fills. Arrian kept in time with the bass and Kulu accented the composition with stunning mystical keyboard effects. They went on for some time and finally wound it down to a stop. The crowd was very pleased with the performance. Before Yosemite could return to the microphone, the crowd started chanting "Sierra, Sierra, Sierra." Yosemite looked toward the back of the stage where Shasta Varium stood. She gave him a nod and he turned back toward the audience. Stepping over to his microphone, he cleared his throat.

"Maranadda is happy to be here tonight with Frozen Solstice and Enchanted Resonance. Whether you are from here on Salinarr Nevis or if you've traveled across the Syrenthian Galaxy to see our show, we appreciate it. Unfortunately, we have some bad news. We know how much you all love Sierra. She would have loved to be here tonight, but had to respond to a galactic emergency on Shar Nefalis in the Industrial Sector. As some of you know, she is also a Galactic Emergency Medical Technician. So, in her absence, we would like to play an instrumental set for you," Yosemite said.

The crowd was silent for a moment.

"Fuck that shit, man!" someone shouted.

"We wanna hear Sierra!" another voice called out.

The crowd quickly became a negative group and people shouted and were taken aback with disappointment.

"We flew all the way from Exandra!"

"We paid a lot of credits to see *all* of you!"

It became very evident they were not happy. Some of them began to throw things and many of them started to exit the hall. Several people along the back right of the hall became violent and grabbed trash cans, throwing them against glass windows and doors.

Shasta Varium walked out onto the stage to try and calm down the crowd. It did not work. The violence started spilling out into the corridor of the casino. Shasta saw one of the fans inadvertently get struck with a chair and fall to the ground. The victim's friend began beating the aggressor senseless.

"Oh fuck!" Yosemite said.

The band stared on in disbelief as the crowd became a massive angry mob. The security officers stood their ground along the front of the stage and at the sound booth. The band members from Frozen Solstice and Enchanted Resonance came out from backstage to witness the commotion.

"This is fucking crazy," Sanarith said.

"I think we may have a riot on our hands," Shasta said.

The first medical shuttle lifted from the surface of Shar Nefalis, heading for the *Deliverance*. The second medical shuttle team prepared another triage center for the miners. Madison's unit and the second unit headed for the mine shaft, near the front of the structure. They all helped remove rubble from the mine entrance. Soon, there was an opening large enough to accommodate them. One of the members from the second unit retrieved LED illuminators from the medical shuttle and gave one to each of them. The mine was dark and damp. They slowly descended down the wet slope, gripping a handrail along one side.

"A lot of the water from the firefighters came down here," Madison said.

"Are you sure?" Sierra asked, stepping in a puddle with her boot.

Madison turn around and was about to say something to Sierra, but refrained.

"Help!" a distant cry echoed.

"We're on our way," Madison yelled.

They continued down the incline until it plateaued. Ahead of them stones had fallen and blocked the tunnel. One by one, the teams moved the rocks aside until an adequate opening was available. One of the miners popped through the opening, an LED illuminator attached to his helmet.

"I am so glad to see you guys," he said.

"Are you hurt? Are there others?" Sierra asked.

"I'm fine. The other four miners are farther down the tunnel. There was a large explosion sound and the shaft collapsed. Our air is getting a bit thin down here. I think the oxygen exchange was destroyed. When I heard you guys moving the rocks, I came to investigate. I'm glad I did," the miner said.

"So, the others are okay?" Madison asked.

"Yeah, we're all okay, just a little shaken up. We need water, if you have any," he said.

"We certainly do," Blaze said.

"Let me take you to the others," the man said.

They followed him through the opening and down the tunnel. It opened up into a large cavernous area. To the right, a large rock surface sloped up on an angle toward the ceiling. Two large metal beams were positioned on a perpendicular angle to support the tunnel rock above. Several metal bins sat along the right, below the rock slope, all filled with the unprocessed element to make thermal cubes. To their left, a mine shaft that led to yet lower levels was filled with water that had leaked down from the firefighters. Ahead of them, the tunnel narrowed again and began to slope downward once more. Not far from the wide cavernous area, a small hollowed area opened up on the right. Four men sat on a rock there, waiting for their co-worker to return.

"Well, look what you've brought back," one of them said gleefully.

The others made shouts of joy and stood up, smiling at the unexpected rescue.

"Okay, let's get you guys some water," Blaze said.

Blaze and Alex both pulled water bottles from their EMT bags and handed them to each of the miners.

"So, what happened up there?" one of the other miners asked.

"Your thermal cube facility was bombed by Xenolfan terrorists. Many of the personnel up there are dead. We will be taking you guys up to the *Deliverance* hospital ship for evaluation," Madison said.

The dim light revealed a look of shock and sadness on the miners' faces.

"Let's head up to the surface. You'll want to wear these," the second unit leader said. He handed each of the miners a respirator mask.

They put them on and started back toward the surface, avoiding puddles of water along the way. After they reached the surface, the miners were led to the second medical shuttle. Bradford Smith stood near the shuttle entrance, giving each of the miners his condolences for the loss of their fellow co-workers. Soon, the shuttle lifted from the surface of Shar Nefalis and joined the first medical shuttle aboard the *Deliverance*. By the time Sierra returned to the surface, Braxton had gone on to continue his investigation. Madison's unit boarded the remaining medical shuttle and they proceeded toward the sky. Bradford Smith was left with the coroner's team to help identify the deceased.

As the shuttle flew above Shar Nefalis, Sierra stared out the observation window next to her seat, her face emotionless. The silence on the trip back to the *Deliverance* spoke volumes of the toll the run, with all of its carnage, had taken on the team. They were exhausted. As Sierra sat in silence, thoughts of her bandmates drifted through her mind.

Madison received a message over the comm. "Riots? Are you serious?"

Chapter Ten

Things quickly escalated when the audience at the concert on Salinarr Nevis began to cause riots and disorder, and it was considered an emergency. The incident commander, Elliss Millott, decided to have the *Deliverance* set a course for Salinarr Nevis at once.

They're rioting because I'm not there singing? Whoa! Sierra thought.

She didn't know if she should feel loved and wanted by the fans or pissed at them for acting like idiots. Didn't they understand her situation?

What a bunch of Jinkins! she thought.

Salinarr Nevis was not far from the Industrial Sector, so the *Deliverance* arrived in a timely manner. En route to the gambling planet, Madison had received reports of the disorder spreading into some of the nearby casinos, but that most of it was taking place in the concert hall and outdoors near the hall. Vandalism was rampant and many people were being struck with flying objects. Elliss Millott sent three medical shuttles down to the surface of the planet in several locations near the riots.

The medical shuttle that Madison's unit was in settled near the

Silver Star Concert Hall, in the middle of one of the many landing pads. Many ships of various sizes and maintenance conditions were parked on the landing pad.

"Okay, there are a lot of people that need medical attention. But this is a dangerous situation, so be careful out there. And no, Sierra, we can't have our laser rifles with us this time. Have your comms on and stay in communication with me," Madison said.

"Umm, I wouldn't have suggested that, anyway," Sierra said, scowling.

They exited the medical shuttle and stood next to the ship, staring at the restless crowd. There were shouts of disappointment and actions of aggression. At that moment, another shuttle settled next to theirs. Soon, the incident commander, Elliss Millott, stepped out of the shuttle and walked over to Madison's unit.

"I brought some extra help. With four units, I hope to manage the injured. Madison, go ahead and start through the crowd, looking for victims of this madness," Elliss said.

"You heard the man, let's go," Madison said.

Madison, Blaze, Rachel, and Alex started in one direction. As Sierra and Aurora began heading in another direction, Elliss got Sierra's attention and she walked over to him.

"What's up?" she asked.

"I have something for you in another unit, if you are interested," Elliss said. "You'll be working near the edge of the galaxy, including the Shardaa Sector."

Sierra's heart skipped a beat as she stared at him in disbelief.

"I am interested," Sierra said.

"Good. We can talk more after this crisis," Elliss said.

Sierra smiled and ran off toward Aurora who was waiting for her near the crowd.

"What was that all about?" Aurora asked.

"Elliss found a position for me in another unit. I'll be transferring out of Madison's unit. I'm kind of relieved and anxious at the same time," Sierra said.

"I'll miss you," Aurora said.

Sierra looked up into her brown eyes. Aurora's blond hair was draped over one shoulder of her uniform and an EMT bag was over the other.

"I'll miss you too, Aurora. I'll still be around, though. Actually, this might give me the opportunity to get to know you better. We should hang out," Sierra said.

"Umm, that thing on the shuttle when we were heading toward the Industrial Sector...I felt something between us. To be honest with you Sierra, you kind of made me a little wet," Aurora said.

"And you have always aroused me, Aurora. You know I swing both ways, right?"

"Yes, I know," Aurora said.

Sierra smacked Aurora's ass hard. "We've got work to do. Let's get to it," she said.

They moved into the crowd, looking for anyone who needed medical assistance. As they neared the side of the building, a small Xenolfan boy ran up to them, shouting. He was talking so fast, it was difficult to decipher what he was trying to say.

"Calm down. Talk slower. I can't understand you," Aurora said.

"It's my sister, she's hurt...over there," the boy said, pointing.

They quickly followed him toward the metal barricades along the building entrance. A young Xenolfan girl lay still on the ground. Red blood trickled down the side of her bluish-gray face.

"You gotta help her," the boy cried.

All GEMS teams were trained in both human and Xenolfan anatomy. Although there were many differences, they both shared many of the same basic life functions. Sierra set her bag down next to the girl. Aurora knelt down where Sierra was and began to get the girl's vitals. The normal vitals for Xenolfans were slightly different than humans, but the little girl's were not where they should be.

"She's unconscious and she's lost a lot of blood. We need to get her to the medical shuttle immediately," Sierra said.

"What happened here?" Aurora asked the boy.

"Some human man pushed her hard against that metal bar. I hate him!" He sobbed.

"We can't wait for a transfer board," Sierra said.

She picked up the little girl and turned toward the medical shuttles.

"Aurora, take her brother's hand. Let's get them to the shuttle," she said.

"This is Aurora, we have a little Xenolfan girl with head trauma. She has lost a lot of blood. We are on our way back to the medical shuttle now. Tell me we have a Xenolfan blood supply on the shuttle."

"We do," Madison said. "Drop her off and Elliss's team will handle it. I need you two back out here."

They brought the two Xenolfan children to the medical shuttle and the team from Elliss's shuttle quickly went to work. Sierra and Aurora headed back toward the madness. Alex called over the comm about an injured man they were bringing back to the shuttle. Sierra and Aurora made their way along the building, near the entrance to the concert hall. A human woman sat on a ledge, just inside the doors, her nose bleeding.

"Would you like an ice pack?" Aurora asked the woman.

"Yes, please," she said calmly.

Sierra pulled an ice pack from her EMT bag and activated it.

"Okay, hold this on for ten minutes and then off for ten minutes, and repeat. And here is something for the pain," Sierra said.

As Sierra and Aurora moved on inside the building, the Xenolfan military began to show up in several areas of the concert hall with laser rifles in their gloved hands. Sierra could see her band safe and secure up on the stage as they looked out at the crowd in disbelief. She suddenly realized she was in a unique position.

Wait a minute! I have the power to stop this entire fucked-up insanity, Sierra thought.

Sierra turned on the comm. "This is Sierra. I can solve all of this disorder by simply singing. That's why the crowd is pissed off in the first place," she said.

"Sierra, if you stand down from your duties as a Galactic EMT and go sing, you will be done with my unit. You need to be out helping these victims," Madison said.

It was another ultimatum from Madison. She was torn between her job and her band. It was a tough decision, but Sierra made it quickly. She decided to disobey Madison's order.

"Aurora, I need you to find the rest of your unit and continue to help those in need. I can stop this madness and if I don't, more people are going to get hurt. I'm done with this unit. I will keep in touch with you," Sierra said.

She handed her EMT bag to Aurora and headed for the stage.

"I am done with your unit, Madison," Sierra said over the comm.

In the past, Madison had told her not to get used to her office at the GEMS headquarters on Relistorr. Madison always kept Sierra's office at an uncomfortable temperature. Sierra hadn't received a pay increase in years, but the others in the unit certainly had. Madison micromanaged everything Sierra did and made her feel like she had to walk around on egg shells just to do her job. Sierra was never included in unit meetings and there was no good communication. The atmosphere had become very draconian. Compared to the other Galactic EMTs in the unit, Madison had a different set of rules when it came to Sierra. Sierra could not understand Madison's double standard. She had been unfair to Sierra and had singled her out for a long time.

What a hypocrite! Sierra thought as she walked toward the stage. *I don't need this extra stress in my life. It's not worth it. Since I'm that much of a burden to her, then I should do both of us a favor and leave her unit. I'm thankful Elliss came through for me.*

When Sierra approached the barricades, the security personnel along the front of the stage saw her Galactic EMT uniform and let her pass onto the stage. She sprinted around to a small set of steps and walked up onto the stage. At first, the rest of the band didn't recognize her, but then Yosemite saw her and his eyes opened wide in surprise.

"Sierra!" Yosemite shouted.

The rest of the band suddenly took interest in this person in the Galactic EMT uniform. They all greeted her with a warm welcome. Shasta Varium walked over to where they were all gathering onstage.

"It's unfortunate that I wasn't here when you needed me. I was saving lives, and that is something that I hope you all can understand. I certainly didn't expect this chaos! I just helped a little Xenolfan girl who had her head knocked into a barricade by a grown man. This has got to stop. My boss told me to keep helping the victims and that I better not leave and sing, but I can stop all this crazy madness, simply by singing. I told her that I am leaving her unit. I was already offered a job in a different unit anyway. And I'm extremely disappointed with our fans right now. So, let's put a stop to this shit right now. Arvon, I want you to signal Vincent at the sound booth and have him crank up the subwoofer. And then give me a steady bass drum beat so that we can get the attention of the crowd. I'll begin singing some melodic vocalise. When you all feel it is working, we'll start playing Dissimulate. Does that work for you guys?" Sierra asked.

"That's a wonderful idea, Sierra. By the way, you look exhausted," Shasta said.

"You have no idea..." Sierra said.

Sierra looked off to the right and saw Shaslin and the others safe in the box seating. Arvon had Vincent increase the subwoofer volume. He began a steady beat on the bass drum that sent thunderous thuds reverberating throughout the building. The sound could be heard outside and in the nearby casinos. The roar of the angry crowd became quiet as their attention was drawn to the concert hall stage.

Outside, the violence stopped as the crowd returned to the concert hall. The crowd departed the outside area and the nearby casinos and left the injured victims very visible to the Galactic EMT teams. It sped up the medical attention they desperately needed. As they quickly stepped in to help those on the ground, Madison knew Sierra was right.

Sierra stood in front of her microphone at center stage and saw the thousands of fans return into the hall. Her long black hair was in a ponytail, which she typically did not do during performances. The Galactic EMT uniform looked a bit awkward, but she planned to use it to her advantage after they played Dissimulate. She began her melodic vocalise and Arvon ceased the bass beat. The beautiful a cappella vocalise emitting from Sierra's voice pierced through the hall. It didn't take long for the crowd to realize the woman with the Galactic EMT uniform was Sierra. There was a deafening cheer throughout the concert hall. She continued the vocalise for a short time and then the rest of the band began to play Dissimulate from their third album, Discord. Another loud cheer came from the crowd. Sierra raised her right arm and gave the fans the metal horns hand sign. The slow, heavy beat quickly transitioned through a time change and went into a fast thrash section. As Sierra sang, she saw a much different crowd before her than just minutes before. When the song came to an end, the crowd applauded. She stood there and waited until it became fairly quiet.

"Well, Maranadda fans, we need to have a discussion," she finally said. The audience became very quiet. "You see, when I'm not singing for Maranadda, I'm busy as a Galactic Emergency Medical Technician. I'm always on call to respond to galactic emergencies and disasters. Today—the very day of our largest show ever—I got a call and I had to go save lives. These victims are people, just like you. It could be your mom, your sister, your dad, anyone. It's my job and I'm not going to apologize for saving lives. We received another call for the emergency here on Salinarr Nevis, the one caused by our fans. So, GEMS arrived and we began to help the victims. To the human male that pushed the little Xenolfan girl's head into the metal barricade outside of the concert hall, you should be ashamed of yourself. She has head trauma and has lost a lot of blood. And that is just one victim. Never before have I seen our fans act like animals. I know all of you fans did not participate in the riots. I also know you have traveled from far and wide across the Syrenthian Galaxy to see this show. And I'm sure Frozen Solstice and Enchanted Resonance gave stunning symphonic metal performances. If I wasn't standing here right now, just those two bands alone would have been worth your journey to Salinarr Nevis. Yet here I am…exhausted from saving lives and I'm going to give you what you want. But I ask one fucking thing from you fans in return, just one fucking thing. Be civil to one another, don't be a fucking Jinkins! Do we have a deal?"

There was a very distinct confirmation from the audience.

"Are you ready for a killer show?" Sierra asked.

More cheers filled the hall. Sierra turned back at the rest of the band and smiled. They began the playlist for the rest of their set.

"If you're not ready for a fast-paced adventure, you might want to move over to the slow lane. This next song is from our first album, Esoteric. It's called Red Jacket. It's about the rich history of copper mining on the planet Red Jacket," Sierra said.

The band began to play the beautiful musical composition with stunning riffs and pounding drum rolls. Soon, Maranadda began to play another song from the Esoteric album, the dark theme song Alchemy. That was followed by Tales of Shardaa from the same album. As Sierra sang Tales of Shardaa, she felt a bit odd because of her recent experiences in the Shardaa Sector. From there, they went right into the song Dissolution, from their second album, Novels. By the time Dissolution ended, Sierra gazed out at a crowd and saw them behaving as would be expected. She prepared herself for a song that she wrote about her personal struggles with Madison. Ironically, it had come to fruition. Sierra knew that many fans could empathize with the song Blacklisted, from their Discord album.

"This next song is one I wrote about a personal struggle. It's called Blacklisted," Sierra said.

The crowd clapped and cheered as the music kicked in with a very heavy and melodic rhythm.

"I gave you years of loyalty.

I chalk it up to lost opportunity.
I was taken advantage of.
That has created a cause and effect.

"I exposed the truth.
You gave a title to justify the greed.
You justify your differing weights.
You rationalize your dishonest scales.

"Nothing will be held over me.
Your secret honor code of hate...
The sands burst forth.
The hourglass has been crushed.

"Forever blacklisted, I stand.
My head is held up high.
There is only a transitory endurance.
I rearrange the master plan.

"I will be in this fixed state no more.
Forging upward, I'm on to success.
Only now as I exit, do you understand.
No, your arrogance has blinded you!"

Members of the Galactic Emergency Medical Services had already treated the victims from the earlier riots and the area was clear of all medical shuttles. Several of the victims had to be transported up to the *Deliverance* hospital ship for further treatment and surgery, including the little Xenolfan girl.

As Maranadda's performance continued, they played many more songs. By the time the show was over, Sierra walked backstage and collapsed onto a couch, extremely exhausted.

I need sleep, she thought, closing her eyes.

An hour and a half later, Vincent woke Sierra. "Hey, sexy! Can we offer you a ride back to your ship that—I assume—is on Relistorr?" he asked.

She rubbed her eyes and wiped the drool from the corner of her mouth. Sitting up on the couch, she looked around the backstage area.

"You guys already packed up?"

"Yes. I believe we're the last ones here in the hall, actually," Vincent said.

"Yeah, my ship is on Relistorr and I would appreciate a ride. I quit Madison's unit today. She's such a Jinkins. I will be starting with a new unit soon. I need to talk to Elliss Millott, our incident commander, for the rest of the details. I will be assigned to the outer edge of the galaxy," Sierra said.

Shaslin noticed another person in a Galactic EMT uniform appear from around the black stage curtain. They all looked over toward the side of the stage crossover area.

"Aurora!" Sierra gasped. "What are you doing here?"

"Madison knows you were right. She had me come back in my ship to make sure you had a ride back to Relistorr to get the *Tenebris*," Aurora said.

Sierra stood up from the couch and gave Aurora a hug.

"Aww, that's sweet of you," Sierra said. She turned to Vincent and Shaslin. "Well, it looks like you guys don't have to go out of your way after all. I appreciate you staying and looking out for me, though."

"No problem. It was a nice gesture for her to come back for you. We will see you around soon," Shaslin said.

Shaslin and Vincent both gave Sierra hugs and left the hall.

"Well, shall we go?" Sierra asked.

"Hey, did you know the Xenolfan military were about to fire on the crowd before you calmed them down?" Aurora asked.

"Seriously? That would have *really* fucked things up," Sierra said.

"I think you handled it much more beautifully," Aurora said. "I love your voice."

Aurora turned to Sierra, leaned in, and kissed her soft lips. Sierra breathed deeply and kissed her back, their tongues merging together with a surge of passion. Sierra looked at the beautiful blonde, took another deep breath, and smiled. They kissed again for a long time, playfully exploring each other's smooth tongues and lips.

Aurora took Sierra's hand and led her back to the couch. She began to remove Sierra's uniform top.

"I really need a shower," Sierra said.

"I don't care. I want you the way you are," Aurora said.

Soon, Aurora had Sierra's breasts out and gently massaged them.

She alternated between each, sucking the tits as she massaged them. Sierra became very aroused and removed her pants. Aurora looked down at the smooth vulva and reached in with her fingers to stroke it.

"Lie down," Aurora said.

Sierra was quick to oblige as she lay on the couch with her tan legs parted for Aurora. Sierra was concerned about the sweat and musky odor from her exhausting day, but it didn't bother Aurora in the slightest. She began licking Sierra's pussy, her wet tongue sending surges of bliss to Sierra's core. As Aurora repeatedly licked around the wet folds, Sierra moaned. Aurora flicked her tongue across Sierra's clit and sent her arching back into the couch. She elevated her hips up off the couch, shoving her pussy against Aurora's mouth.

"Oh fuck. Ahhh!" Sierra moaned.

Aurora continued for some time before Sierra exploded, convulsing into an incredible orgasm. Sierra looked up at Aurora and saw her wipe her mouth with the back of her hand.

"Sorry that I'm sweaty," Sierra said.

"You're fine," Aurora said.

"Okay. Well, you are overdressed for the occasion," Sierra said.

"Yes, I am," Aurora said.

She removed her uniform and switched spots on the couch with Sierra. Sierra looked between Aurora's legs at this new pussy. The smooth lips were moist and parted. One thing that Sierra enjoyed about being a bisexual was the taste of another woman's juices. She kissed along Aurora's thighs and made her way to the beautiful pussy that was displayed before her.

"You're so hot, Aurora. And you have a beautiful pussy," Sierra said.

She began to reciprocate the act by licking and sucking at the folds of Aurora's labia. Her clit was well pronounced and very sensitive to the tip of Sierra's tongue. Aurora breathed heavily and moaned with great pleasure.

"That feels so nice, Sierra. You're really good at that."

Sierra's tongue danced around Aurora's pussy until she screamed with pleasure and erupted into an orgasm. Sierra inserted her tongue inside Aurora's vagina and licked at the thin secretions of cum.

"Mmm," Sierra uttered.

Chapter Eleven

Light came through the window from the morning sun on Asparr Celtarious, brightening Sierra's bedroom loft. She slowly opened her eyes and yawned.

What a wonderful night's sleep…and finally in my own bed, Sierra thought.

She removed the covers and sat up on the bed. She looked over at the time and realized she had overslept. She was supposed to meet with Priscilla on Exandra to go over their sexual freedom speeches together. She certainly did need the extra sleep. She stood up from the bed and observed her nude body in the mirror, her black hair draped over her right breast.

Absolutely gorgeous, she thought, smiling.

Sierra placed the shower towel she had used the night before into a basket and threw on her robe. She went downstairs to make breakfast. As she put a little something together from the limited items in her kitchen, her thoughts returned to the other night with Aurora.

She recalled what Aurora had told her when they reached GEMS headquarters on Relistorr to get the *Tenebris*. Aurora had told Sierra that it was the first time she had been with another woman, and she wouldn't mind repeating the act, but that she definitely needed cock in her life. Sierra had told Aurora that the need was definitely mutual. Sierra had asked her if she was interested in swinging and that it was a lot of fun. Aurora had told Sierra that she would keep that in mind. Sierra smiled and wondered if they would ever hook up again.

She turned off the stove burner, placed her concoction on a plate, and sat at the table. As she ate her meal, she realized that she needed to purchase more food supplies for the house. The comm sounded and Sierra looked over to the living room. She stood up from the kitchen table and walked over to answer it.

"Hi, Priscilla."

"Umm, you're not here," Priscilla said.

"Sorry, I'm running late. I certainly needed the extra sleep."

"Oh, no problem. I just wanted to make sure you're all right."

"Well, thanks for checking, sweetie. I'll be on my way shortly."

"Okay. I'll see you soon."

Sierra turned off the comm and returned to the table to finish her breakfast. After breakfast, she took her monthly contraceptive pill. Soon, she was dressed and heading for the door with a printed copy of her sexual freedom speech in her hand, which she had grabbed from her office. The seminar would be held soon and they needed to be prepared. After locking the door, she made her way to the *Tenebris*.

In the darkness of space, Sierra flew the *Tenebris* at lightspeed toward Exandra. She gazed at the beautiful blue stars in the distance. She wondered what her new Galactic Emergency Medical Services unit would be like. Anything could be better than working under Madison Stephard.

Suddenly, intense blue beams of laser fire surrounded her ship.

What the hell? she thought.

She turned to look out the side of the canopy, but could not see behind her. Another set of beams pierced through the darkness of space, coming very close to hitting the *Tenebris*. She pulled up on the controls hard and the old fighter ship looped around in an arc. She was then able to see another ship nearby. The ship looked like a custom piece of junk. A blue marking was displayed across the side of the ship with strange white text.

Who the hell is that? she wondered.

The next shot hit the *Tenebris* on the starboard side, scorching the metal surface slightly. It wasn't enough to cause any serious damage, but the next shot could. Sierra quickly enabled the deflector shield, which she usually did only if there was concern of asteroid dust and fragments in certain areas of the Syrenthian Galaxy. She maneuvered around in another arc and engaged the thrusters. The odd looking ship was now in front of her and she opened a plastic cover for her own laser trigger switch. It was time to see if Flux Ship Mods came through for her. She pressed and held the red button. Blue beams of laser fire penetrated the ship in front of her and it exploded, sending a shower of shrapnel in every direction. She immediately flew to the right and just missed the drifting beams and panels of twisted metal. She had no idea why the ship was firing on her, but she was very thankful that she had her old fighter ship recently modified with laser weapons. Most civilian ships did not have weaponry on them, so the attacker had a little surprise of their own. Still, she wondered who it could have been and she was very nerved-up because she had never killed anyone before. She wondered how many people were on the ship.

I don't know what else I could have done, she thought, her mind racing.

She made a few adjustments on the navigation computer and continued on toward Exandra, increasing the ship to lightspeed-plus.

Sierra landed the *Tenebris* on Exandra at Braxton and Priscilla Stryderr's house, just outside of the capital city. Exiting the ship, she was greeted by Priscilla, who walked over to the landing pad and gave her a hug.

"You'll never believe what just happened to me," Sierra said.

"What the hell happened to the side of the *Tenebris?*" Priscilla asked.

"That's what I'm talking about. I was attacked by another ship. It kept firing at me and hit my ship."

"Damn! How did you get away?"

"Well, I recently had the *Tenebris* modified with lasers, like these fighter ships used to have during the Syrenthian War. And I'm glad I did because I used the weapons to destroy the other ship. I'm a bit on edge right now. I need to report this. I don't even know…I killed them," Sierra said.

Priscilla hugged her again. "You can tell Braxton what happened when he gets home," she said.

"He's not here?"

"No. He's at the administrative building working with some others on his investigation findings, but I expect him home soon," Priscilla said. "So, shall we go in the house and get started on reviewing the speeches?"

"Yes," Sierra said. "And I'm a bit thirsty, so can you grab me a Sevis?"

"Yeah."

Sierra set the printed copy of her speech onto the living room table while Priscilla went into the kitchen and grabbed a bottle of the sweet, carbonated beverage called Sevis from the refrigerator. Sierra looked around the cozy living room and her thoughts immediately went to the previous time she was there when they had a threesome. She smiled as Priscilla walked back into the room.

"What are you smiling about?" Priscilla asked.

"Oh, I'm just reminiscing our last encounter in this very room," Sierra said.

"Ah. That was nice. Maybe when we're done with this speech thing, we can revisit that nostalgia."

"Oh, Priscilla Pussy Lips, you never let me down."

Priscilla grabbed her own printed speech from the side table. Sierra opened the bottle of Sevis with a distinct pop sound and took a long, refreshing drink. They began reviewing both works for the upcoming Sexual Freedom Seminar on Red Jacket. They started with Priscilla's sex-positive health speech and then went into Sierra's sexual freedom speech. After reviewing them, they came to the conclusion that they both sounded fine.

"So, what's been going on with you, Sierra? Braxton said he saw you on Shar Nefalis. What a tragedy that was. I certainly hope Braxton gets to the bottom of this investigation soon," Priscilla said.

"Yeah. What have I been doing? Oh boy…where do I start? Well, my identity was stolen and I saw someone kill the thief right in front of me at an intoxication joint on Volum. I recently switched GEMS units, so I'm no longer working with the bitch, Madison. I've been doing the band thing, as usual. That terrorist attack run we went to on Shar Nefalis was awful. What else? Oh, I had to try and stop the rioting crowd on Salinarr Nevis. Come to find out, the Xenolfan military were about to kill a bunch of the rioting fans…and they would have had I followed Madison's orders and not went onstage to sing. Oh, and do you want to hear something weird?" Sierra asked.

"What?"

"On one of our runs, we went to the Shardaa Sector to rescue a seemingly delusional space traveler. His name was Dennon Cobalt. When we found him, he was unconscious, but woke enough to mention that he saw something out there on the planet S2, like a female or something. I'm not sure what Dennon saw, but we went to investigate it and there was a cave there. There are caves shaped like pussies, Xenolfan pussies. And there are odd feather symbols above them. I wonder if the feathers of Shardaa are supposed to mean something. We went in to check it out and saw no one there. But when we exited, I turned around and looked into the darkness of the cave. I swore I saw blue lights, like bright blue, glowing eyes. I had a strange, eerie feeling come over me for a second time there in the Shardaa Star System and I collapsed. I have no idea what the hell that was. Maybe that's what Dennon Cobalt saw, but I don't know. But my new GEMS unit covers the edge of the galaxy, including the Shardaa Sector, so I'm kind of freaked out. And then on the way here, someone tried to kill me," Sierra said.

"Wow, you've been through a lot lately," Priscilla said.

"Oh, and Vincent, Shaslin, and I saw a hot and arousing show at the Sex Palace Theater. They had both a human sex show *and* a Xenolfan sex show."

"Damn, that sounds hot."

"It was hot. The Xenolfan couple was interesting. I wouldn't mind getting in on that action sometime," Sierra said.

"You would be breaking Xenolfan law, Sierra. Shame on you!" Priscilla said, laughing.

"Yeah, how ridiculous!" Sierra said.

"Well, I may not have a blue pussy, but I have a nice one that you can get some action on," Priscilla said.

Priscilla pulled off her pants and grabbed Sierra's bottle of Sevis. She poured a drop onto her pussy.

"Priscilla Pussy Lips, you are a naughty girl," Sierra said, moving down to lick up the drop of liquid. "Mmm, your pussy tastes like sweet Sevis."

"Am I naughty?"

"You *are* naughty. What am I going to do with you?" Sierra asked. "I think you may need a spanking."

Priscilla turned over and put her bare ass in the air. Sierra smacked both ass cheeks with a hard slap and then repeated it again. The tan skin became slightly flush.

"Do you promise to be a good girl?" Sierra asked.

"How good do you want me to be, Sierra?"

"I want you to be good and take care of me."

Priscilla reached over and grabbed Sierra right in the pussy.

"I'll take really good care of you," Priscilla said.

"Oh, I like that."

She tilted her hips up and pushed her vulva hard into Priscilla's groping hand.

"Now, take off your clothes," Priscilla demanded, in a sudden role switch.

"Yes, ma'am," Sierra said.

She quickly removed her clothing. The two women both stood naked in the living room, each staring at the other. They slowly began to circle each other on the soft, slate blue carpeting. Sierra lunged at Priscilla and they both went down and playfully wrestled on the floor. After rolling around a few times, Priscilla locked Sierra's head between her thighs.

"Now, eat it!" Priscilla ordered.

"Oh, Priscilla Pussy Lips, you are looking good."

She began tonguing the moist pussy lips and clit. Priscilla pushed Sierra's head down hard against her pussy and began to breathe heavily. Priscilla's moans aroused Sierra, and she could feel her own wet pussy begin to tingle. She reached a free hand down and fingered her inner lips and clit, sliding two fingers into her hole. Suddenly, Sierra's pussy vibrated with a loud queef and they both laughed.

"That felt kind of good," Sierra said.

"What your doing with your tongue feels *really* good," Priscilla said.

Sierra continued licking and sucking along the beautiful lips. Soon, they traded places and Priscilla began kissing Sierra's wetness, her tongue flicking up and down the moist slit. Sierra parted her legs a bit more and Priscilla sucked onto her vulva and began to move her head from side to side.

"Ahhh! Ahhh fuck," Sierra screamed with quick shallow breaths.

Her body quivered. "That feels so nice."

Priscilla slowed her tongue movements down and eventually came to a stop and repositioned herself with her vulva against Sierra's in a scissors position. Priscilla braced her arms, gripping the carpeting, and began to push herself against the warm, wet pussy. Sierra slowly rotated her hips in graceful circles, the folds of her labia pressing against Priscilla's. They could each feel the other's radiating heat. The moist sounds of their secretions rhythmically coming together made a music of its own. As they continued tribbing, they could both feel the emerging wave of ecstasy rushing toward them. The surge came closer and they rode the edge of the wave until it splashed over them in a flood of pure rapture. They both collapsed in the most relaxing way.

"You don't know how much I needed that," Sierra said as she lay still on the carpet.

"That was the most healthy, therapeutic orgasm I think we've had together," Priscilla said, leaning up on her elbows.

"I could just stay right here and fall asleep," Sierra said.

"Not me. You just gave me a surge of energy. I'm ready to go again," Priscilla said.

"Well that's good, because I'm home now and watching you two just turned me on like nothing else," Braxton's voice came from the doorway.

Both women looked up in surprise.

"Braxton!" they said simultaneously.

"Hello, ladies," he said.

Sierra suddenly developed a renewed energy of her own.

"Well, would you like to join us?" Priscilla asked.

"Of course!" Braxton said, removing his clothes.

Braxton and Priscilla had an agreement that her and Sierra could engage in sexual activity together without his presence, as long as Priscilla filled him in on the juicy details. He much preferred it when all three of them were together, so he was happy to arrive in time to participate in the playful afternoon. His wife being a bisexual had its perks. Although Sierra was not exclusive with the couple, they were exclusive with her. They didn't fully consider themselves swingers, but the Lifestyle did appeal to them. They were completely satisfied with the threesomes they had with Sierra on occasion.

Braxton lay on the soft living room floor next to the two beautiful women. It didn't take long for his cock to become fully erect. Their three tan bodies added contrast against the slate blue carpeting. Braxton began to kiss Priscilla in a passionate embrace. Her lips were warm against his. He kissed along her neck to her ear. Her shiny, long blond hair emitted the musky fragrance of Sierra's pussy. He kissed down her neck to her breasts. They were soft against his gentle massage. Sierra leaned over and kissed Priscilla's tits as Braxton held them up to her lips. She sucked the nipples, alternating back and forth between the left and the right. Priscilla spread her legs wide as Braxton went down farther and licked her labia. He ran his tongue along the lips and folds, gently sucking on her clitoris. It was already so wet from her sex with Sierra that Braxton could taste the arousing secretions. As Priscilla moaned with pleasure, Sierra went down and took Braxton's hard cock into her mouth. She smoothly sucked along the hot, rigid cock, pumping it with a free hand. They soon switched positions and Priscilla sucked Braxton's firm cock and licked down his shaft to his balls, gently caressing them. Sierra moved around and squatted down onto him. Priscilla guided Braxton's cock into Sierra's pussy, licked her fingers, and then rubbed the wet tips against both of their genitalia in smooth strokes. The sight of his half-inserted cock in Sierra's wet pussy aroused Priscilla immensely. She indulged in fucklicking them, starting at his balls, she flattened her tongue against them and slowly slid up his shaft. She could taste Sierra's cum as it dripped down the underside of his cock with its milky-white flow. Priscilla continued slithering her tongue upward on the shaft to where it disappeared inside Sierra. The tip of her tongue then found the new warm texture of Sierra's inner labia. She flicked against the moist lips and up to Sierra's clit where she lightly sucked. She repeated her fucklicking between the two of them and pulled away when Braxton began pumping faster. The wet, smacking thrusts of his pulsating cock against her moist pussy caused Sierra's white cream to drip even more. Priscilla would occasionally lean in and lick at the cream between their thrusts. Braxton pulled his cock out of Sierra and Priscilla sucked it and kissed along the shaft. She then buried her face in the tasty, musky wetness of Sierra's pussy and quickly moved her head side to side and up and down. She once again guided Braxton's wet cock back toward Sierra and re-inserted it into the pink pussy. Sierra grabbed at a nearby table leg with a clenched fist, letting out a loud, pleasurable moan as her body stiffened and she came to an incredible orgasm. Soon after Sierra came, Braxton pulled out of her and went around behind

Priscilla who was on all fours. Holding her hips tight, he inserted his wet cock into her pussy. She pushed back wildly against his thrusts. She enjoyed the feeling of being filled up with his cock. Sierra lifted her head up and sucked at Priscilla's bouncing tits as she rocked back and forth. Priscilla could feel the wave coming again. She quivered and squeezed the fabric of the carpeting as the wave rushed over her.

"Oooh, oooh," she cried with blissful joy.

Braxton came to an intense orgasm with a loud grunt, his cock rapidly pulsating inside of Priscilla's warm pussy. As he pulled out of her, his cum also dripped out, flowing down her leg. The three of them were tired and coated with a thin layer of sweat. They all fell asleep where they lay on the slate blue carpet of the living room, their arms and legs intertwined and embraced together.

Braxton, Priscilla, and Sierra sat at the table of an elegant restaurant in the capital city of Exandra. They were enjoying each other's company and conversation on a well-deserved night out.

"So, how is the investigation going?" Priscilla asked.

Braxton looked around the dining area and kept his voice low. "When I returned with my findings, I learned that Tellaris Whitestone never returned from Olf Teruda after he went there to confront them regarding the comm chatter we discovered. We have reason to believe they are responsible for his disappearance. A lot of this is pointing right to the Xenolfan Government. So, we will be having a meeting with our leader, Edward Sirlain, on the next steps the Syrenthian Government should take."

"Wow. It seems like they're up to something. Their leader really hates humans," Sierra said.

"Priscilla, I don't know if you have any plans in the works to go back to Olf Teruda for more protests, but I don't want you to. Things are a bit scary right now. I don't trust them and I don't want anything to happen to you there," Braxton said.

"Don't worry. I'm not going back there. All of the petitions we took the time to collect from all across the galaxy didn't seem to matter. They never got back with us. What an incredible waste of our time," Priscilla said.

"I agree with Braxton, you shouldn't go back there…especially if people are disappearing. *Hey,* I wonder if they are trying to kill *me* for being an interspecies sexual freedom advocate," Sierra said.

"What are you talking about?" Braxton asked.

"There was an ugly-looking spaceship that kept shooting at me on my way here to Exandra. They actually hit my ship and now the *Tenebris* has a scorch mark on its starboard side. But I was able to fire back because I had the *Tenebris* modified with lasers. And…" There was a long pause at the table. "…and I shot the ship and it exploded. I don't know how many people were on board. I didn't know what else to do," Sierra said with a worried look on her face.

"Can you describe this ship to me?" Braxton asked.

"Yeah. It was like a custom-made piece of junk. It had modified pieces and parts sticking out everywhere," Sierra said.

"Did it have a distinct blue marking across the side with some odd white text across it?" Braxton asked.

"Yes."

Braxton started laughing, uncontrollably. It drew the attention of people sitting at some of the other tables.

"Sierra, there was no one on board. So, you didn't kill anyone. That was a preprogrammed drone ship that we've been trying to track down for months. There were others, but we've already destroyed them. The group of people responsible for creating and controlling them are already in prison. They were programmed to continue flying in space to random locations and automatically firing on moving objects. We couldn't seem to pin down the last one. Ha! You did us a great favor. I will let the team know. I'll just need the approximate coordinates of the wreckage," Braxton said.

"Okay. I can get that for you from my ships navigation computer. Well, I'm happy I didn't kill anyone," Sierra said.

"The group of people behind those remote ships are now in prison because their ships fired on several ships, killing three people. You are lucky that it didn't blow up the *Tenebris*. Congratulations on the shot. Even if there were people aboard, you would've had every right to fire on it because it fired on you first. I'm glad you modified your ship with lasers," Braxton said.

"Me too," Sierra said. "There's nothing like being able to defend yourself against an aggressor."

Chapter Twelve

The missiloid flight was fairly uneventful. Other than crossing paths with a small, dark gray ship, there were no other witnesses. From the distance of space, the missiloid would have looked like an ordinary asteroid. Besides, if the ship's pilot happened to see what it actually was, it would be too late by the time the space traveler reported it. Garrious sat at the controls in the quietness of the cockpit. On two separate occasions, the pilot cockpit itself had shifted on the asteroid. Garrious thought the rock may have cracked slightly, but was not concerned. The engineers equipped the cockpit with just enough air supply to reach Aamaress. He had a lot to think about during the silence and he wondered what the missiloid controllers from back in the Syrenthian War were like.

Were they just like me, with no family of their own? he thought.

Having no family is probably why Aaranix Tuvelless had chosen him for the mission. Sure, he had other relatives, but no one close, like a family of his own. He said his goodbyes to those relatives on Olf Teruda before departing for the asteroid in space. He knew he was going to die.

Why does Aaranix Tuvelless hate the interspecies unions so much? he wondered.

Garrious did not have an issue with interspecies relationships himself, but he was loyal to the Xenolfan leader, Aaranix. Following the orders was the proper military thing to do. In a way, he felt honored and dignified that he had been chosen for such a mission. It was something to be proud of…but it would be his last mission. That fact brought so many memories of his life to the surface. He remembered going on picnics with his parents when he was a child. They would always pick a spot near the multiple waterfalls on Olf Teruda, not far from the government palace. Looking up at a picture he had mounted on the control dash, his eyes watered. It was a picture of him with his parents, who had died years before. The caption read: "We love you, Garrious." Memories of a few Xenolfan women he dated came to mind…relationships that had come and gone. He really did wish he had a family of his own. Maybe then, he would not be in his current situation. Many of his other military missions came to mind. The team that went to the Industrial Sector were all a part of Aaranix's overall scheme.

He felt the pilot cabin lift from the surface of the rocky asteroid once again and began to doubt the integrity of the construction. At that moment, he heard something hit the side of the metal cockpit and saw a piece of rock from the asteroid float up into view and drift away as the missiloid flew onward. The rock had a metal threaded stud through it with a metal anchor plate on one end, fastened with a nut. Garrious realized it was the left front anchor plate where the cockpit had been fastened to the asteroid.

Oh shit! he thought.

He hoped he would be able to complete his mission to Aamaress, but either way he knew he was going to die. Either the cockpit would break loose from the asteroid and he would drift in space until his air ran out—at which point the remote signal to the ion engine would be lost and he would subsequently lose control of the asteroid—or he would die during the missiloid crash on Aamaress. He hoped for the later so that he would not die for his mission in vein. The missiloid would not make it to Aamaress without him controlling it. Garrious checked the distance to the resort snow planet of Aamaress.

Almost there, he thought.

Soon, the bright white planet could be seen ahead through the canopy observation window. The planet had a bluish tint to it. Two light gray satellites orbited Aamaress, one slightly larger than the other. The background of space in that sector was a light blue color, decorated with many beautiful stars. As the planet loomed before him, he began to imagine what his death would feel like. The missiloid entered the outer atmosphere of Aamaress. Garrious adjusted the controls and maneuvered the asteroid toward the nearest populated area. He realized it was not the main resort, so the smaller Winterfest would have to do. As the imminent collision course approached, Garrious could sense the low air pressure in the controller cabin. Heat from the atmospheric entry could be felt through the heat shield glass coating. Garrious closed his eyes and waited for death. Turbulence from the atmosphere ripped at the canopy. Garrious heard additional metal pieces break free from the asteroid. Suddenly, the cockpit tore away from the rock, completely separating. Opening his eyes, he could see the asteroid continue down toward its destination. The separated cockpit began to rotate in a dizzying spin. As it spun, a strobe-light effect was displayed inside the cockpit, rapidly alternating through the canopy between sky light and ground shadows. Garrious blacked out from the G-force. As the cockpit descended toward the mountains of Aamaress, it began to stabilize. Garrious opened his eyes and suddenly felt nauseated. He noticed he was on a collision course with the brown peak of a mountaintop. Snow covered the rest of the mountain. Garrious grabbed the side of the canopy as the front observation window smashed into the brown peak. It crushed the glass and made a small opening, a few glass particles flying in onto his uniform. A cold, snowy breeze blew in at his face through the opening. The impact changed the trajectory of the cockpit and it began to slide down the side of the snowy mountain at a high rate of speed, straight toward a group of rocks at the edge of a cliff. The distant explosion of the asteroid impact suddenly brightened the sky before him for a brief moment. Garrious vomited. He wiped his mouth on his arm as he watched the rocks getting closer. The cockpit swiftly curved on a slope underneath the snow and missed the rocks by a few meters, flying off the cliff. Garrious saw the rock wall cliffs pass by far below. Abruptly, the pilot cabin landed on another slope farther down the mountainside. The snow was much deeper on the lower slope. As the pilot cabin slid farther down, Garrious could barely see out the top of the window because of the deep snow. He noticed it begin to rapidly slow down, until it finally came to a stop. He sat there for a long moment, high winds passing by from the impact of the asteroid.

I'm not dead... he thought.

Xenolfan males with human females and human males with Xenolfan females could be seen having a wonderful time in the Winterfest town square. The remote town was part of The Avalanche Resort in the Northern Territories region of Aamaress. A long and rugged snowmobile trail connected the main lodge to the remote lodge in Winterfest. The smaller lodge was also warm and cozy with a stone fireplace. A stroll down the lodge corridor where the guest rooms were located would fill one's ears with moans and high-pitched reverberations of orgasmic bliss. In addition to the many warmer indoor activities and intimacies, the interspecies couples also enjoyed outdoor activities during their stay in Winterfest with snowmobiling, skiing, and snow hiking in the wilderness. An outdoor cross-country skiing activity near the town square is exactly where one interspecies couple found themselves looking up at the clear blue sky at a fiery object that appeared to be heading straight at them. Others started to look up at the incoming asteroid. Panic quickly followed with screams and people running toward the edge of the forest.

The fiery impact engulfed the entire town of Winterfest. Red flames and black smoke immediately consumed the pine forest around the area. A shockwave followed the impact with high velocity winds and snow flying high into the sky. The shockwave could be felt as far away as the main lodge of The Avalanche Resort. Avalanches are exactly what took place afterward on several of the surrounding mountains. Part of the ship docking bay at the main lodge collapsed, crushing several ships.

Everyone at the main lodge could feel the ground shake beneath them. The cracking sound of impact was deafening. Many of the guests and workers ran outside into the cold to see what had happened. They could see the black smoke and blazing fire in the far distant Northern Territories. Many of them gasped and started to panic. They turned around and looked at their immediate vicinity with the collapsed portion of the docking bay. Eyes turned toward the sky, looking for any clues of what could have caused the explosion. They only saw a blue sky, which was a rare occasion on Aamaress. It was usually gray and cloudy. Suddenly, a very strong wind came at them from the Northern Territories region and drove them back into the lodge.

"Contact the Syrenthian Government!" Mauve shouted.

Max ran to the back room to turn on the communicator. It was dead.

"The comm's dead. We have no communications. What the hell just happened?" Max asked.

The high-velocity winds suddenly broke a window in the front of the grand foyer, causing further panic.

"From what I can tell from outside, it looks like something happened in Winterfest, like an explosion or something," Mauve said.

At that point guests started exiting their rooms and filled the grand foyer, all wondering what had taken place. Gathin and Eslarr proceeded down the stairs toward the front counter. Gathin didn't have time to put a shirt on.

"What's going on?" Gathin asked.

"Yeah, what the hell just shook our room?" Eslarr asked.

"I don't know. We think something happened in the remote town of Winterfest, like an explosion. Part of our docking bay collapsed too," Max said

"And the high winds just broke out our front window," Mauve said, pointing to the front of the grand foyer. "When I get a chance, I'll go grab some thermal cubes to try and keep it warm in here."

Gathin could feel the cold breeze blowing against his bare chest. It sent goosebumps all over his body.

"Cool wolf tattoo, by the way," Max said, looking at Gathin's left side.

"Eslarr, I'm going to put a shirt on. I'll be right back," Gathin said.

As he left the counter, other guests started asking Max and Mauve many questions. It didn't take long for the two young resort workers to become overwhelmed.

"Where is your boss? Maybe he'll know more than you two," one guest spouted.

Max and Mauve looked at each other with sudden concern.

"He was up at Winterfest," Max said.

Suddenly, a man came in the main entrance of the grand foyer.

"I saw what happened! It was an asteroid that hit," he said.

"Fuck!" Mauve said.

• • •

As the winds from the asteroid impact ceased, Garrious tried to open the cockpit canopy, but the snow was too heavy for him to lift it. He began kicking at the broken observation window until there was an opening large enough for him to escape. Although it was cold, the sudden fresh air was very welcome, as the cabin air had virtually depleted. Garrious slowly climbed out of the cockpit and noticed the faint burning scent of the distant asteroid impact. As he climbed out onto the front section of the cockpit, his left leg slipped on the snow, causing his right thigh to come down hard on the broken glass edge of the observation window. Sudden agony began to radiate down his leg. He screamed in pain as blood started to drip down the outside of the cockpit, disappearing into the deep snow. Garrious managed to pull his right leg free from the cockpit and slid down into the deep snow, grabbing at his wound. He pulled a small piece of the heat-resistant glass out of his thigh and limped away from the wreckage, a red blood trail following him through the snow. He noticed the cockpit canopy had come to a stop near a flowing stream of water at the foot of the mountain. The stream disappeared in either direction. Garrious made his way down to the flowing water. Large stones decorated the side of the stream. As he approached one of the stones, he sat down and dipped his hands into the fresh, icy water. He continued to scoop the water up into his mouth to quench his thirst. Garrious swished around the remaining vomit taste and spit to the side. After a few more drinks, he cleaned up his uniform the best he could. He tore at his sleeve to create a bandage for the bleeding thigh. Garrious managed to rip off a small piece of fabric and tie it around his leg. It didn't help much, but did slow the bleeding slightly. He looked around his immediate vicinity and saw nothing but mountainous terrain and pine trees. Garrious stood up and limped toward a rock wall that was located along the stream. To his surprise, around the corner of the rock wall, there was a breathtaking view of the mountains and pine forest, all covered in a beautiful blanket of snow. He found an area of the stream with many rocks across it and was able to cross to the other side. Garrious didn't know where he was or which direction to go…and he was very cold. He sighed and trudged through the snow toward another rock outcrop, drips of red blood behind him. Garrious came across what looked like a trail of some sort. It ran along a cliff and turned around the corner of the mountain. He made his way around the bend, to find the trail disappearing into the pine forest. Garrious knew he could not walk that far and began to look for a place to rest.

A quick and fiery death would have been better than freezing to death while I bleed out, he thought.

Between two brown rock outcrops, he noticed a snowy inlet next to a single white pine tree. He slowly made his way toward the opening. To his amazement, it opened up into a small cave. The brightness of the white snow illuminated the cave, giving him enough light to see adequately.

I'm tired, so tired. I just want to lie down and rest, he thought, making his way into the cave.

As he entered, a remaining piece of fabric from his sleeve caught onto a branch of the white pine tree and ripped off from his outfit. It was a few degrees warmer inside the cave, but still dangerously cold for him to survive for an extended period of time. To one side, there were small rocky pebbles where he lay down and rested.

Perhaps, if I can make it to where the main resort is located, I can get help. But why would they help me? Wait, they don't know that I was the missiloid controller. As far as they know, I am just a Xenolfan guest here on Aamaress with a human female... I'm never going to make it to the resort. I'm never even going to make it back out of this cave alive, Garrious thought.

Closing his eyes, tears began to roll down his bluish-gray, patterned face, their liquid form freezing next to his ears.

"What have I done?" he asked himself.

Chapter Thirteen

As Rastall settled the *Cosmic Disturbance* onto the landing pad, he could see his local sex health clinic was not very busy. Like most of the clients at the sex health clinic, Rastall had a high sex drive. It had been a while since he received sex and he was incredibly horny. He had not received sex since he was on Aamaress with the Xenolfan couple, Shalarr and Fioness. He looked up on the wall of the ship at the poster the Xenolfan couple had given him of their risqué theater pose. Rastall exited his ship and walked toward the building. He was thankful the cost of the clinic was covered in full by the government, thanks to that beautiful, black-haired woman he had met at the Sex Palace Theater on Salinarr Nevis. He recalled her name was Sierra Shalinsky.

The sex health clinics that were set up across the Syrenthian Galaxy separately for both humans and Xenolfans provided basic sex therapy sessions of education, mandatory STI testing to maintain an STI-free population, manual genital stimulation, and oral sex. The most popular appointments were for oral sex. It was against policy and thus prohibited to have vaginal sex or anal sex at the clinics.

Entering the building, he made his way to the check-in desk. The waiting room was practically empty, except for a woman with short, brown hair who sat reading a magazine. Like the one she held, many of the magazines had sexual imagery as well as sexual health articles. Rastall sat in one of the comfortable, cushioned chairs and waited for his name to be called. Picking up one of the magazines from the table next to him, he began thumbing through it. He came across a sex-positive health article written by Priscilla Stryderr. As he started reading it, the woman across the room was called in for her appointment. He looked up at her as she went through the door into the patient rooms. His attention shifted back to the article. The article went deep into the therapeutic benefits of sex. It was followed by another article from the same author that covered the story of how the Syrenthian Galaxy became virtually STI-free because of the implementation of the sex clinics. The article even gave credit to Sierra Shalinsky for her roll in the effort. Rastall closed the cover and put it back onto the table. He walked over, grabbed the magazine the woman had been looking at, and then sat back down. As soon as he opened it, he realized she must have been aroused going into her appointment. The vivid imagery of couples in various sexual acts was exciting. Just as he turned the page, his name was called. He looked up at the nurse, laid the magazine down onto the table, and headed for the patient rooms.

"How are you, Rastall?" the nurse asked.

"Good. Better, now that I'm here," Rastall said.

"We'll be in room five here," she said.

She stepped aside to let him in first and then followed in behind him, closing the door.

"So, what's new?" she asked.

"Not a lot. On my way here, I saw the most bizarre thing. In the distance of space, I saw what looked like a missiloid—you know, the kind from the history books—which the Xenolfans used to use back in the Syrenthian War. I know what I saw," Rastall said.

"That *is* strange. Did you report it to the Syrenthian Government?" she asked.

"No," he said. "They would probably think I'm crazy. Maybe I should..."

"Well, you never know," she said.

"I missed you last time I was here. They had a male nurse cover for you," he said.

"Ah, yes. And how was that experience for you?" she asked.

"Well, it was a nice experience, but I prefer a female nurse," he said.

"Well, I'm back. So, let's get you undressed and up on the table."

Rastall removed his clothes and set them neatly on the nearby counter. The room was nice and warm. He lay flat on his back and looked over to the nurse. She pressed a device against his upper arm to check for STIs. He was clean.

"Have you ever had that device show a positive?" he asked.

"Nope. Well, not since the galaxy was declared STI-free a while back," she said. "When everyone came to the clinics and had been checked and treated around the same time, that fixed the problem," she said.

Setting the device on the counter, she walked over and began massaging his flaccid penis. It didn't take long for him to get a full erection. She gently caressed his balls and began to lightly pump his cock with her hand. There was a distinct orgasmic moan from one of the other patient rooms.

"You always know how to handle my cock with care," he said.

"You have a very nice cock, Rastall," she said.

The nurse leaned over and began fellatio. Her lips felt so wonderful on his cock. He could feel her tongue slowly slide down his shaft and slither at his balls.

"Mmm, that's nice," he said.

Bobbing her head up and down, she sucked on his cock with smooth motions. She continued for a long while, changing it up a bit by sliding her lips and tongue down and then back up. The ebb and flow of his approaching orgasm started to plateau. He soon began to peak and he could feel the nerve endings in his toes quickly make their way up his legs to his cock. She could feel the pulsing flesh around her lips and moved away. She jacked his cock with quick motions as the feeling of pleasure flooded his entire body. He ejaculated high into the air and it came down onto his stomach with an audible splat. His loud groan could be heard throughout the patient rooms.

"Oh, I needed that," Rastall said.

"I can tell you needed that. Next time, don't wait so long," she said, handing him a towel.

Rastall cleaned up the cum and threw the towel into a laundry hamper next to the counter. He went into an adjacent bathroom and washed himself up. After returning to the patient room, he got dressed. The nurse went in after him and rinsed her mouth out with a minty solution.

"I will definitely not wait as long next time," he said.

"I hope the rest of your day is as wonderful as your visit here," she said.

"I can't guarantee that," he said, laughing.

The nurse opened the door and followed him out into the corridor. The woman he had seen earlier from the waiting room also exited her patient room at the same time, followed by another female nurse. The two patients made their way toward the clinic exit.

"Come again," the nurses said.

"You've got to be joking," Yosemite said.

"No. I'm sorry, but your ATV shipment is delayed until further notice. There was a terrorist attack in the Industrial Sector on Shar Nefalis and a lot of the ATVs at Ticrisuda Powersports took collateral damage. It's now on backorder," CJ Whitmann said.

"Well, that sucks. I was hoping to hit the trails with my new ATV real soon here," Yosemite said.

The gray-haired man behind the counter shrugged. Yosemite McFarlin sighed deeply and turned from the counter toward the front door of the old hardware store. As he turned, his shifting weight caused the wooden floorboards to creak.

"I'm sorry, Yosemite. I'll keep you updated on the situation," CJ said.

"Okay. Thanks for checking into it," Yosemite said.

Yosemite left CJ Whitmann's Hardware & Supply Co. and walked down the old, gray, wooden steps toward his anti-gravitational transport. He flew toward his home, very disappointed. The red and orange landscape of Red Jacket was breathtaking, even for a resident who saw it on a daily basis. As Yosemite passed the Civie Arena—where Shasta Varium had scheduled a forthcoming concert—his disappointment was replaced with excitement. Another big show was coming up. Sierra and her friend Priscilla were also scheduled to speak at the venue, just before the concert. He was looking forward to both events.

"Sir, we just received a message from a man named Rastall regarding what appeared to be a missiloid sighting," a female voice came over the comm.

Braxton Stryderr's attention was suddenly peaked. He looked up from his desk at the comm.

"Missiloid? Those haven't been used for years, not since the Syrenthian War with the Xenolfans— Oh shit! This isn't good. Where was this sighting located?" he asked.

"Not far from the snow planet Aamaress," the woman said.

"Okay, thanks for the information," he said, his complexion turning pale.

Braxton quickly contacted Edward Sirlain, head of the Syrenthian Government. Edward answered the comm.

"Hello, Edward. I hate to bother you at this late hour, but you need to be made aware of this situation. The sighting of a missiloid has just been reported near Aamaress. As you know, those were used by the Xenolfans during the Syrenthian War to attack human controlled planets. Between this reported sighting, the Xenolfan terrorists on Shar Nefalis, and the disappearance of our very own Tellaris Whitestone after visiting Aaranix Tuvelless on Olf Teruda, I believe we may be on the verge of war with the Xenolfan Government," Braxton said.

"It certainly does not look good. I'll head to your office shortly and we can further analyze this shit," Edward Sirlain said.

A Xenolfan military scout ship disengaged from lightspeed near Aamaress. Its black hull was very stealth against the darkness of space. The sole Xenolfan official aboard finished programming a drone and released it from the scout ship. The black, metal drone traveled down through the cold atmosphere of Aamaress toward the missiloid impact zone. The small, sleek drone was extremely fast. It flew through the pine forest with extreme precision. As it came to a clearing of charred and blackened trees at the forest edge, a smoldering crater was displayed. It transmitted the data from its internal sensors back to the scout ship in the orbit of Aamaress. The devastation of an entire village was revealed, its structures completely flattened. What was left of the small asteroid lay on an angle, impacted into the ground and protruding into the air. Mangled human and Xenolfan bodies could be seen at the outskirts of the epicenter. Farther out, near the far edge of the forest, several of the victims stirred in the dirty snow, crying out for help. After hovering over the ruins, the drone slowly flew in a different direction, across to the other side of the devastation. Similar data was reported back to the Xenolfan scout ship. Soon, the drone ascended past the mountain forest and toward the gray sky, eventually disappearing into space.

"Xenolfan scout ship *X2143*, reporting back to military base Dalaa. We have a confirmed hit with massive casualties. The Aamaress orbit has been decayed ever so slightly, but not enough that it cannot correct itself over time," the Xenolfan official said.

"Roger that. Return to base Dalaa and report to Aaranix Tuvelless on Olf Teruda," the remote voice said.

The Xenolfan official retrieved the black, metal drone from the airlock and set a course for Olf Teruda's satellite, Dalaa.

"Rest in peace, Garrious," he said.

Gathin tried to reach his ship in the collapsed docking bay at The Avalanche Resort on Aamaress so that he could send out an emergency communique. When he arrived at the docking bay, he found the structure to be very unstable. With the cold, blowing wind, it made some very frightening, creaky sounds and he did not trust going into it to get to his ship. He noticed many ships had been crushed underneath the concrete slabs. None of the other owners dared to risk it either. He decided to stick to plan B and try to rig a relay to the comm in the lodge.

With somewhat of a technical background, Gathin went to work on the comm in the lodge and managed to get the communications system back online with a relay, but only with capabilities of transmitting an intermittent signal on a broad frequency range for short distances. As Gathin finished tinkering with the comm, Eslarr entered the back room from the grand foyer.

"Mauve and I just finished covering the broken window with plastic, so it should get warmer out there in the grand foyer," Eslarr said.

"Good. And I have the comm working now…sort of," Gathin said.

Max hovered over Gathin.

"Max, I'll let you sit here and do your thing," Gathin said, standing from the chair.

Max sat in the chair and the comm was lit up before him. They were in the back office, behind the host counter. As Gathin, Eslarr, and Mauve looked on in anticipation, Max pressed the transmit button.

"This is Max from The Avalanche Resort on Aamaress. This is an emergency. We need assistance with what appears to be an asteroid that struck our remote village in the Northern Territories. I repeat, we have an emergency. Please help us," Max said.

They all looked at each other and waited for a response. Nothing was received from the comm. The silence seemed very loud. The faint sound of some guests could be heard out in the grand foyer.

"Well, while we're waiting, I'm going to go mix up a batch of my new Sipathrott aphrodisiac elixir drink that I've been experimenting with," Mauve said as she left the room.

"How can she be in the mood at a time like this?" Eslarr asked.

"Oh, she's always horny," Max said.

Silence filled the small room.

"Maybe you should try it again," Gathin suggested.

"Okay," Max said. He pressed the transmit button on the comm. "This is Max from The Avalanche Resort on Aamaress. Emergency! Emergency! We need immediate assistance. Does anyone copy?"

"Sir, we are receiving an intermittent signal. It seems to be an emergency call for help from the planet Aamaress," a woman said.

She sat at the controls of a large space freighter that traveled the remote space lanes near Aamaress. The freighter was a light gray color with two docking bays and multiple levels.

"An emergency on the resort snow planet Aamaress? That's odd. Perhaps there was an avalanche or something. Contact the Galactic Emergency Medical Services headquarters on Relistorr," the captain said.

"Yes, sir," the woman said.

The woman looked up the information for the GEMS headquarters on Relistorr and contacted them.

"GEMS emergency hotline. What is your emergency?" the GEMS official asked.

"Hi. I'm calling from the space freighter *Aplomb*. We just received an intermittent signal from the planet Aamaress with an emergency call and just wanted to pass it along to you. It sounds like they are having some communications issues as well," the woman said.

"Do you know the nature of the emergency?" the GEMS official asked.

"We do not. We just happened to be passing near Aamaress in the remote shipping lanes and picked up on the signal," the woman said.

"Okay, we will check it out. And since that is Syrenthian Government territory, we will also contact the Syrenthian Government. Thanks for reporting it," the GEMS official said.

The woman at the space freighter controls tried reaching back out to Aamaress. "Hello, Aamaress. This is the space freighter *Aplomb*. We have received your message and relayed it to GEMS."

There was no response. Eventually, the woman on the space freighter gave up on trying to reach them.

"Thank you for contacting GEMS and reporting this. I wonder what's happening on Aamaress," the captain said.

They both looked out the ship's observation window in wonder at the distant bluish-white planet as they drifted by in the remote space lanes.

Elliss Millott met with Sierra in her new, warmer office at the GEMS headquarters on Relistorr. It was located in a different wing of the building, far away from Madison Stephard. The incident commander was reviewing the details of the new unit that Sierra was now a part of. It was a much smaller unit than Madison's, with only three Galactic Emergency Medical Technicians. The other two Galactic EMTs were Rasmond Echeon and the unit's director, Sethain Absoneth. The positive thing about the move to the new unit was that they were both wonderful people. Sierra had known them both for years from the GEMS social circles. Rasmond was a brunette with a heart of gold and Sethain was a man with short, blond hair who was trying to make practical changes in the galaxy, one crises at a time.

Elliss went over Sierra's new role with the unit and exactly where her on-call territory would be located. As he mentioned to her before, it was near the edge of the Syrenthian Galaxy, including the Shardaa Sector and other remote areas. Suddenly, the comm at Sierra's desk rang.

"Hi, Sierra. Is Ellis there with you?" a man asked.

"Yes," Sierra said.

"I'm here. What can I help you with, Sethain?" Elliss asked.

"The emergency hotline received a communication from a space freighter near Aamaress. They have relayed an emergency message from the planet asking for help. Since that is Syrenthian Government territory, I have already reported it to the Syrenthian Government on Exandra," Sethain Absoneth said.

"Thank you, Sethain. It looks like we'll be headed for Aamaress," Elliss said, turning off the comm.

"That doesn't sound good," Sierra said.

"Nope. Okay, let's get your team together and head for the *Deliverance*," Elliss said. "See, with our new policy, this is where you would have normally flown directly from your home planet of Asparr Celtarious, or wherever you happened to be at the time, and traveled directly to meet the *Deliverance* at Aamaress. But since you are already on Relistorr, we will just leave from here."

"Okay, well I better meet up with my new unit," Sierra said. "Thanks again for giving me this opportunity."

"You're welcome," Elliss said.

Sierra stood up from her new desk, grabbed her EMT bag, and followed Elliss out her office door.

Chapter Fourteen

The *Deliverance* disengaged lightspeed and drifted toward the looming bluish-white planet of Aamaress. Two gray satellites could be seen orbiting the planet, a larger one in the foreground and a smaller one on the other side of the planet. Sierra had her uniform on and walked with the two other people in her unit, Sethain Absoneth and Rasmond Echeon. The corridors of the *Deliverance* were busy with personnel hustling to their destinations. As the three of them approached the docking bay from the upper level, they could see their medical shuttle's light gray finish glistening from the docking bay's overhead illuminators.

"We need to stop here at the supply room and gear up for some cold weather. We will each get one thermal cube. Only use it if you have to because there is a galaxy-wide shortage on them right now. We don't have the luxury of each carrying multiple thermal cubes as we normally would have. That's because of the recent terrorist attack on Shar Nefalis in the Industrial Sector," Sethain said.

"I was there with my former unit for that call. It was horrible," Sierra said.

"Yeah, what a tragedy. I hope this isn't worse," Sethain said.

They entered a supply room near the docking bay entrance and began gathering warmer gear and other supplies.

"These look very warm," Rasmond said as she held up a thermal coat.

"I've already been briefed on the lodges and settlements of the planet. Let's stay sharp out there. We are the initial team to go in. We will be landing at The Avalanche Resort's main lodge. There, we will get information from eyewitnesses to see what we are dealing with. We may need to stay and help with any situations at the main lodge or split up and scout the area. Have your comms ready for any urgent communications between us. Once we can assess the situation, I will signal the *Deliverance* if we need other medical shuttles," Sethain said.

"Sounds good," Rasmond said.

They bundled up in the warmer clothes and gathered one thermal cube each. They each grabbed their EMT bag, put the thermal cube inside, and exited the supply room.

"Man, these warm clothes are hot enough to make me thirsty," Sierra said.

"I'm sure you'll cool down as soon as we get to Aamaress," Rasmond said.

Rasmond put her long, brown hair into a ponytail. Sierra adjusted her hair tie as well and snuggled the warm hat over her ears. Turning left, they made their way through another doorway and onto a platform of metal grating, which was painted yellow. It overlooked the docking bay with a connecting metal-grated stairway. As they made their way down the yellow stairs, the distinct metal sound of their boots clomping on the grated steps could be heard throughout the docking bay. Sethain would be piloting this medical shuttle himself. As soon as they were aboard and buckled in, they exited the docking bay of the *Deliverance* and headed for the bright snow planet of Aamaress.

As the medical shuttle settled onto the white ground in front of the main lodge, Sierra could see snowflakes slowly falling from the gray sky. The nearby mountains and snow-covered pines were breathtaking. After Sethain turned off the ship's engines and anti-gravitational units, they exited the medical shuttle and stepped onto the soft, snowy ground. Despite the cool air, Sierra still felt hot wearing the thermal gear. In the distance, the partially collapsed docking bay could be seen. Several resort guests that were outside the lodge stared at the Galactic EMTs as they made their way to the main entrance. When they entered into the grand foyer, Sierra first saw the large plastic covering over the broken window. Her gaze was then drawn to the stone fireplace and guests who relaxed on the soft leather couches. The three of them made their way toward the host counter. There were three humans and a Xenolfan talking at the counter.

"Hi. We are Galactic Emergency Medical Technicians from the Galactic Emergency Medical Services. My name is Sethain Absoneth. I'm this unit's director. This his Rasmond Echeon and Sierra Shalinsky. An emergency signal from here was received by a passing space freighter. They relayed the message to GEMS and we also notified the Syrenthian Government. Who is in charge here at the lodge?"

"Well, Mauve and I…kind of. My name is Max," he said.

"What do you mean?" Sethain asked as he stared at the young man for a long moment.

"Well, we think our boss was killed by the asteroid that hit the remote lodge in Winterfest. Actually, these two guests, Gathin and Eslarr, should be in charge. They have helped out tremendously since the asteroid hit," Max said.

"So, what are we dealing with here?" Sethain asked.

"Apparently, an asteroid hit Winterfest up in the Northern Territories. There is a single main trail that connects the main lodge here to the remote lodge. I think it is very odd that it would hit Winterfest, given the chances of an asteroid striking virtually anywhere else on the planet. We cannot communicate with them, but I was able to get the comm fixed enough to send out a short-range signal. You said a passing space freighter received it? I'm just glad there was a space freighter near Aamaress at the time. Thank you guys for the timely response. You probably noticed the damaged docking bay and broken window. I'm surprised there wasn't more destruction here at the main lodge," Gathin said.

"Yes, the docking bay looks like it could completely collapse at any moment," Sethain said.

"Is there a hospital ship here?" Eslarr asked.

"Yes. The *Deliverance* is in orbit above Aamaress," Rasmond said.

Sierra noticed a glass on the counter and looked up at the four of them.

"Do you mind if I get a glass of water too? I'm thirsty and this warm gear is not helping," Sierra said.

"Oh, not at all. I'll be right back," Mauve said, disappearing to the back room.

"So, you guys don't know how bad Winterfest is?" Sethain asked.

"No, not really," Max said.

"After the asteroid struck, the ground shook and there was a terrible wind storm for a short time. That's how the damage here at the main lodge happened," Gathin said.

"So, you two are guests here?" Sierra asked Eslarr.

"Yes, we came here to be together because my government, the Xenolfan Government, forbids humans and Xenolfans to be together. We love each other very much and damn them for trying to stop us. We were recently married here in the grand foyer and we will be purchasing a log home here on Aamaress. Look around at all these guests. The Avalanche Resort here on Aamaress is the one secret place where we can come together, whether it's for love or sex or both. Our xeno tryst will not be quenched!" Eslarr said.

Her sapphire eyes filled with tears as she looked around the grand foyer at all the other guests. Sierra followed her gaze.

"I love Gathin…and I will fight till death to be with my husband, if need be. You EMTs and the Syrenthian Government that you contacted about this asteroid incident better not inform the Xenolfan Government. They will just come and arrest us…or worse. Please tell me you guys won't inform them," Eslarr said.

Sierra could see the anxiety on her bluish-gray face. Her beautiful white hair flowed eloquently down her back. As Mauve came back with a glass of water and set it on the counter, Sierra put an arm around Eslarr and looked her straight in the eyes.

"Do you know who I am?" Sierra asked.

"No," Eslarr said.

"I'm Sierra Shalinsky, a sexual freedom advocate for human and Xenolfan relationships. I fight for the forbidden interspecies sex. I will have your back more than you can possibly know. In fact, we have collected signatures from all over the Syrenthian Galaxy and given the petitions to Aaranix Tuvelless on Olf Teruda. A good friend of mine has led protests on Olf Teruda. I will be giving a sexual freedom speech on Red Jacket at the forthcoming Sexual Freedom Seminar. In fact, I want you and Gathin to attend," Sierra said.

"Now that I think about it, your name was mentioned to us before by someone we met here named Rastall. He said he met you at the Sex Palace Theater on Salinarr Nevis," Eslarr said.

"Okay, I think I remember him," Sierra said.

She reached into her warm coat and brought out a small satchel. After opening the small satchel, Sierra produced four tickets.

"Here are two tickets to the Sexual Freedom Seminar. And these two are for a concert that will happen afterward at the same venue on Red Jacket. It will be at the Civie Arena. They are for the symphonic metal band Maranadda. I am also the vocalist for Maranadda. I really want you two to be there. I want nothing more than happiness and joy for you two. I am so glad that I have met you both. You two are the reason why I fight," Sierra said in a passionate statement.

Sierra grabbed the glass of liquid from the counter that Mauve had set there earlier. She took a long drink, paused for a moment, and then finished the rest. Setting the glass down, Sierra handed Eslarr the four tickets.

"Like all of our Maranadda concert tickets, they are not for a specific show. Our tickets can be used at any of our future shows. If you miss one, you can catch us at another show," Sierra said.

"Thank you so much...for everything. We will definitely be at both events. I would have never guessed you were all those things. You're an amazing woman, Sierra," Eslarr said.

"Yes, very amazing," Gathin finally said.

"You two have inspired me to write a new song," Sierra said.

The interspecies couple both hugged her and thanked her again.

"Oh shit!" Mauve exclaimed.

They all looked at Mauve as she gasped.

"What's wrong?" Max asked.

"She drank the wrong glass. This is your glass of water," Mauve said, sliding a glass across the counter toward Sierra.

"So, what's the big deal? Weren't they both water?" Sierra asked.

"No! Before you guys arrived, I just got done mixing a triple batch of my experimental Sipathrott aphrodisiac elixir drink. That wasn't water!" Mauve said.

Sierra looked at the young woman with a blank face. She returned the small satchel of event tickets to her inner coat pocket.

"This shouldn't be a problem. I'm usually pretty aroused anyway,"

Sierra said.

"Oh, no, it will be a problem," Mauve said, shaking her head. "You see, it's a triple batch of Sipathrott, mixed with several other aphrodisiacs in a liquid elixir form that I was experimenting with. I was only going to try a small sip myself."

"Oh," Sierra said. "How long before it kicks in?"

"Probably in thirty minutes," Mauve said.

"Nice going, Mauve. Why did you leave it on the counter?" Max asked.

"I'm sorry. I didn't mean to," Mauve said.

"Mauve, I like your style. I'll be fine. Don't worry about me. Okay?"

Mauve looked at Sierra with a worried stare.

"You look like you're about to cry. Seriously, don't you worry about this. I can handle it. Just be careful in the future," Sierra said.

Shaking her head in an affirmative response, Mauve remained silent. Sethain looked at Sierra and Rasmond.

"I didn't want to use the water from my EMT bag in case I need it out in the field," Sierra said.

"So, if you think you'll be fine, let's talk about the plan here," Sethain said.

"Okay," Sierra said.

"I will contact the *Deliverance* and brief them on our situation. Rasmond and I will fly the medical shuttle to Winterfest to assess the damage and call in for more medical shuttles, if necessary. Sierra, I want you to take one of the resort's snowmobiles and search along the trail that connects the main lodge to the remote lodge at Winterfest in the Northern Territories. With the ground shaking, avalanches, and the strong winds, there could be victims on the connecting trail. I'm assuming there is an extra snowmobile Sierra can use," Sethain said.

"Yes, definitely," Max said.

He grabbed a key from below the counter and handed it to Sierra.

"The snowmobiles are across the main court from where your ship is parked. I'm sorry they're older models. We have a large order for new snowmobiles, but they're taking forever to get here. There is only one main trail that connects the main lodge here to the remote lodge in Winterfest, so it should be fairly easy to find. It is quite a distance, however. And you will need to be careful on the trail because there are mountainous cliffs and rock outcrops as well as lots of trees," Max said.

"Okay," Sierra said, taking the key from Max.

"If I find any victims along the trail, am I bringing them back here to the main lodge?" Sierra asked.

"No," Sethain said. "Meet us up at Winterfest where the medical shuttle will be."

Sierra headed for the main entrance of the grand foyer.

"Godspeed," Eslarr called after her.

Sierra stopped and turned toward Eslarr. "Thank you, sweetie," she said before continuing out the door.

Sierra made her way across the snowy court and around the medical shuttle with the strap of her EMT bag draped around her neck. She saw the snowmobile garage ahead of her. She matched the number on the key to the number on the snowmobile.

Number sixty-nine, here we are. It must be my lucky day, Sierra thought.

She opened up the seat and put her EMT bag inside. Removing one of the two helmets from inside the seat, she put it on her head and adjusted it over the hat she wore. The snowmobile was an older Ticrisuda Powersports model. Starting up the snowmobile, she maneuvered it out of the garage and onto the snowy court. She waved at Sethain and Rasmond as they entered the medical shuttle.

I wonder what horrors they will find up in Winterfest, Sierra thought.

She looked in her mirrors and noticed the medical shuttle lift from the snowy, white surface and ascend into the gray sky. Ahead of her the populated area of the main lodge was quickly replaced by a white pine forest at the foot of a mountain. The wide court gave way to a narrow rustic trail. The hardpack snow trail that was behind her transitioned into a less traveled trail of soft, powdery snow. Sierra observed the beautiful wilderness displayed before her. The pines rushed by as she twisted the throttle at full speed. The engine whined with all of its force. The falling snow rushed at her visor like stars at lightspeed. The trail twisted and turned through the pine forest for some distance. The snowmobile seat started feeling very warm. She looked down.

That's odd, she thought.

She suddenly realized it wasn't the seat at all. Mauve's experimental aphrodisiac elixir had kicked in. The warm feeling quickly became an incredibly hot feeling between her legs. Every little bump on the trail, every little twist and turn of the snowmobile sent surges of pleasure straight to her pussy. Sierra began to breathe heavily.

Oh my. This is way more intense than I could have possibly imagined. Ahhh! she thought.

She lifted her bottom up off the seat in a squatting position, which took away the vibrations that she felt.

Ah, much better, she thought.

The extreme arousal subsided, but her legs were getting tired of holding her weight up with the squatting position. In addition, it was more difficult to control the snowmobile while squatting. She finally sat back down and the intense feeling returned.

This is going to make my job very difficult, she thought.

As she made her way up the rocky mountain trail, her mind became focused on a new problem. It looked as if a snowstorm was brewing before her, so she slowed her speed and calculated the course ahead. She came to a stop as she entered into a white-out of blinding snow. It was seamless with the sky for a long moment before letting up. Once the mountainous course became visible again, she continued forward toward a switchback that ascended up the mountainside. Drifts of snow covered the rocky outcrops to her right. Rolling past light brown, rock monoliths, she became nervous when she saw sheer cliffs ahead of her. She slowed down to a crawl as the trail turned to the left in a sharp curve. She took a moment to look over the edge.

Damn, they should put a railing there or something, she thought.

The curvy trail continued upward before plateauing, where it was carved out between two rock walls. As she passed through the ravine, she looked up at the sheer, light brown cliffs. A few snow-capped white pine trees hung over the tops of the rock walls on either side. Ahead of her, the trail ascended upward and straight toward a horizon that she could not see over. The sun peaked through the gray clouds and began to shine on the white snow, sparkling like a million tiny crystals. She slowed down as she came to the crest of the hill. It was a mountain pass in the middle of nowhere. A smaller trail split off from the main trail ahead and curved to the right. It went up and over the main trail with a metal bridge, disappearing into a cave. The main trail started to descend in a straight, downhill slope that went on for some distance. She took the opportunity on the straightaway to squat up off the seat once more. Her pussy was throbbing so much that she could feel her secretions seep out, soaking her cold panties. She briefly closed her eyes with the sense of mounting sexual tension.

I just have this urge to be filled with a big, throbbing cock. Oh, I could just ride it like there's no tomorrow, she thought.

When she reached the bottom of the descent, she followed the trail as it curved to the right and into a valley. She carefully sat back on the seat. A mountain was on her right and a stream of flowing water appeared on her left. Beyond the small stream lay another mountain. Drifts of snow created a multitude of interesting shapes along the stream. Gray clouds, once again, filled the sky. The brief sunshine came and went very quickly. Sierra slowed down as the trail curved around a rock wall to the left. Another drop-off was on her right. She crawled at a very slow speed around the bend. Ahead of her, she noticed a single white pine tree between two rock outcrops. Beyond the rock outcrops was another cliff on the right. As she slowly rode past the pine tree, something caught her attention. Sierra stopped the snowmobile and backed up. A piece of fabric was stuck on one of the white pine tree branches. A small cave was located between the rock outcrops. She pulled the snowmobile off the trail and into the snowy inlet between the outcrops. Sierra removed her helmet, set it on the snowmobile seat, and walked toward the pine tree. Reaching up to the branch, she examined the piece of fabric. She looked back down at the cave entrance as flakes of crystal snow fell from the sky. As she walked toward the entrance, she noticed the footprints she left in the snow revealed drips of frozen blood beneath them. Sierra quickly turned around and ran back to the snowmobile. She grabbed the helmet, opened the seat, and thew it inside next to the other one. Grabbing her EMT bag, she closed the seat and ran back toward the cave. The bright, white snow gave enough light inside the cave for her to see, but she needed to take a moment to adjust her eyes to the dimness. Sierra noticed someone lying on the ground next to the wall on her left. She ran over to them. Sierra discovered that it was a Xenolfan male with his head resting on small pebble stones. A small pool of blood had collected on the cave floor, near his legs.

"Oh my! Hey, can you hear me?" Sierra asked.

There was no answer. She knelt on the floor next to him and felt his bluish-gray skin.

"Oh shit, you're freezing."

Sierra reached into her EMT bag, removed the thermal cube, and activated it. Setting it off to one side, she could feel the heat begin to radiate out from it. It didn't take long for the small cave to warm up to a tolerable temperature. She checked his vitals, remembering the Xenolfan numbers. His blood pressure was slightly low. She examined him and found the wound in his right thigh. The bleeding had stopped on its own because of the fabric that was tied around his leg. Xenolfans were known to heal quickly, but he would still need stitches. That was something they would need to do up on the *Deliverance*. She could, however, bandage it up really nice. She removed the tied fabric and cleaned up the wound. Sierra couldn't help but notice the proximity of the injury to his Xenolfan penis. She smiled as she tried to fight off her extreme arousal. As she applied an adequate bandage, he stirred on the cave floor and she leaned over him and looked at his eyes. To her amazement, they were open, their sapphire color making her smile again.

"Hi. Can you tell me your name?" she asked.

He stared at her for a long moment, his bluish-gray, patterned face motionless. The Xenolfan blinked several times before Sierra heard him struggle to speak. He coughed a few times and Sierra helped him sit up against the cave wall.

"My name is Garrious," a weak voice came from him. "This warmth feels so nice. I'm glad you found me. How did you find me?"

"A piece of your clothing ripped off onto the pine tree outside the cave," she said.

"What's your name?" he asked her.

"Sierra Shalinsky. So, I take it that you were returning to the main lodge of The Avalanche Resort when the asteroid struck up at Winterfest?"

"Yes. Is that what it was? The blast blew me down and I cut my leg on a sharp rock," he said.

"Where is your snowmobile?" Sierra asked.

"It's far back on the trail. It was giving me trouble after the blast. I'm lucky I found this cave," he said.

"I'm going to give you some medicine that should strengthen you and make you more alert. You will need to get stitches up on the hospital ship," she said.

She reached into her EMT bag and removed a specific medication that would stabilize him. She also gave him the bottle of water that was in her bag. The bottle of water was just a reminder of the full glass of experimental Sipathrott aphrodisiac elixir that she had drunk back at the main lodge. Just from the thought, her pussy throbbed once again.

Trying to control the urge, she tightened her fists and closed her eyes until it subsided.

"So, what lucky human female are you with here on Aamaress?" Sierra asked.

"The plan was to hook up with her in Winterfest. I had actually never met her before, only through long distance communications," he said.

"I thought you said you were on your way back to the main lodge when the asteroid hit," she said.

"Well, actually, I was on my way to Winterfest and then turned around when the missiloid struck," he said.

"Missiloid? You mean, asteroid?" she asked.

"I'm sorry, yes, asteroid," he said. "So, you must be here with another Xenolfan male. What is it like to have interspecies relationships with us Xenolfans?"

Does he even realize that I'm a Galactic EMT? Sierra thought.

Ignoring his question, she looked into his eyes and then down toward his alien cock and grew another smile.

"Was this going to be your first time with a human female?"

"Umm, yes," he said.

The moisture between her thighs was incredible.

"Well, I guess today is my lucky day. You see, I've always wanted to be with a Xenolfan male too, but I've never had the opportunity," Sierra said.

What am I doing? I would never do this while on the job. I'm just so fucking horny, I can't take it anymore, she thought.

Garrious felt that if he didn't have sex with the human woman, he would blow his cover and reveal who he really was. He didn't expect to live, yet there he was. Garrious was hesitant at first because Sierra was human and his leader hated the interspecies mix. Garrious, however, was not Aaranix Tuvelless and he really didn't hate humans, like his leader. He began to warm up to her. The heat of the thermal cube felt nice and cozy. Sierra was so horny from the triple dose of aphrodisiac elixir, she thought she was going out of her mind. She had never been so aroused in her life. Taking the opportunity to fulfill one of her longtime fantasies, she slowly seduced Garrious, carefully removing one article of clothing at a time. Soon, they were both nude in the warm cave. Her beautiful, tan body contrasted against his muscular, bluish-gray body. Avoiding the bandaged leg, she parted her legs over his left leg and rubbed her pussy against his thigh. Her plump breasts brushed up against his bluish-gray chest. She could feel the heat of his now warm body against her bare skin. He pushed her back slightly to get a better look at her vulva. She could tell from his expression that she looked a bit different than what he was used to. She, in turn, looked at his reuleaux triangular rod, its bluish-gray tip slightly angled.

"Your pussy opening…it isn't triangle shaped like Xenolfan females are," Garrious said.

"No, but it's very adaptive. Your cock reminds me of an ovipositor, with its large orifice at the angled end," Sierra said.

She reached out and grabbed the rigid, bluish-gray cock. The shape was stepped down in the middle with a section of less girth toward the tip. The tip of the cock itself was shaped on a forty-five degree angle, the orifice quite wide.

"I can assure you, there are no eggs coming out of there. It may look like an ovipositor, but the only thing coming out of there is a hot load of cum," he said, laughing. "But I'm wondering…"

"Yes?"

"You don't expect me to fuck you in your ass, do you?" he asked, looking down at the second hole on her bottom. "Xenolfans don't do that."

Sierra laughed this time. "Ha! That is a very good question. It depends on which human you talk to. I personally don't do anal play of any kind. If shit comes out, it's not involved with any sex I do, so you are safe from that with me," she said. "I'm anti-anal."

"Well, that's good to know," he said.

The attitude that Garrious had toward humans was greatly influenced by the opinions of Aaranix Tuvelless. That inimical attitude was suddenly changing as he opened up to Sierra. Being a sexual freedom advocate for the forbidden interspecies relationships, Sierra knew this type of sexual encounter should have already been a part of her experience.

Finally, I will know first-hand what I'm fighting for, she thought.

Sierra took a medical blanket from her EMT bag and laid it down on the cave floor. Garrious moved over onto the blanket. She was beyond aroused from the effects of the aphrodisiac elixir and it didn't seem to be wearing off in the slightest. The large bluish-gray erection that Garrious sported looked so enticing. Her breasts bounced slightly as she reached down and caressed his smooth member. The sexual tension they both felt was extreme. Sierra could see the excitement in his expression. He reached out with his large bluish-gray hands and softly caressed her breasts. Garrious noticed that her vulva was smooth, the pink inner labia slightly parted. He could see the moist secretions of her arousal. She leaned down toward his cock and released her grip, causing his phallus to spring forth toward her mouth. She took the opportunity to put her mouth around it, slowly sucking up and down the alien shaft.

"Oh, Sierra, that feels so nice," Garrious said.

She sucked up and down his warm, hard cock and then slowly slid her tongue down the smooth, reuleaux triangular shaft to his leathery, bluish-gray ball sack. She remained there for a moment, gently sucking at the two balls, before she started up the shaft again to the angled tip. After flicking her tongue on his most sensitive spot for a long while, she continued to suck him. Sierra felt Garrious's rigid member pulsate against her tongue. She was fascinated by the distinct shape of the Xenolfan's cock. She quickly became accustomed to her lips slipping back and forth over the stepped section of his cock. The angled end was also a fun change-up from the human cock heads that she was familiar with. He groaned with pleasure resulting in a deep reverberating sound. He soon switched places with Sierra, being very careful with his injured leg. She lay on the medical blanket and parted her thighs. Garrious slowly moved his mouth against her smooth vulva, his tongue and lips sliding gently up and down her pink, moist folds. Her extreme arousal was finally being taken care of.

"Ahhh! I love that!" she shouted, the sound echoing in the small cave.

He eagerly continued cunnilingus as he enjoyed the foreign, human pussy. The musky taste of her sexual secretions was quite enjoyable to him. He licked at the arousal fluid and then made his way back up her beautiful lips to focus on her clit.

"Garrious, I'm coming!" Sierra shouted.

She put both of her hands on his white hair and pushed down hard while pushing upward with her hips.

"Ahhh!" she gasped with short, deep breaths.

Garrious felt a spasm against his mouth. Drops of moist, white cream dripped from her pussy. He licked at it, enjoying the sweet taste of her cum. Sierra switched places with him again and began fellatio once more.

"Whoa! Slow down for a second," Garrious said, breathing heavily. "You've brought me to the edge of an orgasm!"

After he cooled down for a moment, Sierra lay on her back with her thighs spread open, exposing her moist vulva. Garrious slowly slid his reuleaux triangular cock into her. He went in shallow at first before backing out and then sliding in shallow again. He drove deeper with each thrust until he was fully inside of her. The strange reuleaux triangle shape of his cock felt interestingly different inside of her. She could feel the stepped section and the angled end. The extreme arousal from the overdose of aphrodisiacs was so intense, so primal that she felt the urge, the need to be stuffed with something, anything. It was so nice to finally be filled with his hard, throbbing cock.

"Oh, your cock feels so good inside of me!" she moaned.

She repeatedly pushed upward, meeting his thrusts. The wet, smacking sounds of coitus created a beautiful rhythm that echoed in the small cave, filling it with a continuous arousing sound. Their sensations were incredible as they continued through the natural motions of carnal desire. Garrious withdrew from her and she turned over on her hands and knees. He moved behind her and slid his bluish-gray cock back between her warm, pink folds. Grabbing her ass, he pushed forward with his deep thrusts. Sierra responded by pushing back toward him. Garrious reached under her with one hand, brushed across her rib cage, and slowly massaged her soft breasts. After fucking in that position for a while, he withdrew again and she turned back over and lay on her back. He kneeled down and gently kissed and licked along her clitoris and labia once again before sliding back into her.

"Oh, I've been waiting to have sex with a Xenolfan male for so long," Sierra said, looking up into his sapphire eyes.

She moaned again and again as her heavy breathing progressed. Garrious maintained a steady thrust until she grabbed his back tight, letting out a loud cry.

"Ahhh!" she screamed.

She wrapped her legs tight around his back and pushed up with all of her strength as she reached an epic orgasm with every nerve in her body tingling from her head to her toes. The warm feeling of her cum gushing against his phallus felt incredible as he continued to pump her. Garrious could feel his own nerves raging to the surface as he burst, his reverberating groan echoing loudly throughout the small cave. He continued thrusting deep into her wet pussy several times before slipping out of her. She stared up at him with a blissful gaze and a smile.

"It's hard to believe this is actually happening to me. If you knew my background growing up, you would know how strange this is. Despite how I was brought up, I seriously enjoyed the feel of a human woman. You're amazing, Sierra," Garrious said as he sighed deeply.

Sierra sat up and his large load of Xenolfan cum poured out from her pussy and onto the medical blanket. Taking one corner of the blanket, she wiped up the remaining cum and reached over to wipe off his cock as well. She tossed the medical blanket to the side of the cave.

"How's your leg holding up?" she asked.

He looked down at the bandage. "It's aching like a mother fucker. Thank you for your help, though. And…thank you for opening my eyes to see humans differently. You've been so helpful, in more ways than one," Garrious said with a smile.

"I need to get you up to Winterfest where I'm supposed to meet the medical shuttle. From there, we will get you up to the *Deliverance* for stitches."

Seeing her uniform in the pile of clothes, it finally dawned on Garrious that Sierra was a Galactic EMT.

"We're going there? But that's where it hit."

"Yes. That is where you will get help and where I need to help."

I don't want to go to Winterfest and see what I have caused, Garrious thought, swallowing hard.

They put their clothes back on and she bundled up in her warm thermal gear. Since he had no warm gear, she grabbed a second medical blanket from her EMT bag and wrapped it around him. She deactivated the thermal cube and let it cool down. The cave became extremely cold once again. When it was at a safe temperature, she put the thermal cube back into her EMT bag and led the way out of the cave.

"By the way, where is your warm gear?" Sierra asked.

He hesitated for a long moment. "Embers from the missil— asteroid blast caught them on fire, so I had to quickly remove them," he said.

Sierra looked back at him with a strange look.

"Why do I find that hard to believe? You seem like you're not telling me something," Sierra said.

He said nothing else as they made their way through the white drifts to the snowmobile. Sierra put her EMT bag in the seat and grabbed her helmet. She handed Garrious the spare helmet and closed the seat. Sierra mounted the snowmobile and started it up as Garrious mounted on behind her, being careful with how he positioned his wounded right thigh. Turning the snowmobile toward Winterfest, Sierra looked back into the darkness of the small cave and gasped. She thought she saw a woman figure with blue eyes. Stopping the snowmobile, she did a double take and only saw darkness through the blowing snow. Whatever she thought she saw was gone. She shook her head from side to side.

"Are you okay?" Garrious asked.

"I don't know. I think I'm seeing things again. Let's go," she said.

She twisted the throttle and headed farther into the Northern Territories toward Winterfest. It wasn't until they were twenty-one kilometers from their destination that she realized the aphrodisiac elixir was indeed still very active in her system. She was unable to lift her bottom off the seat, like she had previously done, since Garrious was on the back. Although it wasn't as intense as what she had previously felt, the feeling was still fairly strong. She just rode it out with clenched fists.

After Sethain and Rasmond had arrived in the medical shuttle on the outskirts of what used to be Winterfest, they scouted the area for survivors. There were many injuries at the outer parameter of the impact zone. Sethain immediately contacted the *Deliverance* to have more medical shuttles sent down to the surface of Aamaress. The devastation was horrifying. They brought the victims back to the medical shuttle, one by one. After bringing back several people as a team, Rasmond remained with the victims at the medical shuttle and treated each of them the best she could. Many victims suffered from burns, head trauma, broken bones, and lacerations. They would definitely need to be brought to the *Deliverance* as soon as possible. They quickly ran out of adequate space in the medical shuttle and it was becoming very crowded. Sethain brought back the wounded as he found them. Finding people alive was becoming more infrequent as he went along the parameter. Scouting the entire area would take time.

Sethain hoped the extra relief would arrive soon. He tried not to let what he saw during the scouting operation affect him. As he slowly walked through the area, there didn't seem to be anyone else alive.

"Sierra, this is Sethain. How are you doing?" he asked over the comm.

"I'm good. I found one survivor. He needs stitches. I have him with me now. I'm almost to your location. I should be there soon," Sierra said over the comm.

"Okay. We could really use your help here. I have more help on the way. It's bad Sierra…really bad," Sethain said.

As Sethain continued the search, he found a wolfdog wandering outside of Winterfest, near a charred pine grove. It looked frightened and ran up to him. Sethain comforted the animal and looked at the name tag on his collar. His name was Stormy. He had a coat of gray and black fur and two beautiful blue eyes. He brought the wolfdog back to the shuttle just as two more medical shuttles swooped around and settled onto the snowy ground next to theirs.

Daylight was quickly fading and Sierra turned on the snowmobile's LED headlight. She could see two medical shuttles settle onto the ground behind a group of burned pine trees ahead of her. As she came to a stop next to the shuttles, she could not help but notice the remainder of the large asteroid sticking out of the ground on an angle. She saw Sethain in the distance, walking back toward the medical shuttle with a wolfdog.

"Let me get you over to the medical shuttle, Garrious," Sierra said.

After they removed their helmets, Garrious looked through the darkness at all the devastation. Glowing embers became noticeable at the impact zone as night set in. Sierra saw his saddened face. Suddenly, he began sobbing.

"Garrious… I'm sorry about the woman you were supposed to meet here. For whatever it's worth, it probably went so quick, she didn't feel anything," Sierra said.

Her words didn't seem to help him. He rubbed his eyes with the back of his bluish-gray hand. She walked him over to one of the medical shuttles that had just arrived. One of the Galactic EMTs from that shuttle quickly brought him aboard.

"He's going to need stitches in his right thigh when you get back to the *Deliverance*," Sierra said to the shuttle's team.

"Thanks again for everything," Garrious said.

"Thank you as well. I hope you heal quickly. It was nice to meet you, Garrious," Sierra said, winking.

She turned around and exited the shuttle. Sethain met her outside.

"I only found one person on the trail, a Xenolfan male. It was pretty much a desolate and dangerous trail of snow and ice. I see you found a wolfdog," Sierra said.

"Yes. According to his collar, his name is Stormy. We will have to bring him back to the main lodge before the *Deliverance* departs. I need you to help scout the area for any more survivors," Sethain said.

"Okay. I see the teams that have arrived are helping Rasmond to transfer some of the patients from the overcrowded medical shuttle," Sierra said.

"Yes. Rasmond has her hands full. I'm glad we got the extra help. Okay, let's split up and do some more searching. Do you have a flashlight in your EMT bag?" Sethain asked.

"I do. I need to grab it out of the snowmobile seat. I'll be right back," Sierra said.

Sethain left the wolfdog at the medical shuttle with Rasmond. As he retrieved an LED flashlight from his own EMT bag, he began walking into the devastating darkness. Sierra walked up to the snowmobile and grabbed her EMT bag. She quickly ran to catch up with Sethain and turned on her LED flashlight.

"This is going to be a long night," Sethain said.

In the early morning hours on Aamaress, a small transport shuttle settled onto the snowy court in front of The Avalanche Resort's main lodge. Sierra stepped out of the shuttle with a wolfdog at her side. They walked through the snow together toward the entrance of the main lodge. Only a few guests were in the grand foyer. A Xenolfan female sat next to the stone fireplace and Gathin and Eslarr sat on one of the other leather couches.

"Stormy!" Mauve shouted.

She ran over to greet the wolfdog and gave him a big hug.

"You know this wolfdog?" Sierra asked.

"Yes. He belongs to our boss. He always hangs around the lodge here. So, our boss must have been there when it happened…"

"I'm sorry, Mauve. There are some survivors. I'm not sure if he is one of them or not. Everyone has been brought up to the hospital ship, *Deliverance,* for medical treatment and surgeries. If he is still alive, I'm sure we'll know soon enough. But I don't want to get your hopes up because the chances are very slim."

"I understand. So, it was an asteroid, then?" Mauve asked.

"Yes. Oddly enough, it landed right on Winterfest," Sierra said.

There was a long silence as Mauve petted Stormy.

"Well, I'm glad we found the wolfdog."

"Yes, me too. So, how are you feeling after the whole aphrodisiac elixir mix-up?"

"Oh shit! That is the worst best thing ever. I'm still feeling it. In fact, I have some downtime before the *Deliverance* takes off, so I'll have time to take care of the little problem in the transport shuttle. I would not recommend drinking that elixir yourself. It's *way* too potent."

"Again, I'm so sorry I left the glass on the counter. I hope you get back to normal soon," Mauve said.

"Sierra!" Eslarr exclaimed from the couch.

Sierra walked over to the lounge area in front of the stone fireplace.

"Hey, it's nice to see you two again," Sierra said.

"It's nice to see you as well, Sierra. How bad is Winterfest?" Gathin asked.

"Very bad. There aren't many survivors," Sierra said.

"And how are you holding up?" Eslarr asked.

"It was a long night, but I'm doing all right. I think Mauve's elixir is starting to wear off, but it's not out of my system yet," Sierra said.

"Well, the comm is fixed properly, they will be getting the window fixed in here, and they have some engineers coming in to repair the docking bay," Gathin said. "I think our two ships are okay. I can't say that for some of them that ended up under the concrete, however."

"They are just material things and can be replaced," Sierra said.

"True," Gathin said.

Sierra looked over at the Xenolfan female who sat alone next to the fireplace. She looked very lonely.

"Did you lose someone up at Winterfest?" Sierra asked.

The Xenolfan woman turned toward Sierra, a few strands of her long, white hair falling in front of her sapphire eyes. The sadness that was revealed on her bluish-gray face was very evident.

"No, I didn't lose anyone to that asteroid. I lost someone to another

Xenolfan woman. My human lover never showed up here to meet me. I found out why. Cheating's been going on with another Xenolfan female and our relationship has ended," the woman said.

"What's your name?" Sierra asked.

"Yttursal," she returned.

"Hi, Yttursal. My name is Sierra. This is Eslarr and Gathin."

Eslarr and Gathin both greeted the woman.

"As far as the Galactic Emergency Medical Services is concerned, the disaster here on Aamaress has been resolved. I have some extra time before we depart, if you'd like to talk about it," Sierra said.

"Thanks for the offer. I just feel like I've wasted my time coming here to this snow planet. It's a beautiful resort, but not if you're alone. All I have now is a forlorn hope for my lover to come back. I feel... I don't know. Can we talk someplace private?" Yttursal asked.

"Sure. Let's take a walk," Sierra said.

Yttursal stood up and they walked toward the stairs. Sierra turned over her shoulder.

"If I don't see you two again before I leave, I hope to see you at the upcoming events," Sierra said.

"Yes, we will be there," Eslarr said.

Sierra and Yttursal walked up the carpeted steps and into the lodge corridor. As they walked together, Yttursal held her head down in sadness. Sierra tried to wrap her head around Yttursal's situation.

"To be honest with you, Yttursal, I have a hard time with the whole monogamy thing. So, I'm not sure if I can totally empathize with you. But I do hate cheaters. If he did this to you, then perhaps he did you a favor. You don't want someone around like that. You are a very beautiful Xenolfan woman and if you're into humans, there are so many more out there than the one that stood you up here. He was a promiscuous betrayer and you can do better than him," Sierra said.

"I didn't say it was a man. No, I'm a lesbian," Yttursal said.

Sierra stopped in the corridor and looked at Yttursal, a smile spreading across her face. Her pussy suddenly began to tingle with excitement.

"Yttursal, I'm a bisexual swinger in the Lifestyle. I'm not monogamous and I cannot replace your lover, but I would like to comfort you, if you'll let me," Sierra said.

Yttursal lifted her head and looked at Sierra. A smile grew on her face as well. She took Sierra's hand, her bluish-gray fingers interlacing with Sierra's tan ones.

"You've inspired me to write a song about cheaters," Sierra said.

"Are you a song writer?" Yttursal asked.

"I write some songs. I'm the vocalist for Maranadda," Sierra said.

"You're joking. I love Maranadda! Oh my...you're Sierra Shalinsky!" Yttursal said.

"That, I am."

"Suddenly, I feel wet between my legs," Yttursal said.

"I know the feeling. I'm still so fucking horny from an accidental overdose of a Sipathrott aphrodisiac elixir that I could scream," Sierra said.

"Well, we'll just have to take care of that," Yttursal said, slapping Sierra's ass.

The two women walked down the empty corridor to Yttursal's room. Shutting the door behind them, Yttursal turned Sierra toward her, pulled her close, and looked into Sierra's blue eyes.

"I want you to know how much this means to me, Sierra, even if it's just this one time," Yttursal said.

"You do realize that you are fulfilling one of my other fantasies?" Sierra said.

"Am I?"

"Yes."

Their lips came together in a long, sensual kiss. Sierra looked into Yttursal's sapphire eyes.

"You're beautiful," Sierra said.

Sierra began to remove Yttursal's clothing. Yttursal, in turn, removed Sierra's uniform. The two stood there for a moment, checking out each other's sexy bodies. Yttursal had much larger breasts than Sierra and was a bit more husky as well. Sierra lifted each breast and sucked at the bluish-purple nipples. Yttursal looked at Sierra's vulva and began stroking it with two bluish-gray fingers. Sierra parted her legs slightly as they stood there in the entryway of the room.

"Let's get more comfortable," Yttursal said.

She grabbed Sierra's hand and led her over to the large bed. They both climbed onto the bed and Yttursal spread her bluish-gray legs apart. Sierra took a moment to examine the foreign looking pussy. For the most part, it looked similar to a human's—other than the color— except the vaginal opening was in the shape of a reuleaux triangle. It reminded Sierra of the caves she saw in the Shardaa Sector.

The shape of Garrious's cock would fit perfectly in there, Sierra thought.

Sierra began licking the bluish-pink folds. For fun, she traced her tongue in circular motions around the reuleaux triangle opening before focusing on Yttursal's clit. The high-pitched reverberations that suddenly came from Yttursal took Sierra off guard. She looked up at her.

"Are you okay?" Sierra asked.

"Oh, I'm very okay. That's just the sound we Xenolfan women make during sex. I'm sorry if it hurt your ears," Yttursal said.

"No. I'm just wondering. Amp feedback on stage can be louder than that," Sierra said, continuing cunnilingus.

Yttursal began pumping her hips against Sierra's mouth. Soon, an intense, high-pitched, reverberating scream came from Yttursal that was so loud, Sierra had to cover her ears.

"Damn!" Sierra said.

A heavy flow of cum dripped from Yttursal's reuleaux triangular opening. Sierra licked at the juices and gave Yttursal's pussy lips one last suck with her mouth.

"You are quite good at that, Sierra. I can't remember when the last time I had an orgasm that intense," Yttursal said.

"Thank you."

They changed positions on the bed and Yttursal made herself comfortable between Sierra's legs. She was familiar with human female pussy and enjoyed Sierra's very much. As Yttursal continually flicked her long tongue against the moist vulva, Sierra reached down and fingered her own clitoris side to side for extra pleasure. It didn't take long for Sierra to explode with delight. After her orgasm, they began tribbing together. Like she had been with Garrious, Sierra was especially excited to see the visual of the two contrasting skin colors come together as they rubbed their pussies against one another. The extreme arousal that Sierra had been experiencing felt like it was finally being quenched. Their second orgasms were simultaneous, the two pussies pressing together hard.

"Oh yes!" Sierra shouted.

"Ahhh!" Yttursal cried.

The loud pitch that came from Yttursal didn't seem to bother Sierra the second time. They separated themselves and both lay on the bed, breathing heavily.

"That was wonderful," Yttursal finally said. "But I'm not done with you yet. I have a surprise for you."

"A surprise?" Sierra inquired.

Yttursal reached into a bag next to the bed and brought out a double-ended Xenolfan male dildo.

"I have an illegal one with a human male cock on one end and a Xenolfan male cock on the other end, if you prefer," Yttursal suggested.

"No, this one is fine. I enjoy the different feeling inside of me," she said.

Yttursal slowly inserted one end into Sierra and moved it in and out. She then put the other side into her own pussy. They both began fucking the dildo together, driving it deep into their holes. Sierra ground her pussy hard onto the dildo. Yttursal rotated her hips in circular motions, pumping the artificial cock. Every move they both made helped the other's sensations. They soon had their third orgasm together. Laying still for a long, relaxing moment with the dildo connecting them together, they could each feel their pussies pulsate onto the bluish-gray toy phallus.

"This has been so relaxing to me. I needed this more than you can know," Yttursal said.

"Well, I'm glad I could help. Remember, you can do better than the woman who took off with someone else. You can find a nice monogamous human female, I'm sure. Don't settle for that type of deception," Sierra said.

"You're right," Yttursal said.

Yttursal slowly slid the dildo out of her pussy. Sierra pumped it in and out a few more times and then slid it out of her own pussy as well.

"I need to get back to the *Deliverance,* or they are going to leave without me," Sierra said.

She stood up from the bed and quickly got dressed.

"Before I go, I would like to give you tickets to some forthcoming events that I will be performing at. One will be for the Sexual Freedom Seminar and the other will be to see Maranadda, both on Red Jacket," Sierra said.

"Oh my! That's awesome. I would love to go to both. Thank you...for everything," Yttursal said.

Sierra reached into her pocket, removed a satchel, and produced the two event tickets for Yttursal.

"Enjoy," Sierra said. "And I will write that song that I promised you."

Sierra quickly left the room and headed back toward her transport shuttle.

I think I finally feel like the extreme horniness is gone, Sierra thought.

Braxton's government ship arrived on Aamaress at the site that once was Winterfest. With the reports the Syrenthian Government had received about a missiloid near Aamaress and the following report of an asteroid hitting the planet, it brought his investigation to the snow planet. There was some concern about Aamaress's orbit decaying because of the impact of the missiloid, but it checked out fine on their scanners.

Dressed in thermal gear, he exited the ship, along with his crew of four. They slowly made their way through the rubble to the asteroid itself. The other crew members searched for clues around the area while Braxton observed how the missiloid had impacted and protruded up toward the sky on an angle. He walked over and began to climb up the massive asteroid, his gloved hands grasping onto the rock. Braxton stopped part of the way up and began taking pictures of the threaded studs that were in a couple of spots along the stone surface. The areas had been flattened around the studs to accommodate a cockpit. The studs were stripped and the metal anchor plates were bent, as if the cockpit came off during atmospheric entry. He noticed a couple of the anchor plates and studs were completely missing. Braxton carefully climbed farther up the asteroid to the top. He snapped pictures of what used to be an engine, all but destroyed from the impact of the missiloid. After climbing down fifteen meters from the asteroid, he approached the other crew members.

"I believe the missiloid cockpit detached itself during the atmospheric entry. Let's get back to the ship and calculate the possible trajectory of where it may have landed, based on the angle of the asteroid itself," Braxton said.

They all headed back to the ship to run the calculations in the computer.

"Depending on when the cockpit became detached, there are several possibilities of where it could have landed. Taking the mountains in the area into account, the most probable ones would be these three spots on the screen…within a diameter of one kilometer," one of his crewmen said, pointing to the screen.

"Let's check out all three of them. I want the scanners on. Let's see if we pick up any unusual metal objects," Braxton said.

The ship lifted from the surface and they flew toward the areas of the Northern Territories that the computer had indicated. The first was a snowy grove of white pine trees. They hovered over the trees for a long moment.

"There is no damage to the trees or any evidence of a landing. The scanners are not picking up any metal objects," the crewman said.

They flew toward the second possibility, slowly flying over a mountainous area. They swooped down into a valley, next to a flowing stream of water. Suddenly, the scanners began to beep repeatedly.

"We have something, Braxton," the crewman said.

It's a bit narrow, but can you set the ship down near that trail?" Braxton asked.

"It's a bit narrow indeed. Part of our wing span will be hanging off a cliff. Do you still want me to try it?" the crewman asked.

"Yes…carefully," Braxton said.

The pilot set the ship down in the snow near the trail and turned off the engines. Braxton quickly grabbed a wall as the ship settled in the soft snow and leaned toward the cliff.

"Whoa!" Braxton exclaimed.

"I think we'll be okay," the crewman said, looking at the others with wide eyes.

They exited the ship and stepped out into the deep snow. Making their way toward the snowy object the scanners had indicated as metal, they came to the stream of water. They were able to find a section of large stones that crossed over the stream. After carefully maneuvering across the stream of water, they walked up a slight grade to the snow-covered object. Braxton wiped the snow from the surface of the cockpit. They all stood there staring at it for a moment.

"Well, the missiloid controller must have survived the fall because the window is busted out from the inside. And look…blood," Braxton said. "Don't we have a blood tracer in the ship?"

"Yes, we do. I'll go get it from the ship," a crewman said.

As the crewman left to retrieve the blood tracer from the ship, Braxton inspected the inside of the cockpit. He pulled out a few of the missiloid controller's personal effects, including a picture with a caption that read: "We love you, Garrious."

"Okay, the missiloid controller was a Xenolfan male named Garrious. Let's run that name in the database when we get back to the ship," Braxton said, putting the picture into his pocket.

The crewman returned with the blood tracer. The crewman turned on the power and began tracing the blood trail at the cockpit window. They followed it toward the stream and across the same stones toward the trail.

"He couldn't have gone far. He wouldn't have been dressed for this weather and he was injured," Braxton said.

They continued to follow the blood along the snowmobile trail toward a small cave near a single pine tree. The tree branch had a torn piece of fabric stuck to one of the branches.

"I think we've found our killer," Braxton said.

They entered the darkness and turned on LED flashlights. The cave was empty. Something caught Braxton's attention. He walked over to the cave wall and picked up a medical blanket. Examining the medical blanket, he realized there was what appeared to be some type of stains on the blanket.

"This is a GEMS medical blanket. These are not blood stains. Take this back to the ship and have it tested for DNA," Braxton said.

They headed back toward the government ship. Upon returning, they ran the DNA testing on the blanket stains and brought the results to Braxton.

"Okay, I've got some information for you, Braxton. The stains are Xenolfan semen and human arousal fluid. The DNA on the human female was crossed referenced to a Sierra Shalinsky. She's a Galactic EMT for Galactic Emergency Medical Services. There is only limited DNA in the database for Xenolfans, but I did get a match for Garrious," the crewman said.

Sierra! Braxton thought.

"Good work. I believe the injured were all brought aboard the *Deliverance* and are now en route to Relistorr," Braxton said.

"It appears that the Galactic EMT had sex with the missiloid controller, sir," the crewman said.

"Umm, yes, it does appear that way. Let's intercept that hospital ship. I will contact Elliss Millott, the GEMS incident commander, and let him know we will be on our way," Braxton said.

. . .

The flight back to Relistorr was uneventful. Sierra lay on a bed in a private cabin aboard the *Deliverance*. She took the time to reflect on the last couple of days on Aamaress. Sierra felt for the survivors of the tragic event. Their lives would never be the same again. She wondered what would become of Garrious and the other patients who were currently in another part of the hospital ship. The Galactic Emergency Medical Services protocol stated that when patients were released from the hospital ship, they would have a choice to be picked up, have a courtesy shuttle ride home, or if their ship was salvaged by the salvage team and operational, they could fly home themselves. As Sierra lay there in the quiet of her cabin, she was inspired to write a few songs. She began writing a song called Stormrider about her snowmobile trail experience on Aamaress. Some time later, she also wrote a song for Eslarr and Gathin called Forbidden Lovers and a song for the beautiful Yttursal called Promiscuous Betrayer. Perhaps Maranadda could incorporate them into their playlist and on their forthcoming Surefire album. Sierra had already written one other song for the new album. She set her writing pad down and closed her eyes.

The comm sounded at her side, startling her.

"This is Sierra," she answered.

"Sierra, this is Braxton. I'm concluding our long investigation and I need to see you right away. I'll meet up with the *Deliverance*. It's urgent," he said.

"Okay. I guess I'll see you soon," she said, turning off the comm.

Sierra yawned, lay back down, and closed her eyes. Suddenly, she opened her eyes wide and gasped.

Why is he coming here? This can't be good, she thought.

She stood up from the cabin bed and headed for the docking bay.

Sierra watched from the observation deck as the Syrenthian Government ship settled into the *Deliverance* docking bay and came to a halt. She went down the metal stairs to meet Braxton. Several crew members exited the ship followed by Braxton.

"Give us a moment," Braxton told the crew members.

"I realized this *must* be urgent, if you are intercepting this ship," Sierra said.

"Indeed, it is. Let's take a walk," Braxton said.

They slowly walked along the docking bay wall.

"I have concluded my investigation. The Xenolfan Government sent terrorists to destroy the thermal cube factory on Shar Nefalis in the Industrial Sector. They also attempted to destroy Ticrisuda Powersports, but did not succeed. They did this to prevent the shipment of those items to Aamaress. We believe they are responsible for the disappearance and possible murder of my colleague, Tellaris Whitestone, who went there to confront them on some comm chatter we discovered. And now I have concluded they are responsible for sending the missiloid to Aamaress, which killed all those people in Winterfest. That is exactly how the Xenolfan Government used missiloids back in the Syrenthian War one hundred years ago. We discovered the missiloid controller's cockpit had detached itself from the asteroid on the atmospheric entry to Aamaress. Just like back in the war, it was intended to be a suicide mission, but it broke apart instead. We found the cockpit at the foot of a mountain. The controller broke out of the canopy after it crashed in the snow and apparently cut himself on the glass. We traced his blood to a cave. And that is where we found both of your DNA on a GEMS medical blanket," Braxton said. "You're a horny girl, Sierra."

"The fucking Jinkins! Damn it! I knew his story didn't add up. As far as my horniness, I accidentally drank a glass of potent aphrodisiac elixir that one of The Avalanche Resort workers left on the counter. I thought it was water. I have never been so aroused in my life. Normally, I would have not done that while on the job… So, he is the one who killed all those people in Winterfest?" she asked.

"Yes," Braxton said.

"Let me take you straight to him. Patients with the least severe injuries had to wait the longest, but he's now in one of the recovery rooms," she said.

Braxton motioned for the four crew members to follow. Sierra led them up the metal stairs and through a long corridor. They came to a corridor intersection and Sierra turned right. They followed along to an elevator. After entering a security access elevator, Sierra brought them up to the patient section of the hospital ship. She received Garrious's room number from the nurses station. Braxton led the way from that point.

"Stay behind me," he told the others.

He pulled a laser pistol from the inside of his jacket and they entered the room. There was an empty bed.

"Where is he?" Braxton asked.

Sierra quickly made her way back to the nurses station.

"Where is Garrious, the patient with stitches in his right thigh…from that room?" Sierra asked.

"I just got here. Let me check the computer," the woman said. "It looks like he scheduled a ride from GEMS to Olf Teruda, but I don't think the shuttle has left the *Deliverance* yet. They're in the salvage docking bay."

"Okay, let's go," Sierra said.

They all ran for the salvage docking bay. Heading back down the elevator and down several corridors, they came out into a different docking bay. The *Mossenberg* salvage ship sat to one side of the large docking bay. A shuttle was fixed in the center of the bay, ready to depart. They ran over to the shuttle as it slowly moved toward the docking bay exit. Braxton stepped in front of it and pointed his laser pistol at the pilot. His four crew members motioned for the pilot to stop. Sierra looked at the pilot through the window. The shuttle came to a stop and the pilot exited with a questioning look.

"What's going on?" the pilot asked.

"She'll explain," Braxton said as he stormed the ship along with his four crew members.

The pilot looked at Sierra.

"Apparently, he is responsible for the destruction on Aamaress. It was a missiloid, like the Xenolfans used during the Syrenthian War," Sierra explained.

"Oh wow. I would have been responsible for him getting away," the pilot said.

"You didn't know. He seems to have fooled a lot of us," she said with a frown.

Moments later, Braxton and the four crew members came out of the ship with Garrious in handcuffs. They stopped in the center of the docking bay where Sierra and the pilot stood.

"How could you? How could you kill all those innocent people? You fucking bastard! You lied to me. I knew there wasn't something right with your story. I really wish you would have died, like you were supposed to. It's what you deserve," Sierra said, a tear rolling down her cheek.

Garrious looked at her with a blank face.

"I wish I would have. I'm sorry. I was never against interspecies relationships. I was just following a military order from Aaranix Tuvelless. He's the real human-hater. You actually opened my eyes to see that all I was told about humans was not true. I'm sorry I hurt you," he said, tears rolling down his own bluish-gray, patterned face.

"I assume your ship is in the main docking bay. I'll show you a shortcut," the pilot said to Braxton.

Under armed guard by the Syrenthian Government officials, Garrious was led by the pilot toward a corridor at the opposite end of the docking bay.

"I'll talk to you later, Sierra," Braxton said.

Sierra didn't respond. She stared at them as they left the salvage docking bay. The only thing she felt was betrayal and sadness. She slowly walked back to her cabin, tears flowing down her face. Most of her sadness was for the people Garrious had killed.

Chapter Fifteen

Edward Sirlain's long, grayish-blond hair was slicked back and braided in a ponytail down his back. The Syrenthian Government leader stood at a podium before an emergency security council. The conclusion of Braxton's investigation lay before him.

"I appreciate you all coming to the administrative building at this hour to read the investigation and cast your votes. The night sky of Exandra remains peaceful. I'm not sure how long that will last if the Syrenthian Government does nothing about this. To that end, you and I have voted to declare war on the Xenolfan Government. You've all read the investigation results that you have there in front of you. We cannot stand by idle while Aaranix Tuvelless attacks our sovereign territories. The deaths on Shar Nefalis and Aamaress are catastrophic. The suspected death of our own investigator, Tellaris Whitestone, is another cause for alarm. He's been missing since he was sent to Olf Teruda. We have in custody the Xenolfan missiloid controller responsible for the Aamaress disaster. He has given us information that sums up the investigation. We have no choice but to assemble our warships and prepare for a confrontation with the Xenolfan

Government, both at Olf Teruda and Salinarr Nevis. We will also put an embargo on the alien worlds indefinitely," Edward said. "I know there are a few of you that did not vote for this. I will do my best to keep this as peaceful as possible. I don't want any more bloodshed than you do. We will have updates on the progress of the situation posted on the government board. Thank you again for your attendance."

As Edward Sirlain left the room, he heard murmurs among the members of the emergency security council.

I had no choice than to call the meeting, Edward thought as he left the room.

He immediately contacted the Syrenthian Government military and put into motion the plan. Within hours, five Syrenthian Government battleships began the flight to Olf Teruda at lightspeed-plus. In addition, another three battleships flew toward Salinarr Nevis. Edward sent a communique ahead to the Xenolfan Government informing them of the investigations, the embargo, and the war declaration.

"Aaranix, we just received a communique from Edward Sirlain, the leader of the Syrenthian Government. He has declared war on us," the dignitary said.

A look of shock came across Aaranix's bluish-gray, patterned face.

"They can't prove anything. Damn it! I want you to ready the *Deltarr* battleship from Dalaa. And summon the *Oldstaff* from the Montoraania Star System. Our secret mining operation on Montoraania will just have to be left unguarded for the time being. The Syrenthian Government doesn't suspect that we're mining in their territory anyway," Aaranix said with a deep sigh.

"We have reports of five battleships en route here to Olf Teruda and three more on their way to Salinarr Nevis. Do you want our ship from the Montoraania Star System to go to Salinarr Nevis?" the dignitary asked.

"Screw Salinarr Nevis. I want both of our battleships here at Olf Teruda as quickly as possible," Aaranix said.

"I'm on it, sir."

Aaranix Tuvelless suddenly realized he had made a poor decision by not increasing the number of his military battleships. With all the wealth pouring in from the casinos on Salinarr Nevis, the Xenolfan Government was certainly financially capable of investing in their military. They only had two older battleships in their arsenal.

Aaranix stood up from his desk, picked up a large cabinet and threw it across his office. It came crashing down with papers flying out of it and slowly gliding back and forth to the floor.

"Damn the humans!" he said, kicking a trash can across the room.

When word of the embargo and war declaration reached the businessmen at the casinos on Salinarr Nevis, they became outraged with Aaranix Tuvelless for carrying his forbidden interspecies law too far. As a result, all humans were restricted from traveling to Salinarr Nevis and Olf Teruda. Any humans on either planet were encouraged to leave immediately. The loss of revenue at the casinos on Salinarr Nevis would be staggering. Countless credits would just be gone. Many of the business owners sent messages of their displeasure to the Xenolfan Government on Olf Teruda.

Shortly after five Syrenthian Government battleships appeared at Olf Teruda, two Xenolfan Government battleships exited lightspeed within seconds of each other. The positions of the *Deltarr* and the *Oldstaff* were facing the five ships in a standoff. Aaranix Tuvelless was in the government palace war room, staying abreast of the situation. It was a room that had not been used in many, many years. Dust covered most of the equipment. Aaranix pressed several buttons on the old console.

"Fire on those Syrenthian Government warships…now!" Aaranix commanded.

Laser fire erupted from the two Xenolfan Government battleships. The intense blue beams struck the deflector shields on two of the five Syrenthian Government battleships, *GrayMar* and *Sanctuary Star*. After a short time the deflector shields on the two Syrenthian Government battleships began to weaken, allowing the destructive beams to scorch their reinforced hulls. When all five Syrenthian Government battleships began firing their laser cannons back at the two Xenolfan battleships, a maelstrom of blue beams followed. There was no sign of the Syrenthian Government battleships letting up on their intensity. Suddenly, the *Deltarr* exploded with a blinding light.

Small explosions erupted in two areas along the surface of the *Oldstaff*. Its stabilizers were damaged and the ship began to skew sideways. A small area of the *Oldstaff's* aft section broke free, its twisted and melted metal frame drifting in space. Damage to the Syrenthian Government battleships was minimal. The two older Xenolfan battleships were no match for them. The damaged *Oldstaff* had ceased fire and drifted awkwardly sideways in space above Olf Teruda. After several minutes, two fighter ships were launched from each of the Syrenthian Government battleship docking bays. The ten sleek SG302 fighter ships split up. Eight of the ten fighter ships flew toward the military base on Olf Teruda's single satellite of Dalaa. The other two SG302s flew to the surface of Olf Teruda, heading for the government palace. The fighter pilots assigned to the government palace target were instructed only to cause superficial damage as a stern warning and then maintain a presence in the airspace above the palace. The same could not be said on Dalaa, The eight SG302 fighter ships were only met with minimal resistance from surface cannons. The Xenolfan military did manage to destroy one of the fighter ships, however. The surface cannons were swiftly taken out of commission.

Three Syrenthian Government battleships maintained an orbit above Salinarr Nevis, their presence visible from the planet's surface. As they had been ordered to do, they simply remained present until they were further instructed. Many of the casino businessmen were further upset with Aaranix Tuvelless and made demands that he resign. Threats were made to cut off financial transactions to the Xenolfan Government capital on Olf Teruda. Since a large amount of credits was sent to the Xenolfan Government from casino profits, the lack of financial support would have a strong impact on government operations.

"An emergency communique is coming in from Olf Teruda, sir," a man said in the war room on Exandra.

"I'll take it," Edward Sirlain said, walking over to the comm. "This is Edward Sirlain."

"Hi, Edward. My name is Phensiarr Charseaa. I am contacting you from the Xenolfan Government to inform you that Aaranix Tuvelless has been forced to step down as leader. With the displeasure of multiple businessmen on Salinarr Nevis and our own people here on Olf Teruda, he didn't have much of a choice. I have been a remote part of his staff for some time and I have seen things with Aaranix Tuvelless that are disturbing. I've seen him disregard petitions that were collected from across the Syrenthian Galaxy as well as many other disregards for peace. He has a hatred for humans that I will never understand. It especially bothers him when Xenolfans and humans become involved together, for a reason that he has yet to share. His top dignitaries, who were loyal to no end, have also stepped down. I have conducted a full investigation into the Shar Nefalis incident and the Aamaress incident as well as the disappearance of the government official that you sent here. I will review the report when it is available. Upon review, I will share the results with you. As of right now, I have taken his place as leader of the Xenolfan Government. My first act as the new leader will be to repeal the absurd law the forbids our species to be together. All I ask of you is to call off your warships," Phensiarr Charseaa said.

"I see. Consider them called off. I would like to meet with you to sign a ceasefire agreement and a peace treaty," Edward said.

"I will definitely do that as well as share the investigation results with you regarding the agent you sent here," Phensiarr said.

"Well, congratulations on your new position. I look forward to working with you to resolve the tensions that have risen between our people as of late," Edward said.

"Thank you," Phensiarr said.

Edward Sirlain ordered a ceasefire and recalled all of the Syrenthian Government military ships back to Exandra.

Phensiarr Charseaa sat in her new office reviewing the investigative report that she had initiated regarding the missing Tellaris Whitestone and the two attacks on sovereign Syrenthian Government territory. With surveillance footage and interviews, it had been concluded that Tellaris was murdered and his body placed in the flooded lower levels of the government palace. She read further and learned about the missiloid and the bombing in the Industrial Sector. She closed the folder in front of her and rested her bluish-gray hand on her forehead, sighing heavily.

"This is bad," she said to herself, breathing deep.

I'm trying to retain the respect of the human government here, and this…this is not helping at all, Phensiarr thought.

Phensiarr Charseaa quickly left her office and immediately ordered Aaranix Tuvelless and his top dignitaries to be arrested. She accompanied the security team that was responsible for locating Aaranix Tuvelless. He was apprehended and put into handcuffs not far from the government palace.

"Aaranix Tuvelless, you are charged with the murder of Tellaris Whitestone as well as the murders on Aamaress and Shar Nefalis," Phensiarr said.

"You don't understand! I'm warning you of the consequences of repealing the forbidden interspecies sex law. The results of the interspecies unions will create monsters! It was all in that book, *Anathema Strain,* that I read before the archives were flooded," Aaranix said.

Phensiarr Charseaa immediately traveled to Exandra to meet with Edward Sirlain and a Syrenthian Government council with the results of Tellaris Whitestone's disappearance, as she had promised she would. It was an anxious flight. She felt so embarrassed and ashamed of what the previous leader had done that she wasn't sure if she could repair things.

Her ship settled at the administrative building on Exandra. She was led by armed guard to a conference room where Edward Sirlain and a Syrenthian Government council sat at a long table. She sat down at the remaining empty seat. Being the only Xenolfan in the room made her feel even more uncomfortable, given the circumstances.

"Good afternoon, ladies and gentlemen. My name is Phensiarr Charseaa. I am the new leader of the Xenolfan Government. The investigative report that I mentioned revealed that Tellaris Whitestone's body was found in the forbidden lower levels of the government palace, which had been flooded from years before. He was murdered by Aaranix and two of his dignitaries. Furthermore, Aaranix was responsible for the attack on Shar Nefalis. He was attempting to destroy snowmobiles and thermal cubes that would have been shipped to Aamaress. He is also responsible for the missiloid attack on Aamaress. As he discovered, The Avalanche Resort on Aamaress was home to the secret xeno tryst of our two species. He went too far in enforcing his forbidden interspecies sex law and the law has now been repealed.

"When Aaranix Tuvelless was arrested, he warned of the consequences of repealing the forbidden interspecies sex law and he said the results of the interspecies unions would create monsters. He apparently read that in a book down in the archives before they were flooded. I have also ordered a psychological assessment for Aaranix, to be performed while in prison, because it's common knowledge that our two species cannot breed together. For him to create all this death and destruction based on a phantom book…it's insane.

"During this whole investigation that I had initiated, there is one other thing I found out. Apparently, Aaranix was mining on the planet Montoraania, which is Syrenthian Government territory. For some reason, he had one of the two battleships we had, *Oldstaff,* guarding that operation. I have ordered all mining operations to cease and all equipment to be removed from the planet."

"Do you realize a compound called Toraanium is found on Montoraania? It is toxic only to humans. It doesn't sound like he was up to any good there," Edward said.

"No, it doesn't. I will make a public apology on behalf of the Xenolfan Government for the death of Tellaris Whitestone and for the attacks and deaths on Shar Nefalis and Aamaress. Aaranix Tuvelless and two of his top dignitaries have been arrested for murder and sent to prison to await the death penalty. The Montoraania incident will be added to his sentence. I am very disappointed in our former leader and I look forward to working with the Syrenthian Government now and in the future," Phensiarr said.

"Thank you for presenting the results of the report. Other than Montoraania, we concluded as much, but could not prove that Tellaris Whitestone was murdered. I'd like to schedule a time to send in a team and retrieve his body," Edward said.

"Yes, we can do that right away," Phensiarr said. "When I return to Olf Teruda, I will make a public announcement with an apology and the current status of our galactic situation. There have been rumors circulating around Salinarr Nevis about a war, but officially, nothing has yet been stated regarding this whole confrontation that our two governments have had."

"Very well. If you could sign the ceasefire agreement and peace treaty here, it will officially end this New Syrenthian War," Edward said.

Phensiarr picked up the pen, looked over the documents, and signed them.

"There we go," she said.

"Thank you. It was nice to meet you in person. I had never actually met Aaranix Tuvelless in person," Edward said.

"You weren't missing much," Phensiarr said. "It was nice to meet you and, again, I look forward to us working together."

She stood from the conference room chair and headed for the door.

Gathin and Eslarr traveled from Aamaress to the Sexual Freedom Seminar and Maranadda concert at the Civie Arena on Red Jacket. They were delighted that Sierra had given them tickets for the events. Yttursal arrived on Red Jacket as well, after traveling a great distance across the Syrenthian Galaxy to attend the back-to-back events. There was a huge turnout that filled the entire arena. Two women approached the stage.

"Hello. Welcome to Civie Arena here on Red Jacket. Thank you for attending the Sexual Freedom Seminar. My name is Sierra Shalinsky and this is my colleague, Priscilla Stryderr."

Sierra stepped back and Priscilla stepped over to the microphone and cleared her throat. "Some of you have traveled from far across the Syrenthian Galaxy to attend the Sexual Freedom Seminar. Among you, there are both humans and Xenolfans alike. Most likely you either would like to be in an interspecies relationship without repercussions, or you know someone who would. Or you may be here today because you feel blacklisted as a swinger in the Lifestyle. Well, this seminar is for you. After Sierra's speech, I will be discussing the importance of a healthy, sex-positive lifestyle. Some of you may wonder why Sierra doesn't cover all of the different sexual orientations or preferences. She is only one person. She can only advocate for those things that she feels extremely passionate about, otherwise it is not genuine or watered-down at best. There are already so many other advocates for the other orientations and preferences that you don't need that from her. I'm sure there is another seminar being held right now for whatever letter they are adding to the acronym this week. Okay, I'm being sarcastic, but do you get my point? Sierra is laser-focused on the things that she is passionate about, and she cannot be all things to all people. Sierra is responsible for both the human and Xenolfan sexual health clinics that we now benefit from across the Syrenthian Galaxy. Because—"

The audience erupted in a round of applause.

"Thank you. Thank you all so very much. Because of her efforts, both species are now sexually healthier and free from sexually transmitted infections. I work in the healthcare industry and have written articles on this. I can assure you, it has helped tremendously. Sierra and I have worked together on interspecies relationship freedom for some time. We have gathered countless signatures in a galaxy-wide petition that I personally delivered to the Xenolfan Government on Olf Teruda. I have protested on Olf Teruda on two separate occasions. We must not give up our fight for sexual freedom. Ladies and gentlemen, I give you Sierra Shalinsky."

There was another round of applause as Sierra returned to the microphone.

"Thank you, Priscilla. So, I was sitting backstage before the seminar thinking about some of the things I won't be discussing, like homosexuality. Like Priscilla mentioned to you, I simply cannot be all things to all people, or it will just end up sounding generic. One thing I do know about the different orientation groups is that we don't always get along with each other, yet we get lumped into the same growing acronym. I know *some* heterosexuals aren't always friendly with bisexuals or homosexuals. I know *some* homosexuals aren't always friendly with bisexuals or heterosexuals. I've seen homosexuals and heterosexuals wanting bisexuals to pick a side. There's this big misconception that anyone who is not heterosexual all just get along together, but from my experiences throughout the Syrenthian Galaxy and through my own studies, that is so not true. Also, there are many swingers, polys, and BDSMers that don't understand each other, so it's not just the vanillas who don't understand the different sexual practices. The lack of community isn't always the case, but unfortunately, it does happen. That is why I stick to what I am passionate about: interspecies relationships, the Lifestyle, and bisexuality.

"Think of sexual orientation as a continuum…a scale. I call it the sexual orientation continuum. On one side, you have homosexuals and on the other side, you have heterosexuals. In the messy middle, you have bisexuals. I can tell you that it is a fluid continuum. Our feelings change, our moods change, and they can change often. That isn't necessarily unusual. One day, we may feel closer to one end of the spectrum and the next day, we may feel closer to the other end. Bisexuality can change along this scale, whether it is acted upon or not.

"Many of you are here because of the forbidden love that you find yourself in. You may have been treated unfairly or even been arrested, deported, or banished because of it. You may feel blacklisted. You know, I've been feeling down lately… I've felt blacklisted because I'm a bisexual unicorn swinger in the Lifestyle. There have been times when we've all felt it. No matter where you are at on the sexual orientation continuum on any given day, you can't please everyone. Whether you are in a human-only relationship, a Xenolfan-only relationship, or an interspecies relationship, you can't please everyone. Whether you are monogamous, polyamorous, a vanilla, a swinger in the Lifestyle, or are into BDSM, you just can't please everyone. Someone is always going to be offended by something. There will always be those out there that look down on others, that look down on interspecies relationships, that look down on those in the Lifestyle. The judgment of others can be frustrating, but we can't let it get us down.

"Don't pursue sexual acts that aren't mutual. Whether you are in an interspecies relationship or not communication, compromise, and commitment are very important. Listen…don't cheat on each other. Be sure to meet your partner's emotional and sexual needs. Everyone has different emotional needs. Don't act on impulse without thinking. Pay attention to warning signals. You may have a high sex drive. That is a great reason why the sexual health clinics across the galaxy are so necessary. One of our emotional needs is sexual desire. It is a very powerful and intense feeling and often involves lust and passion. It can lead to poor judgment at times. Sexual desire can be aroused by beauty, by chemistry, or by novelty…or too much aphrodisiac. Unlike the desires at the dawn of a relationship, desires in a mature one can fade. Cheating can occur when one partner surrenders to their sexual desire for another. An opportunity may come along, some occasion or situation may occur that results in sexual excitement for a new adventure, but there really is no excuse for cheating. Harboring secrets and hidden desires are what squelch the fire of a great relationship. Because I care about your sexual freedoms and because I care about interspecies relationships, it would break my heart to see it get ruined by cheating. Please, communicate with each other in all things and don't let it happen to you.

"It has been determined that neither humans nor Xenolfans are monogamous by nature. They can still choose to be monogamous, if that works best for them. Over time, many vanilla couples find that to enhance their sexual relationship, swinging in the Lifestyle is helpful and therapeutic. While threesomes, foursomes and swinging may occur, there is great significance in a special love for a specific partner. That partner must be the focus of the relationship, and swinging should be secondary. If both partners agree that non-monogamy is more pleasant than cheating, then it is probably best for the relationship. It's only fair that everyone gets to play and have fun. What bothers some people sexually may not bother other people. In areas of vagueness, it comes down to understandings and personal convictions. When exercising your sexual freedoms, be sure they don't cause others to stumble. The leader of the Xenolfan Government, along with his top dignitaries and some Salinarr Nevis casino owners and businessmen have mentioned that interspecies sex is disgraceful and immoral on many occasions. What is sexual disgrace and immorality? Sexual immorality has been used as a catch-all phrase in modern times, but Aaranix Tuvelless won't give a reason why the law exists. It is a prejudice that he harbors for some reason.

"There have been many studies about all the different aspects of human and Xenolfan sexuality. There are many different interpretations and opinions about sex. There is a multitude of possible sexual activities that people can be involved with. Think of it as your own sex world. Your world needs to be protected from sexual activities that may be bad for your relationship. On your world, there are many enjoyable sexual engagements. Every relationship's world is slightly different. Perhaps try something new that can be mutually agreed upon to add spice to your world. Our tastes change over time. If you together as a couple choose to let some select people into your world to play with, whether it is a unicorn, another couple, or a group, be very selective and cautious. This world of yours—your committed relationship—is very precious and worth protecting at all costs. Even in the interspecies relationships and Lifestyle relationships, communication regarding what is okay and what is not okay is of the utmost importance."

Some woman from the crowd yelled, "Slut!"

Heads turned to try and discover the source of the heckler. Sierra was silent for a moment, but decided to use it to her advantage.

"Sluts are people too. Do you associate the term 'slut' as a sex-positive word that empowers us with the freedom of sexual pleasure? If not, why? We are all smart sexual creatures with the ability to make sex-positive choices. Do you let your own sexual choices and actions make others stumble? If so, why? Be responsible. Key to our sexual freedom is consent and responsibility. We all express ourselves differently. I personally enjoy being a unicorn in the Lifestyle. Everyone is different and what each person consensually does is their business. We all have our own comfort zones and safety bubbles. There shouldn't be an issue between the humans and Xenolfans having sexual interactions. It's a well-known established fact that it is impossible for us to breed together. So, it's strictly for pleasure anyway. We all live in an imperfect galaxy. We all must make the best use of our lives in a repressed society. You can be the light in someone else's darkness. Go make a difference for yourself and for others in the galaxy. Bless you all. Priscilla Stryderr is up next with a healthy, sex-positive speech."

The audience stood up, applauded, and gave whistles and shouts of gratitude. A man from backstage took the opportunity and walked up to Priscilla, who stood behind Sierra, and whispered something into her ear for a long time before returning backstage. Priscilla quickly walked up to Sierra at the microphone and whispered the same lengthy message into her ear.

"Oh my!" Sierra said into the microphone.

The crowd suddenly became quiet. Sierra turned from Priscilla to the audience. An expression of surprise was revealed on her face.

"We have just learned of some breaking news. Because of the recent attacks on Aamaress and in the Industrial Sector by the Xenolfan Government, the Syrenthian Government had initially restricted all human travel to Salinarr Nevis and Olf Teruda. Also, both planets initially had a full embargo by the Syrenthian Government. Apparently, that, along with a war declaration by the Syrenthian Government, did not set well with casino owners, so Aaranix Tuvelless was recently forced to step down as leader, along with his top dignitaries. And he based this forbidden interspecies sex law on a book he read once, which stated we would breed monsters. How ridiculous... The new leader is Phensiarr Charseaa and she did see our petitions before they were destroyed. Her first act as the new Xenolfan Government leader was to repeal the forbidden interspecies sex law. You are now all sexually free!"

The room exploded with shouts of joy. In the crowd, Gathin and Eslarr stood, looked into each other's eyes, and hugged each other tight.

"Despite this wonderful news, Priscilla will still be giving her healthy, sex-positive speech," Sierra said.

The crowd applauded once more as Priscilla took the microphone.

There was a short time between the Sexual Freedom Seminar and the Maranadda concert. The concert itself was in a different section of the Civie Arena. After the speech, Sierra took a moment to reflect on the breaking news that was announced. She walked in the back of the arena to an open overhead door. The orange desert of Red Jacket was quite a contrast from the snowy surface of Aamaress. She thought the Sexual Freedom Seminar went very well. Priscilla Stryderr had already joined Braxton in the box seats for the concert. The family members and friends of all the bands were also in box seats. Other inspiring symphonic metal bands were opening for Maranadda, including Frozen Solstice, Enchanted Resonance, and Cosmic Shit. Sierra left the dusk desert view behind and headed for the changing room to put on her black leather outfit.

It didn't take long to change. When she came out of the changing room, she heard Frozen Solstice playing in the distance. She headed for a room where the other members of Maranadda were lounging.

"Hey, guys! Are you ready for this?" Sierra asked.

"Yes. And it's nice to have you here at the start this time. This is going to be a phenomenal show," Yosemite said.

"By the way, Sierra, your sexual freedom speech was excellent," Arvon said.

"Well, thank you. I think it went well and the audience loved it…well except for one heckler," Sierra said.

"Don't worry about that one person, or even several. You can't please everyone, so don't even try," Sanarith said.

The door opened and Shasta Varium popped her head in.

"Frozen Solstice is sounding good. How are you guys doing?" she asked.

"We are fine. This will go much better than the last show, so don't worry," Arrian said.

"Worry? I'm not worried," Shasta said.

She left and closed the door behind her.

"She's worried. But you can't blame her after the Salinarr Nevis incident," Kulu said.

"Look, I'm here now, guys. This is going to be a great show," Sierra said.

"Vincent said the sound here at the Civie Arena is so much better than the Silver Star Concert Hall on Salinarr Nevis," Yosemite said.

"Awesome," Sierra said. "Hey, it sounds like Enchanted Resonance is about to start. I'm going to check out the crowd."

They all ended up following Sierra to the left wing of the stage. The house was full. Sierra gazed over the crowd. She spotted Eslarr and Gathin toward the back center of the arena. She noticed Yttursal was not far from where the couple sat. Sierra smiled when she saw them. Peering up on the right balcony section, she noticed a little boy in a wheelchair. He wore a cap on his head. It took her a moment, but she recognized him from right there on Red Jacket. It was Benjamin, the boy who always loved to watch Yosemite and the other band members ride by on the quads along the Red Jacket trail.

"Hey, look. It's Benjamin!" Sierra said, pointing to the upper balcony.

"Ah, yes. It's nice to see Benjamin Whitmann made it here to see the show. We gave him tickets a while back. That's his mom and dad next to him. His dad is CJ Whitmann. He owns the hardware store not far from here," Yosemite said.

"Very cool," Sierra said.

"If I ever get my new ATV, I plan on giving him a ride on the new one," Yosemite said.

Shasta walked up behind them as they looked at the crowd.

"Okay, I'm officially not nervous anymore," Shasta said.

The six band members turned around and smiled at their manager.

Maranadda soon took the stage and the cheering of the audience became extremely loud. Sierra walked over to her microphone stand in her sexy, black leather outfit. Her long, black hair trailed down her back and her beautiful, blue eyes stared at the crowd. She gave the metal horns sign.

"If you're not ready for a fast-paced adventure, you might want to move over to the slow lane," she said with her usual opening line. "This first song is called Red Jacket from our Esoteric album. It's a song about the rich copper mining history from right here on Red Jacket."

The clean guitars at the beginning of the song were stunning. They suddenly gave way to a crunchy thrash sound and a fast double bass beat. It was accented from the melodic keyboard sounds as the song took the audience on a journey into Red Jacket's past.

When the song ended, Sierra looked out at the cheering crowd with the biggest smile.

What a difference from the madness at the last show, she thought.

They began to play a much darker song called Alchemy from the Esoteric album. Then came Tales of Shardaa, also from the Esoteric album. Since Sierra had actually been to the Shardaa Sector, every time they played that song now, it gave her the creeps. It was followed by Dissolution from the Novels album. When Sierra began to sing Blacklisted from their Discord album, she reflected on the years working with Madison.

What a waste, she thought.

Next came the very heavy and melodic rhythm of Dissimulate from Maranadda's Discord album. It was a song about Aaranix Tuvelless and his contempt with humans.

> "Our galaxy's fate,
> Dissimulate.
> Syrenthian's fate,
> Dissimulate.
>
> "If you're so diverse, then what's wrong?
> Can't we all just get along?
> You twist our words and fabricate lies,
> Deceiving the galaxy and drowning its cries.
>
> "All things that are good, you reject.
> Your unjust laws, you force in effect.
> You deny freedom and all that is right.
> Your evil motives, our galaxy's plight.

"You label our beliefs as a crazy thing,
As if your beliefs were king.
Politically corrupt, you're so refined.
A prejudice hypocrite against our kind.

"Your agenda's based on idiocy.
We won't tolerate your audacity.
Don't mess with our sovereignty.
Don't push your fucking shit on me!

"Your ignorant intentions are so ill.
You cannot change our will.
Strategic plans are revealed to the wise.
We anxiously await your demise.

"Our galaxy's fate,
Dissimulate.
Syrenthian's fate,
Dissimulate."

By the end of Dissimulate, the vibe from the crowd was a glowing aura that spread to the stage. All the members of Maranadda were gleeful and it showed in their performance. The crowd cheered for a long time after the song had ended. The applauding became quiet as Sierra took the microphone from its stand and put one leg up on a monitor.

"You're looking good. How are you doing?"

The crowd went wild with cheers and whistles.

"Soon, Maranadda will be releasing our forthcoming album called Surefire. Be sure to pick up a copy when it's released. These next several songs will be on the album. I have recently wrote a few of these songs and we've been practicing hard to include these new songs in todays playlist. This next song I wrote from a recent experience on the snow planet Aamaress. It's called Stormrider. I hope you like it," Sierra said.

She turned to Kulu and smiled as the song began.

"This wilderness is a beautiful place.
Pines rush by as I race.

One more switchback, here I go!
Another trail through blinding snow.

"Sitting on a hot machine,
Feeling everything between.
Full speed through the snow,
Dangerous trails, here I go!

"A whiteout, seamless with the sky…
Sheer cliffs as I pass by…
Drifts cover this mountainous course.
My engine whines with all its force.

"Sitting on a hot machine,
Feeling everything between.
Full speed through the snow,
Dangerous trails, here I go!

"Many have traveled this road before.
After me, there'll be many more.
Help is needed just ahead.
I'm full throttle on my sled.

"Sitting on a hot machine,
Feeling everything between.
Full speed through the snow,
Dangerous trails, here I go!"

The symphonic metal composition was a fast-paced sound with extreme drumming and excellent guitar solos. The bridge was a fascinating change up before it went back into the speed metal sound. Sierra was a little worried about the reception of the song, but from the reaction of the audience, it must have been a hit.

"This next song was written by our drummer, Arvon Estivant. It's called Landlubber."

The melodic orchestral sound of string instruments that Kulu provided on the keyboards was outstanding. The sound of every instrument from the violin family could be distinctly heard. The song built up and was accented by flute sounds, alternating with crunchy guitars. Piano was also prominent in the build.

"In this sea of madness,
Seasoned captains should understand.

"New sailors make mistakes,
As they navigate these vast waters.

"While some whisper suggestions of the plank,
Others counsel to chart a new course.

"If the entire crew was taken into account,
We'd all be blacklisted from this ship."

Although Landlubber did not have a chorus, the song was very well received by the fans. When the song ended, Sierra turned around, winked at Arvon, and then looked back toward the cheering crowd. The endless sea of fans extended far back into the arena. Metal horn signs were proudly displayed and fists were in the air. These headbangers were a wonderful sight to see.

"You metal heads look good tonight! I wrote this next song for a Xenolfan woman I met on Aamaress. She was betrayed by someone that she put her trust in. I know she's here tonight. This song goes out to you, Yttursal. It's called Promiscuous Betrayer."

It began with a trudging drum beat and soon became quite heavy, with a symphonic sound that was incorporated into the mix, interweaving its way through Yosemite's distorted guitar playing.

"She endlessly searches for victims to trap,
Stealthily intending deceit.
Be warned of her evil actions;
Awaiting a chance to cheat.
Her dark soul feeds on other's attention.
The evil daughter has won their approval.
The promiscuous whore is at it again,
With loyalty and trust removal.

"You'll give her all you've got.
But she'll want more.

You're only one Xenolfan.
But she's a filthy whore.

"The promiscuous slut has spread her thighs.
Lusting yet another cunt.
Lips secreting, she begins her betrayal.
A parasite on the galactic hunt.
She's a bitch full of twisted lies.
Don't you take her as your own.
Her soul is destined to rot.
She's not worthy of love you've shown.

"You'll give her all you've got,
But she'll want more.
You're only one Xenolfan,
But she's a filthy whore.

"Look deep into those deceiving eyes.
See the darkness of her lost soul.
The tempting demon wants to feed.
She'll plunge you into a burning hole.
When she's had her fill, she'll take you down.
But justice will be done.
Her soul will eternally rot.
By avoiding her, you will have won.

"You'll give her all you've got,
But she'll want more.
You're only one Xenolfan,
But she's a fucking whore."

The audience exploded with applause.

"I might've been a little passionate when I wrote that song, a little angry. Did I mention that I hate cheaters and their deceitful shit. The fucking Jinkins! You can do better, Yttursal."

Yttursal looked onward from the audience at Sierra.

I love you, Sierra. Thanks for that song, she thought.

"I will do better!" Yttursal yelled through the crowd's cheers.

"We have one more song for you tonight. This is another song that

I recently wrote. It's about a special interspecies couple that I met on Aamaress. It was for couples like them that I have fought hard for, advocating the forbidden interspecies sex. And now, with the recent changes in Xenolfan Government policy, it appears that my fight is over. This is for you Gathin and Eslarr. I love you guys. This is called Forbidden Lovers."

The song began with a full orchestra sound. Arrian's bass fell in line next with a trotting rhythm. As the song transitioned into a beautiful and stunning performance, it was syncopated by the addition of Sanarith's guitar work.

> "Shining through the murk,
> Our love has endured.
> With refined wisdom,
> Our love has adapted.
>
> "Forbidden Lovers…
> Can't they see our love?
> Forbidden Lovers…
> Our true love remains.
>
> "Collective essentials are nurtured,
> And equity is in pair.
> An esoteric lifestyle,
> Pure love lucid at its core.
>
> "Forbidden Lovers…
> Can't they see our love?
> Forbidden Lovers…
> Our true love remains.
>
> "Affirmation in beauty resounds.
> Aplomb abounds in the decree.
> This amorous disposition,
> Is truly an alluring contingency!
>
> "Forbidden Lovers…
> Can't they see our love?
> Forbidden Lovers…

Our true love remains.

"Our true love remains."

Sierra sang the last line of the chorus a second time a cappella after the rest of the music had ceased, her beautiful voice piercing through the arena. Gathin and Eslarr gazed across the crowd toward Sierra and smiled. They felt very special and they were glad to have met Sierra Shalinsky.

As Maranadda concluded the show, Arrian, Yosemite, and Sanarith threw guitar picks into the crowd. Arvon tossed drum sticks into the crowd. The six of them gathered at center stage and bowed before the audience. They waved as they walked off stage.

"What an awesome performance. You guys were fantastic," Shasta said. "Listen to that crowd."

"Thanks. At least we don't have far to go with our equipment," Yosemite said.

They walked backstage to relax after the exhausting concert. They each grabbed a bite to eat and began to discuss the new Surefire album. As Sierra excused herself to use the rest room, they continued talking about recording the new album.

After using the rest room, Sierra left her bandmates backstage and walked to a secluded section of the arena where shipping crates were stacked. A forklift and a shipping container sat along one side. The container had the logo of a logistics company displayed across the side of it. Most of the crates contained amplifiers, heads, cabinets, and other musical equipment from a previous show, waiting to be shipped off-world.

Sierra was so drained and exhausted from the back-to-back Sexual Freedom Seminar and Maranadda concert that she just wanted some peace and quiet. She sat on one of the crates and leaned against another wooden crate, closing her eyes. Oh, the silence sounded so good. For once, things seemed to be going smooth for her. She was so happy with her new unit at the Galactic Emergency Medical Services. Her new director, Sethain, was awesome. Things were settling down with all the galactic chaos that had been happening as of late. Oh, the silence was nice. She heard the faint sound of someone walking. As the steps became louder, she figured another bandmate was going to bother her. Sierra opened her eyes to see a woman walking toward her. She was very tall with a tan complexion and white hair. Her outfit was extremely sexy, with tight leggings and a revealing top that accentuated her breasts. A large backpack was fastened to her back. As she approached, her pace slowed until she stood before Sierra.

"Hi Sierra. My name is Estrus. I attended your Sexual Freedom Seminar and I saw the Maranadda concert. I've been following you. You are absolutely beautiful and awesome! You are just what we've been searching for."

"Umm…you're not supposed to be back here. How did you get past security, especially with a backpack?" Sierra asked.

"Like this," Estrus said, lifting the front of her shirt up over her boobs.

A pair of very nice, tan breasts bounced out from beneath the top. Sierra was suddenly aroused and smiled at Estrus. She looked very unique with sexy white hair and sapphire eyes.

That sure is some security we have, Sierra thought.

"Do you want to touch them?" Estrus asked.

"I would love to," Sierra said.

Sierra gently caressed her soft, tan boobs. After playfully massaging them, she moved her hands toward the leggings and slowly rubbed the smooth labia from the outside of the fabric. Sierra shifted slightly on the crate that she sat on and slowly pulled the woman's leggings down. To her surprise, above a shaved pussy was a tattoo of two crossing feathers, one of which was broken. Looking farther down the vulva, below the tattoo, a reuleaux triangular vaginal opening was revealed. Sierra recognized the feather symbol from the Shardaa Sector, above the caves. The vaginal shape was that of a Xenolfan, not a human of tan skin. A familiar eeriness suddenly overwhelmed her. She looked up at Estrus in surprise. The sapphire eyes suddenly began to glow with an intense brightness, like she had seen before in the caves. The large backpack fell to the floor and a massive pair of black wings sprung forth, extending upward toward the ceiling.

"What the fuck?"

To be continued…

Appendices

Benjamin
A Short Story of Benjamin Whitmann

Benjamin is a disabled boy who doesn't have many friends, but loves to watch the quads race by. His mother wishes nothing more than to see him smile. She may just get her wish when he is given an unexpected opportunity.

"Be sure to take the sunscreen with you, Benjamin," his mother said from the kitchen.

"I know, Mom. I have it," Benjamin said. "And I'll be careful."

She came out from the kitchen, handed him two bottles of water, and gave him a kiss on his forehead. He reached up from his wheelchair and hugged her neck.

"I hope you smile today. I love you," she said.

"I love you too, Mom."

After tucking the bottles away in a pouch at the side of his wheelchair, Benjamin slowly rolled toward the front door. He grabbed his cap from a side stand and put it on his head. The cap was one of the gifts he recently received for his twelfth birthday. He made his way out the front door and down the ramp, carefully maneuvering around the corner. As he wheeled toward the front sidewalk of the house, he could feel the heat of the sun beating down on him. He adjusted the bill of his cap to keep the sun out of his eyes. Opening the bottle of sunscreen, he applied a small amount to his exposed skin. He wiped the excess residue on his shorts. Returning the sunscreen to the pouch at the side of his chair, he began wheeling his way down the street toward the trail. He looked at his destination in the far distance. It was a desert area, but had many rocks and outcrops decorating its surface.

I hope they are running the quads today, Benjamin thought.

Several times a week, Benjamin would wheel himself a great distance from his home to the top of the ridge that overlooked a trail where the quads would run. He would sit there on the top of the stone slab that overlooked the trail for many hours waiting and waiting in the hot, desert sun. Often, he would see the 4-wheelers zoom past on the rocky trail below. He always waved at them as they passed by. It really made him feel good when they waved back at him. Some days they didn't run at all and he would slowly wheel himself the great distance back home, very disappointed.

The rusty colored rocks of the desert reminded Benjamin of the history lesson he had learned about that area of the desert. Many years before, it was a copper mining community. The colorful rocks also reminded him of his ever-growing rock collection he had on his shelf back in his room. Benjamin didn't have many friends. It was very difficult for him to make friends. He hated being disabled and tried to make the best of it. He was born without the use of his legs. He remembered the doctors calling it some strange name, but didn't remember what that name was. His parents knew what it was called. He missed his dad a lot. He was always gone at work, but Benjamin understood why. His father owned the local hardware store and had to be there most of the time. When his father did have time to spend with him, he cherished it greatly.

Benjamin maneuvered his wheelchair carefully along the rocky path that led toward the ridge ahead. As he got closer, he looked up at the steep, rocky incline. Although he had wheeled himself up the rocky hill many times, it always made him nervous. One time, he lost it and rolled down the hill backwards and tipped over at the bottom. After brushing the loose stones off, it took him about an hour to tip the wheelchair back up and pull himself back up onto the seat. He never told his mom because he knew she would freak out. Then, he wouldn't be able to see the quads anymore. Somehow, he thought his dad knew, however. Perhaps it was the stone scrapes that were on his arm at the time that gave it away. But his dad never said anything about it. He only advised him to be careful around the ridge.

By the time he reached the large slab of stone at the top of the ridge, his arms were exhausted. He applied the brakes and sat there for a long moment, recovering. The heat was relentless. He removed one of the water bottles from the pouch at the side of his chair. Condensation dripped down the bottle and moistened his hand. He opened it and took a long drink. As he held the bottle, he looked around at the familiar scenery. The brilliant blue sky was beautiful. All was very quiet, except the noise of a slight breeze and an occasional insect flying by. After taking another long drink of his water, he placed the cap back onto the bottle and returned it to the side pouch. He adjusted his cap and looked down at the trail below.

I hope they're running today, Benjamin thought.

After more than an hour, he thought about going back home. Suddenly, he heard the faint sound in the distance. As it grew louder, Benjamin smiled.

They are *running today!* he thought.

Soon, Benjamin could see them getting closer on the rocky trail. He noticed there were five of them this time. As they drove past the ridge, one of them looked up at Benjamin and waved. Benjamin excitedly waved back. His smile remained for a long time as he saw them disappear into the distance. Just that quick, they were gone. For Benjamin, it was worth the wait. Besides, he knew that sometimes they would go by twice.

Although his father was an acquaintance with them, Benjamin didn't really know them that well. He knew they were all in a symphonic metal band together. Once in a while, their vocalist would ride with them, her long, black hair flowing out from the back of her helmet. Benjamin had recently met the kids of the band's keyboardist. He couldn't remember their names, however. He hoped to become friends with them, if he saw them again.

• • •

After waiting for them to pass a second time, Benjamin came to the conclusion that they were only going around once that day. He sighed. As he looked down, a cool rock caught his eye. He reached down and stretched his arm, grasping the rock. He raised it to his lips and blew the dust from its surface.

Awesome!

It had an interesting blue and rust colored pattern. He dropped it into his side pouch. He then finished his last water and put the empty container back. He took one last look at the scenic view across from the trail. The other side had a rusty colored rock wall with a desert tree overhanging from the top. A few green plants decorated the wall. As he began to release the wheelchair brakes, he saw the quads returning, except this time they were coming back from the way they had disappeared earlier.

That's unusual, Benjamin thought.

All five of the quads slowed down and came to a stop just below the ridge. The lead driver looked up at the boy.

"Benjamin, would you like a ride on the quad?" the man asked.

Benjamin grew the biggest smile.

"Yeah!"

That evening during dinner, Benjamin told his father all about his day.

"I got to go for a ride on the quad! And I made some new friends. The band's keyboardist has two kids that I met before and now they want to come over here and play. Plus, the band signed my cap—well, except for the singer. She wasn't there yet. But they said they would get me some concert tickets too," Benjamin said. "Oh, and I found a cool rock."

"Yes, he ask if he could give you a ride today when he stopped by the hardware store. I'm glad you finally had a good day," his father said.

"You know what?" his mom asked.

"Hmm?" Benjamin asked.

"It makes my heart sing with joy that you are so happy and smiling," she said.

"Oh, Mom..."

Maranadda Band Information

Band
Sierra Shalinsky - Vocals
Yosemite McFarlin - Guitars
Sanarith Raastarr - Guitars
Arrian Trodder - Bass
Kulu Avolium - Keyboards
Arvon Estivant - Drums

Other Information
Shasta Varium - Manager / Booking Agent
Vincent Macenburg - Sound
Home Planet - Red Jacket

Select Discography
Esoteric
  Red Jacket
  Alchemy
  Tales of Shardaa
Novels
  Dissolution
Discord
  Blacklisted
  Dissimulate
Surefire
  Stormrider
  Landlubber
  Promiscuous Betrayer
  Forbidden Lovers

SELECT LIST OF CASINOS ON SALINARR NEVIS

Aaranix's Gold
Auracon's Game
Blue Sapphire
Casino 21
Golden Oasis
Lightyear's Treasure
Lucky Stone
Sex Palace
The Ascent
The Wolf's Den

Terminology Glossary

Chapter references are where the term first appears in the novel.
(Some terms may contain slight spoilers.)

A

Aamaress - (Chapter 2) A snow planet located in the Aamaress Star System, within the Syrenthian Government's territory. Aamaress was the location of The Avalanche Resort.

Aamaress Star System - (Chapter 2) A star system in the Syrenthian Galaxy, within the Syrenthian Government's territory.

Aaranix's Gold - (Chapter 2) A casino on the planet Salinarr Nevis.

Absoneth, Sethain - (Chapter 13) He was a unit director and Galactic Emergency Medical Technician for Galactic Emergency Medical Services. Sethain had short, blond hair.

Affelum, Siiteper - (Chapter 5) He was a Xenolfan who lived in the Xenolfan Government palace on the planet Olf Teruda. Siiteper had been the leader of the Xenolfan Government one thousand years earlier. He was the author of the book *Anathema Strain*. Siiteper had long, white hair and sapphire eyes. He also had large, black wings.

Alchemy - (Chapter 1) A song by Maranadda from their first album, Esoteric. Alchemy was a dark theme song.

Alex - (Chapter 4) He was a Galactic Emergency Medical Technician for Galactic Emergency Medical Services. Alex had brown hair.

Anathema Strain - (Chapter 5) A book written by Siiteper Affelum who was an ancient leader of the Xenolfan Government. *Anathema Strain* warned about a host of problems caused by relationships between Xenolfans and humans.

Aomium Swith - (Chapter 6) A planet located in the Shar Nefalis Star System, within the Syrenthian Government's territory. Aomium Swith was part of the Industrial Sector and was the planet that gave the Industrial Sector its name from the large industrial empire that was first developed there.

Aplomb - (Chapter 13) A space freighter whose crew contacted Galactic Emergency Medical Services after receiving an intermittent emergency signal from the planet Aamaress.

Ardellia - (Chapter 6) A planet located in the Shar Nefalis Star System, within the Syrenthian Government's territory. Ardellia was part of the Industrial Sector.

Ascent, The - (Chapter 2) A casino on the planet Salinarr Nevis.

Asparell coin - (Chapter 7) Coins that had been used in ancient times and were worth about 2000 credits each. There was only one group of people who currently used Asparell coins in the galaxy, the Syrenthian Brotherhood Knights of Darkness.

Asparr Celtarious - (Chapter 1) A planet within the Syrenthian Government's territory.

Auracon's Game - (Chapter 2) A casino on the planet Salinarr Nevis.

Aurora - (Chapter 4) She was a Galactic Emergency Medical Technician for Galactic Emergency Medical Services. Aurora had blond hair and brown eyes.

Avalanche Resort, The - (Chapter 2) A secret resort on the snow planet Aamaress. The Avalanche Resort catered to forbidden relationships between humans and Xenolfans.

Avolium, Aaron - (Chapter 1) He lived on the planet Red Jacket. Aaron had blond hair. He was the son of Misty and Kulu Avolium.

Avolium, Kulu - (Chapter 1) He lived on the planet Red Jacket. Kulu was the keyboardist for the band Maranadda. He had long, blond hair. Kulu was the husband of Misty Avolium and the father of Aaron and Shanda Avolium.

Avolium, Misty - (Chapter 1) She lived on the planet Red Jacket. Misty had long, blond hair. She was the wife of Kulu Avolium and the mother of Aaron and Shanda Avolium.

Avolium, Shanda - (Chapter 1) She lived on the planet Red Jacket. Shanda had blond hair. She was the daughter of Misty and Kulu Avolium.

B

Blacklisted - (Chapter 10) A song by Maranadda from their third album, Discord. Blacklisted was written by vocalist Sierra Shalinsky about personal struggles she had with her Galactic Emergency Medical Services unit director, Madison Stephard.

Blaze - (Chapter 4) He was a Galactic Emergency Medical Technician for Galactic Emergency Medical Services. Blaze had brown hair.

Blue Sapphire - (Chapter 2) A casino on the planet Salinarr Nevis.

C

Calbrifae, Marion - (Chapter 1) He was a business entrepreneur who pioneered the copper mining industry on the planet Red Jacket.

Casino 21 - (Chapter 2) A casino on the planet Salinarr Nevis.

Celestial Frost - (Chapter 3) A spaceship owed by Shalarr and Fioness.

Charseaa, Phensiarr - (Chapter 5) She was a Xenolfan who lived on the planet Olf Teruda. Phensiarr was a Government officer on the staff of leader Aaranix Tuvelless and eventually replaced him as leader after he was forced to step down. She had long, white hair and sapphire eyes.

Chelliss - (Chapter 6) A planet located in the Shar Nefalis Star System, within the Syrenthian Government's territory. Chelliss was part of the Industrial Sector.

Civie Arena - (Chapter 13) A venue on the planet Red Jacket.

CJ Whitmann's Hardware & Supply Co. - (Chapter 1) An old hardware store on the planet Red Jacket that was owned by CJ Whitmann.

Cobalt, Dennon - (Chapter 4) He was a seeming delusional space traveler who was rescued from the Shardaa Sector by Galactic Emergency Medical Services.

comm - (Chapter 1) A communicator device that had multiple functions.

Cosmic Disturbance - (Chapter 3) A spaceship owned by Rastall.

Cosmic Shit - (Chapter 15) A symphonic metal band.

D

Dalaa (military base) - (Chapter 5) A Xenolfan Government military base located on the satellite Dalaa.

Dalaa (satellite) - (Chapter 5) The single satellite of the planet Olf Teruda. Dalaa was the location of a Xenolfan Government military base of the same name.

Deliverance - (Chapter 4) A large hospital spaceship owned by Galactic Emergency Medical Services. The *Deliverance* had multiple levels and numerous facilities. A state-of-the-art surgical center was one of its many features. The ship was continually staffed by a multitude of doctors, surgeons, nurses, therapists, and emergency personnel. Most staff worked in shifts, but others worked on an on-call basis. Part of the emergency services division had some military personnel in the mix, as well as a salvage unit.

Dellagg - (Chapter 2) He was an informant for the Xenolfan Government. Dellagg worked on the planet Salinarr Nevis.

Deltarr - (Chapter 15) A Xenolfan Government battleship that was stationed at the Dalaa military base. The *Deltarr* was destroyed in a battle at Olf Teruda during the New Syrenthian War.

Discord - (Chapter 1) Maranadda's third album.

Dissimulate - (Chapter 10) A song by Maranadda from their third album, Discord. Dissimulate was a song about Aaranix Tuvelless's contempt with humans.

Dissolution - (Chapter 10) A song by Maranadda from their second album, Novels.

Doraa, Keddaa - (Chapter 5) He was the lead engineer for the Xenolfan Government military base on the satellite Dalaa who was responsible for creating a missiloid. Keddaa had long, white hair and sapphire eyes.

E

Eccentric Elixir - (Chapter 7) An intoxication joint and cafe on the planet Volum.

Echeon, Rasmond - (Chapter 13) She was a Galactic Emergency Medical Technician for Galactic Emergency Medical Services. Rasmond had long, brown hair.

Enax Port - (Chapter 3) A planet within the Syrenthian Government's territory.

Enchanted Resonance - (Chapter 8) A symphonic metal band.

Enelra, Jacquelyn "Jackie" - (Chapter 1) She lived on the planet Red Jacket. Jacquelyn was the girlfriend of Aarian Trodder and the mother of Sophie Enelra. She had long, brown hair.

Enelra, Sophie - (Chapter 1) She lived on the planet Red Jacket. Sophie was the daughter of Jacquelyn Enelra and Aarian Trodder.

Eslarr - (Chapter 2) She was a Xenolfan originally from the planet Olf Teruda. Eslarr had long, white hair and sapphire eyes. She was in a forbidden relationship with a human named Gathin.

Esoteric - (Chapter 1) Maranadda's first album.

Estivant, Arvon - (Chapter 1) He lived on the planet Red Jacket. Arvon was the drummer for the band Maranadda. He had long, brown hair, tattoos, and piercings.

Estrus - (Chapter 15) She was a mysterious woman who followed Sierra Shalinsky. Estrus had long, white hair and sapphire eyes that glowed. She also had large, black wings, and a feathers tattoo on her lower abdomen.

Exandra - (Chapter 3) A planet that was the seat of the Syrenthian Government.

F

Fioness - (Chapter 3) She was a Xenolfan who lived on the planet Salinarr Nevis. Fioness was a performer for the Sex Palace Theater. She had long, white hair and sapphire eyes. Fioness was married to Shalarr. They owned a spaceship named *Celestial Frost*.

Flux Ship Mods - (Chapter 4) A company that specialized in modifying spaceships.

Forbidden Lovers - (Chapter 14) A song by Maranadda from their fourth album, Surefire. Forbidden Lovers was written by vocalist Sierra Shalinsky as a tribute to her friends Gathin and Eslarr, who were in a forbidden relationship.

Frozen Solstice - (Chapter 8) A symphonic metal band.

G

Galactic Emergency Medical Services (GEMS) - (Chapter 1) An emergency medical services company serving the entire Syrenthian Galaxy with headquarters on the planet Relistorr.

Galactic Emergency Medical Technician (Galactic EMT) - (Chapter 1) A specially-trained medical professional and generally a first responder during galactic disasters and crisis.

Garrious - (Chapter 5) He was a Xenolfan who lived on the planet Olf Teruda. Garrious was a Xenolfan military officer who accepted a missiloid suicide mission. He had long, white hair and sapphire eyes.

Gathin - (Chapter 2) He had shoulder-length, brown hair. Gathin had a wolf tattoo on his left side. He was in a forbidden relationship with a Xenolfan named Eslarr.

Ghost and the Pumpkin, The - (Chapter 1) A children's book about a ghost who befriended a pumpkin.

Golden Oasis - (Chapter 2) A casino on the planet Salinarr Nevis.

GrayMar - (Chapter 15) A Syrenthian Government battleship. The *GaryMar* was one of five Syrenthian Government battleships that was involved in a battle at Olf Teruda during the New Syrenthian War. It sustained minimal damage.

I

Industrial Sector - (Chapter 2) A sector in the Syrenthian Government's territory that included the entire Shar Nefalis Star System with the planets Shar Nefalis, Aomium Swith, Chelliss, and Ardellia. Manufacturing, mining, and other productive facilities were abundant on all four planets.

intoxication joint - (Chapter 3) A drinking establishment.

J

Jinkins (committee) - (Chapter 1) A committee comprised of members of the Superior Mountain Club on the planet Asparr Celtarious. The Jinkins committee made decisions regarding many aspects of the Superior Mountain Club property.

Jinkins (insult) - (Chapter 1) An insult used by Sierra Shalinsky that derived from her discord with the Jinkins committee of the Superior Mountain Club on her home planet Asparr Celtarious. Sierra owned adjacent property across Lake Serenity from the Superior Mountain Club. She defined the insult of Jinkins as meaning idiot.

L

Lake Serenity - (Chapter 4) A lake on the planet Asparr Celtarious that was surrounded by white pine trees. Lake Serenity sat below the Superior Mountains.

Landlubber - (Chapter 15) A song by Maranadda from their fourth album, Surefire. Landlubber was written by drummer Arvon Estivant.

lightspeed-plus - (Chapter 1) A general term used to reference spaceship speeds beyond that of light.

Lightyear's Treasure - (Chapter 2) A casino on the planet Salinarr Nevis.

Lucky Stone - (Chapter 2) A casino on the planet Salinarr Nevis.

M

Macenburg, Shaslin - (Chapter 1) She lived on the planet Red Jacket. Shaslin had long, brown hair. She was the wife of Vincent Macenburg.

Macenburg, Vincent - (Chapter 1) He lived on the planet Red Jacket. Vincent was the sound technician for the band Maranadda. He had long, brown hair. Vincent was the husband of Shaslin Macenburg.

Malanaa - (Chapter 5) She a Xenolfan who lived on the planet Olf Teruda. Malanaa had long, white hair and sapphire eyes. She was one of the many polyamorous lovers of Xenolfan Government leader Aaranix Tuvelless.

Maranadda - (Chapter 1) A popular symphonic metal band whose home planet was Red Jacket. Maranadda had a lineup of Sierra Shalinsky on vocals, Yosemite McFarlin on guitars, Sanarith Raastarr on guitars, Arrian Trodder on bass, Kulu Avolium on keyboards, and Arvon Estivant on drums. Their manager and booking agent was Shasta Varium and their sound technician was Vincent Macenburg.

Mauve - (Chapter 4) She was a host at The Avalanche Resort on the planet Aamaress. Mauve had blond hair. She was the girlfriend of Max.

Max - (Chapter 4) He was a host at The Avalanche Resort on the planet Aamaress. Max had brown hair. He was the boyfriend of Mauve.

McFarlin, Yosemite - (Chapter 1) He lived on the planet Red Jacket. Yosemite was one of the guitarists for the band Maranadda. He owned the house and studio where the band practiced. Yosemite owned several all-terrain vehicles that the band used on Red Jacket trails. He had short, spiky, brown hair.

Meshtief, Garnell - (Chapter 6) He was the owner of Ticrisuda Powersports on the planet Shar Nefalis. Garnell had black hair.

Millott, Elliss - (Chapter 4) He was the incident commander for Galactic Emergency Medical Services. Elliss had gray hair.

missiloid - (Chapter 1) A type of weapon used by the Xenolfan Government against humans durning the Syrenthian War. A missiloid was also used by the Xenolfan Government 100 years later to attack the planet Aamaress, which contributed to the brief New Syrenthian War. The weapons were made from a small asteroid mounted with a cockpit and an ion engine that controlled its direction. Missiloids had no additional weapons and only served the purpose of a suicide mission of mass destruction on a planet.

Montoraania - (Chapter 15) A planet located in the Montoraania Star System, within the Syrenthian Government's territory. Montoraania was known for its compound Toraanium, which was toxic only to humans.

Montoraania Star System - (Chapter 15) A star system in the Syrenthian Galaxy, within the Syrenthian Government's territory.

Mossenberg - (Chapter 4) A salvage spaceship based on the hospital ship *Deliverance*. The *Mossenberg* was equipped with a ship extractor, a tractor beam, and other technologies used by its team to retrieve and haul ships.

N

New Syrenthian War - (Chapter 15) A brief war between the Xenolfan Government and the Syrenthian Government. The New Syrenthian War included a space battle at Olf Teruda and a Syrenthian Government presence in space at Salinarr Nevis.

Northern Territories - (Chapter 2) A remote northern area on the planet Aamaress that included the town of Winterfest.

Novels - (Chapter 1) Maranadda's second album.

O

Oldstaff - (Chapter 15) A Xenolfan Government battleship. The *Oldstaff* was involved in the New Syrenthian War and took extremely heavy damage at a battle at Olf Teruda.

Olf Teruda - (Chapter 1) A paradise planet that was the seat of the Xenolfan Government.

P

Priscilla Pussy Lips - (Chapter 1) A Nickname given to Priscilla Stryderr by Sierra Shalinsky.

Promiscuous Betrayer - (Chapter 14) A song by Maranadda from their fourth album, Surefire. Promiscuous Betrayer was written by vocalist Sierra Shalinsky for her friend Yttursal after finding she had been cheated on.

Q

Quillexx - (Chapter 2) A popular meat from the planet Olf Teruda.

R

Raastarr, Arcashia - (Chapter 1) She lived on the planet Red Jacket. Arcashia had long, blond hair. She was the wife of Sanarith Raastarr.

Raastarr, Sanarith - (Chapter 1) He lived on the planet Red Jacket. Sanarith was one of the guitarists for the band Maranadda. He was bald. Sanarith was the husband of Arcashia Raastarr.

Rachel - (Chapter 4) She was a Galactic Emergency Medical Technician for Galactic Emergency Medical Services. Rachel had brown hair.

Railler, Captain Linex - (Chapter 4) He worked for Galactic Emergency Medical Services and was the captain of the hospital ship *Deliverance*.

Rastall - (Chapter 3) He was a patron of the Sex Palace Theater. Rastall had short, black hair.

Red Jacket (planet) - (Chapter 1) A planet within the Syrenthian Government's territory. It had once been the location of a large copper mining industry.

Red Jacket (song) - (Chapter 1) A song by Maranadda from their first album, Esoteric. Red Jacket was a song about the copper mining history on the planet Red Jacket.

Relistorr - (Chapter 1) A planet within the Syrenthian Government's territory. Relistorr was the headquarters of Galactic Emergency

Medical Services. The planet was extremely secure and only medical and other emergency personnel had access to and from its surface.

Rosheil - (Chapter 8) She was a girlfriend of Arvon Estivant.

S

S2 - (Chapter 4) A desolate planet located in the Shardaa Star System, within the Syrenthian Government's territory. S2 was part of the Shardaa Sector. It had an atmosphere of air.

S3 - (Chapter 4) A planet located in the Shardaa Star System, within the Syrenthian Government's territory. S3 was part of the Shardaa Sector.

S4 - (Chapter 4) A planet located in the Shardaa Star System, within the Syrenthian Government's territory. S4 was part of the Shardaa Sector.

S5 - (Chapter 4) A planet located in the Shardaa Star System, within the Syrenthian Government's territory. S5 was part of the Shardaa Sector.

S6 - (Chapter 4) A planet located in the Shardaa Star System, within the Syrenthian Government's territory. S6 was part of the Shardaa Sector.

Salinarr Nevis - (Chapter 1) A planet within the Xenolfan Government's territory. Salinarr Nevis was filled with casinos across its surface. Years before, the human-controlled Syrenthian Government and the Xenolfan Government agreed that gaming facilities could be developed on the planet Salinarr Nevis to help the Xenolfans compensate for the previous damages done from the old Syrenthian War.

Sanctuary Star - (Chapter 15) A Syrenthian Government battleship. The *Sanctuary Star* was one of five Syrenthian Government battleships that was involved in a battle at Olf Teruda during the New Syrenthian War. It sustained minimal damage.

Sevis - (Chapter 1) A sweet carbonated beverage.

Sex Palace - (Chapter 2) A casino on the planet Salinarr Nevis. Sex Palace featured sex-themed games, the Sex Palace Theater, and an adjacent shopping sex mall.

Sex Palace Theater - (Chapter 3) A theater within the Sex Palace casino that featured live sex performances of both humans and Xenolfans

Sexual Freedom Seminar - (Chapter 6) A seminar held at the Civie Arena on the planet Red Jacket. It featured speakers Sierra Shalinsky with a sexual freedom speech and Priscilla Stryderr with a healthy, sex-positive speech.

SG302 - (Chapter 15) A Syrenthian Government military fighter ship.

Shalarr - (Chapter 3) He was a Xenolfan who lived on the planet Salinarr Nevis. Shalarr was a performer for the Sex Palace Theater. He had long, white hair and sapphire eyes. Shalarr was the husband of Fioness. They owned a spaceship named *Celestial Frost*.

Shalinsky, Sierra - (Chapter 1) She lived on the planet Asparr Celtarious. Sierra was a Galactic Emergency Medical Technician for Galactic Emergency Medical Services. She was the vocalist for the band Maranadda. Sierra was also an advocate for sexual freedom between humans and Xenolfans. She had long, black hair and blue eyes. Sierra owned a spaceship named *Tenebris*. Sierra was best friends with Priscilla Stryderr.

Shar Nefalis - (Chapter 6) A planet located in the Shar Nefalis Star System, within the Syrenthian Government's territory. Shar Nefalis was part of the Industrial Sector.

Shar Nefalis Star System - (Chapter 6) A star system in the Syrenthian Galaxy, within the Syrenthian Government's territory.

Shardaa - (Chapter 4) A desolate planet located in the Shardaa Star System, within the Syrenthian Government's territory. Shardaa was part of the Shardaa Sector. It did not have an atmosphere.

Shardaa Sector - (Chapter 3) A sector in the Syrenthian Government's territory that included the entire Shardaa Star System with the planets Shardaa, S2, S3, S4, S5, and S6 as well as other celestial objects.

Shardaa Star System - (Chapter 4) A star system in the Syrenthian Galaxy, within the Syrenthian Government's territory.

Silver Star Concert Hall - (Chapter 3) A venue on the planet Salinarr Nevis.

Sipathrott - (Chapter 4) A potent aphrodisiac.

Sirlain, Edward - (Chapter 6) He lived on the planet Exandra. Edward was the leader of the Syrenthian Government. He had long, grayish-blond hair.

Smith, Bradford - (Chapter 6) He was the owner of a thermal cube factory and mine on the planet Shar Nefalis. Bradford had gray hair.

Stephard, Madison - (Chapter 3) She was a unit director and Galactic Emergency Medical Technician for Galactic Emergency Medical Services. Madison had long, curly, red hair.

Stormrider - (Chapter 14) A song by Maranadda from their fourth album, Surefire. Stormrider was written by vocalist Sierra Shalinsky about her experience of riding a snowmobile through a snow storm on Aamaress.

Stormy - (Chapter 14) He was a wolfdog owned by the owner of The Avalanche Resort.

Stryderr, Braxton - (Chapter 1) He lived on the planet Exandra. Braxton was a Syrenthian Government investigator and administration official. He had short, brown and gray hair. Braxton was the husband of Priscilla Stryderr.

Stryderr, Priscilla - (Chapter 1) She lived on the planet Exandra.

Priscilla worked in the health care industry at a hospital on the planet Exandra. She was an advocate for sexual freedom between humans and Xenolfans. Priscilla had long, blond hair. She was best friends with Sierra Shalinsky.

Superior Mountain Club - (Chapter 4) An exclusive club located in the Superior Mountains on the planet Asparr Celtarious. The club was run by the Jinkins committee. Members of the club acquired a large amount of property in the Superior Mountains. They were known to be snobs, hypocrites, and rude to others on the planet.

Superior Mountains - (Chapter 1) A mountainous region in the northern territory on the planet Asparr Celtarious.

Surefire - (Chapter 1) Maranadda's fourth album.

Syrenthian Brotherhood Knights of Darkness - (Chapter 7) A mysterious group of people in the Syrenthian Galaxy who were known to be badasses and not to be messed with. The group were the only ones in the Syrenthian Galaxy to still use Asparell coins.

Syrenthian Galaxy - (Chapter 1) A galaxy controlled by two governments. The Syrenthian Government was home to humans who controlled most of the galaxy. The Xenolfan Government was home to Xenolfans who controlled the planets Olf Teruda and Salinarr Nevis.

Syrenthian Government - (Chapter 1) A government within the Syrenthian Galaxy that had mostly human citizens; however, there were some Xenolfans who lived in Syrenthian Government territory. The seat of the government was on the planet Exandra.

Syrenthian War - (Chapter 1) A war that took place about one hundred years earlier. The Syrenthian War was fought between the Xenolfans and the humans. The humans had become aggressive against the aliens for unjust causes. When the Xenolfans started to fight back, it turned into a terrible galactic war. In retaliation, the Xenolfans had used controlled asteroids, dubbed missiloids, to assault human-occupied planets.

T

Tales of Shardaa - (Chapter 3) A song by Maranadda from their first album, Esoteric. Tales of Shardaa was a song about an uncharted, desolate, and mysterious region of the Syrenthian Galaxy called the Shardaa Sector.

Tenebris - (Chapter 1) A spaceship owned by Sierra Shalinsky. The *Tenebris* was about one hundred years old and was once a fighter ship in the Syrenthian War.

thermal cube - (Chapter 2) A device that was designed to warm up an area in cold weather. Thermal cubes contained an element that heated up when activated and cooled back down when deactivated by its electronic circuit.

Ticrisuda Powersports - (Chapter 1) A company on the planet Shar Nefalis, in the Industrial Sector, owned by Garnell Meshtief. Ticrisuda Powersports manufactured snowmobiles, all-terrain vehicles, and other recreational sport vehicles.

Toraanium - (Chapter 15) A compound found on the planet Montoraania that was toxic to humans.

Trodder, Arrian - (Chapter 1) He lived on the planet Red Jacket. Arrian was the bass player for the band Maranadda. He had long, brown hair. Arrian was the boyfriend of Jacquelyn Enelra and the father of Sophie Enelra.

Tuvelless, Aaranix - (Chapter 2) He was a Xenolfan who lived in the Xenolfan Government palace on the planet Olf Teruda. Aaranix was the leader of the Xenolfan Government. He had long, white hair and sapphire eyes.

V

Varium, Shasta - (Chapter 1) She was the manager and booking agent for the band Maranadda.

Volum - (Chapter 7) A planet within the Syrenthian Government's territory.

W

Whitestone, Tellaris - (Chapter 6) He was a Syrenthian Government investigator. Tellaris had grayish-white hair.

Whitmann, Benjamin - (Chapter 1) He lived on the planet Red Jacket. Benjamin was a disabled young boy who enjoyed watching the ATVs race along the trails. He had brown hair. Benjamin was the son of CJ Whitmann.

Whitmann, CJ - (Chapter 1) He lived on the planet Red Jacket. CJ owned a hardware store on Red Jacket named CJ Whitmann's Hardware & Supply Co. He had gray hair. CJ was the father of Benjamin Whitmann.

Winterfest - (Chapter 2) A town in the Northern Territories on the planet Aamaress.

Wolf's Den, The - (Chapter 2) A casino on the planet Salinarr Nevis.

X

X2143 - (Chapter 13) A Xenolfan scout ship.

Xenolfan - (Chapter 1) One of the two known intelligent species in the Syrenthian Galaxy, other than humans. Xenolfans had white hair, sapphire eyes, and bluish-gray skin. Male Xenolfans had a patterned face. One thousand years earlier, the species had large, black wings.

Xenolfan Government - (Chapter 1) A government within the Syrenthian Galaxy that had Xenolfan citizens. The seat of the government was on the planet Olf Teruda.

XT-B5 - (Chapter 3) A robot owned by Shalarr and Fioness.

Y

Yort, Remywian - (Chapter 7) He was a bartender at the Eccentric Elixir intoxication joint and cafe on the planet Volum. Remywian had gray hair.

Yttursal - (Chapter 14) She was a Xenolfan. Yttursal had long, white hair and sapphire eyes.

A NOTE FROM THE AUTHOR

Thank you for your interest in this WymerNovels title. If you enjoyed this novel, consider helping other readers discover it by leaving a review online. If you have any questions, please contact me at www.WymerNovels.com.

—Troy D. Wymer

Troy D. Wymer is a science fiction space opera novelist from Michigan, US. He started writing in 1984, but it wasn't until 2016 that he formed the WymerNovels imprint and began to publish novels. Troy enjoys reading, writing, and listening to various subgenres of metal music.

www.ingramcontent.com/pod-product-compliance
Lightning Source LLC
Chambersburg PA
CBHW020756310726
48969CB00002B/565